D1193311

The Book of Joshua II

BELIEVE

East Baton Rouge Parish Library
Baton Rouge, Louisiana

Books by Iris Bolling

THE HEART SERIES
Once You've Touched The Heart
The Heart of Him
Look Into My Heart
A Heart Divided
A Lost Heart
The Heart

NIGHT OF SEDUCTION SERIES
Night of Seduction/Heaven's Gate
The Pendleton Rule

GEMS & GENTS SERIES
Teach Me
The Book of Joshua I - Trust
The Book of Joshua II - Believe

Copyright © 2014 by Iris Bolling
All rights reserved.

No part of this book may be reproduced in any form
or by any electronic or mechanical means including
information storage and retrieval systems, without
permission in writing from the author. The only
exception is by a reviewer, who may quote short
excerpts in a review.

Printed in the United States of America
ISBN-13:978-0-9913426-0-0

Library of Congress Control Number: 2014905577

This is a work of fiction. Names, characters, places
and incidents are with the product of the author's
imagination or are used fictitiously, and any
resemblance to actual persons, living or dead,
business establishments, events, locales is entirely
coincidental.

SIRI ENTERPRISES
RICHMOND, VIRGINIA
www.sirient.com

Prologue
Mexico

As a CIA operative, few things surprised Joshua Lassiter. As a man, many things disgusted him. Those were his thoughts as he pulled sheets of paper from the container he was holding. Inside were several documents with a letterhead he knew well. The documents were from the White House with the seal of the United States of America at the bottom. It wasn't the Presidential Seal, he knew for he had several documents with that seal himself. No, the document he was holding held another prominent seal in the center. Glancing at the document, the signatures of the Secretary of Defense and the Vice-President glared back at him in bold black ink.

Joshua shook his head not wanting to believe what he was reading. Pulling out his handheld, which he affectionately called Sally, he scanned the document then sent it electronically to Ned, his handler. He knew the original had to be authenticated, however, this would at the very least, give him an idea of the true source of the evidence he'd found.

Tucking Sally in his breast pocket, he pulled out a long thin item that resembled a pen. He held the document up, clicked the top of the item, shining a black light over it. There were certain security features in the paper used by the White House that could not be seen with the naked eye. The features were there. Someone from the White House gave immunity to this man. Joshua looked around at the weapons of mass destruction. "Who in the hell would allow these weapons on U.S. soil?"

He folded the paper and placed it inside a covert section of his coat pocket, near the small GPS button. If something happened to him, Ned would be able to locate the coat using the GPS. The document would be found. He quickly scanned through the other five documents in the file, sending a copy of each to Ned, then placed them back.

This was not his mission. He was in Mexico City to deliver a secure message to the President of Mexico without being detected. Afterwards, he stopped in Monterey to see an old friend, Alejandro Mateo.

Mateo was the head of the Mexican Cartel, but from time to time, he had proven to be a friend to him and the United States. Never hurt to have friends on both sides of the law in his line of work. It would not serve him or Mateo any good if a CIA agent were seen leaving his estate. Joshua used a back way to return to his chopper, which he'd landed at the tail end of Mateo's property some ten miles away. He was about to turn into the densely wooded area where his chopper was, when he heard gunshots, then loud cheers. Turning away from the chopper, he walked towards the sounds and found men taking target practice with M2 Browning machine guns. Sitting next to them on the ground, was an open case of the weapons. He heard the men talking and knew this was an arms deal going down. Joshua thought it was one of Mateo's deals and was about to turn away when he heard the man say, Mateo would have him killed if he knew about this. The other man testing the weapons turned, causing Joshua to pause. Standing not fifty feet away was a face from the past. The last time Joshua saw the man was outside a window in Richmond, Virginia with the scope of a rifle, firing at the police chief.

Jonas Gary, what in the hell are you doing here?

Joshua listened a little longer and discovered Gary had been granted immunity from the highest level in the U.S. He mentioned the documents were in his safe. Joshua was shocked.

"I'll take all you have. Come with me," Gary said as he turned towards the building.

Using the trees as cover, Joshua followed the men to a log cabin style house, with a warehouse type building to the left. The man placed his hand on a panel to the right of the door, to unlock the building. Another man backed a truck up to the door. Using Sally, he took pictures of the men unloading weapons from the truck and carrying them to the warehouse. He made himself comfortable next to a tree. He wanted to see what was in that building.

It was hours later, when he deactivated the sophisticated alarm system, then walked through the door at the back of the building. He couldn't believe his eyes at the sight of the stockpile of weapons of mass destruction. The M2s were only the tip of the iceberg. He sent Ned a message. *We have an issue.* He sent pictures of semi-automatic rifles, AK-47s, AR-70s, Uzis, AR-15s, MAC 11s, even his favorite, grenade launchers. From the floor to the ceiling, there were crates stacked across the room. Walking through the building, he had the feeling someone was preparing for a war with a small country.

"Whew," he murmured as he stood there in disbelief. A few thoughts crossed his mind. Was Mateo aware these weapons were on his property? Were the weapons taken from Mateo without his knowledge? The last thought sent a shiver through his spine. Were these weapons meant for the United States? It was the last thought that caused him to survey the room a little closer. There was a door to what appeared to be an office. Walking over, he tested the door. It was locked. Using Sally, he pushed a few buttons. In a matter of seconds the lock clicked. He deactivated the alarm on the office door, then entered.

The office wasn't large, maybe twelve by twelve. There was a desk with a chair against the wall and two chairs in front of it. Against the wall near the door was a metal file cabinet. On the opposite wall, there was a tall glass case with an assortment of rifles displayed. On the far wall, there were pictures that caught his attention. Joshua stood looking at pictures of Jonas Gary shaking hands with several people he recognized. There were two in particular, that triggered an alert. One was the man named to lead the United States Military, Admiral Mark McGary. If that didn't scare him shitless, the next picture did. Smiling and shaking hands was a picture of Jonas Gary and the Vice President of the United States, Jerry McClintock. Both the Admiral and the Vice President are advisors to the President of the United States.

It was a fact that Joshua himself hadn't been too fond of the United States for the past three years and had wanted to blow up a few places himself. In fact, he had, but that island in Southwest Virginia had been used to imprison young boys in that area and needed to be destroyed. Him blowing up crap was acceptable, but he'd be damned if he would allow anyone to put weapons of mass destruction on the grounds of his homeland.

Looking around, his curiosity was piqued. "What are they doing in a picture with a man like Gary?" He walked over to the file cabinet, then sifted through the files. Not much, records of sales mostly. Not what he was looking for. The man mentioned a safe. Using Sally, he activated the sensor. If a metal safe existed, Sally would find it. And she did. It was in the floor under the two chairs and the carpet in front of the desk. That's where he found the papers he was reading.

Now, standing in the warehouse with his arms folded over his chest, he knew there was no way he could allow these weapons to move from this location. With Gary involved, his gut told him the weapons were slated for the United States. Smiling, as a thought occurred, he nodded his head. "Why the hell not?"

He took the walk back to his chopper, activated the stealth mode, then took off in the direction of the building. Using night vision glasses, he flew in the dark. Before emerging from the trees, he saw activity on the ground. Something must have alerted the occupants of the house, for two men were standing outside of the building and another was running back into the house.

"Oh hell, sorry guys. I wanted to destroy the weapons, but since you are there, I guess you have to go too."

Just when Joshua was about to fire a missile to destroy the weapons below, the sensor on the chopper panel went off. A missile had locked on to him. He looked out the window to see a man standing with a land-to-air missile pointed at him. His first thought was how in the hell did they detect him? His second was anger. "No, you did not fire at me."

He swung the chopper around.

"BOOM." He dropped the missile, then flew away from the explosion.

Flying in the direction of the Mexico and Texas border, Joshua was using every evasive maneuver he knew, but the missile had locked on him. He could not shake it. The only thing he could do, was find a dense area with no population and go low. A second explosion ricocheted below, but he could not celebrate, for he still had a missile on his tail. He flew towards a mountainous area, headed towards one, then pulled up, right before hitting it. The missile nipped the tail end of the chopper sending it into a tailspin, before exploding into the mountain.

The chopper was out of control. Joshua sent a message to Ned. *Going down.* He was still in Mexico, not far from the first explosion. The monitor on the dashboard of the chopper indicated his location was close to Laredo, Texas, just not close enough. He knew the men on the ground would get to him before anyone from the United States could. Moments later, just before his chopper crashed, his last thought was, he never gave his mother grandchildren. Sally was going to be pissed

Chapter One
Washington, D.C.

President Jeffrey "JD" Harrison sat in the lone chair at the top of the oval shaped carpet surrounded by his national security team. On a sofa, to the right of the President sat the Vice-President, Jeremiah "Jerry" McClintock, Secretary of Defense, Harry Armstead, General Gerald Ashton and Admiral Mark McGary. On the sofa to the left sat the President's Political Advisor, James Brooks, Chief of Staff, Calvin Johnson and Royce Davenport, the President's appointee as the Secretary of Homeland Security.

The tension in the room was thick enough to cut with a knife. The topic at hand, a CIA Operative caught behind enemy lines, injured. If it was any other operative, the discussion would be moot, an operative would never be left behind enemy lines. However, they were not discussing a normal operative.

"Everyone in this room knows he will find a way out. He always has." General Ashton huffed. "Hell, the man has nine lives. He should have been dead years ago during that fiasco in Nickelsville, VA."

"Our concern should be the repercussions if we are detected behind enemy lines," the Vice-President stated.

The Secretary of Defense spoke. "We don't want to chance a war with Mexico over this."

"We leave no man behind," Secretary Davenport stated. "We know he is alive. We have the means and the resources to bring him home. I say we go in. I don't give a damn if it's life number one or twenty. We leave no man behind."

President Jeffrey "JD" Harrison had been in office for two years. In that time he had brought the kind of leadership that was inclusive of all, but above all else, a level of respect and admiration from other countries. He turned to his Chief of Staff, Calvin Johnson and his top advisor, James Brooks, men who he trusted with his life for advice. "Scenario, gentlemen?"

"The area is hot. Our presence, if detected, could ignite instabilities. We cannot afford a war in that region," Calvin stated. "With that said, you have a good relationship with the Mexican President. I say give the President a call. Let him know we are coming to get our man. If we are detected, we will hold his confidence and maintain that he knew nothing of our plans to enter his country."

"Lassiter knew the risk." General Ashton voiced his opposition. "He has survived worse. We don't jeopardize our position in the region to save one."

JD stood, then walked over to the window, looking out into the rose garden. It didn't feel right. Joshua was a friend, more like family. With all his crazy antics, he was one of the best weapons at the United States' disposal and someone he cared about. Even if all of that wasn't at play, you don't leave a man behind in enemy territory. "Is he being tortured?"

"With no military background you wouldn't understand, that is an acceptable course of action,"

General Ashton quipped. "Any military man knows he puts his life on the line everyday."

The comment angered JD. Keeping his cool was a part of his job. Even with those who openly disrespected him. Be it with foreign or domestic enemies. He turned, walked back to where everyone was seated and spoke directly to General Ashton. "Look down at the carpet, General." The General looked down, then looked back up at him. "That—is the seal of the President of The United States of America. That would be me. The President is your Commander in Chief. That would also be me. While in this office you will respect the man and the position." His eyes narrowed. "When I ask you a question, I don't want your commentary. I want an answer. Shall we try it again?" JD held the man's eyes to ensure he understood.

"Yes, Sir." The General sat up straight. "Lassiter has knowledge that would dictate extraction. Any country that captures him would be traitorous if they did not attempt to extract that information."

"We never leave a man in enemy territory." JD held the man's glare. "I want him home in forty-eight hours."

"Mr. President, that request could have international repercussions," the General continued to protest.

"Yes, it could. Leaving him will have domestic implications," the President replied.

The President turned his back, walked back over to the window that over looked the Rose Garden. When he placed his hands in his pockets, those in the room that knew him, understood his decision had been made. He turned back to the group. "Secretary Davenport, who can we send in undetected to bring him out?"

Royce stood to hand the President a folder. "Forty-eight hours from go and we will have him home."

JD glanced over the plan, then passed it on to Calvin to review. "Royce, I need you and Admiral McGary to remain. Dead or alive, I want him brought home." Looking up at the other men in the room he nodded his head dismissing them. "Thank you for your counsel gentlemen."

As the men walked out of the Oval Office, Admiral McGary, Calvin, James and Royce remained. "Calvin," the President spoke. "Place a call to the President of Mexico. Tell him with or without his support we're coming to get our man. Secretary Davenport, who are we sending in?"

Secretary Davenport handed a second folder to the President. "I've contacted our top medical retriever."

JD glanced at the file, nodding. "You were that certain of my decision?" He gave the file to Calvin.

"Just being prepared," the Secretary replied.

Calvin looked over the file and chuckled. "If Joshua isn't dead already, this will kill him for sure." He passed the file to James.

"If he's dead, this should bring him back to life," James jested.

"Roc has indicated forty-eight hours would be sufficient for the mission. Unfortunately for Joshua, who is known for his antics, Roc is one of our more dangerous operatives. If Joshua gets out of line, she will kill him."

"Mr. President," Admiral McGary cautioned, "I don't always agree with General Ashton, however, in this situation, I believe he may be correct. Going after Lassiter may be more trouble than he is worth. For the last three years, he has been unmanageable. I don't think I need to remind you of the death of King

Tarik in Asmere, or the island in Nickelsville, Virginia he blew up."

"The President made his decision, Admiral. It's not up for discussion," James stated.

"Admiral, you are correct," the President intervened, knowing James did not care for the Admiral. "I no more need to be reminded of those incidents than I need to be reminded that it was Joshua Lassiter who stabilized the region in Asmere and Emure. Nor do I need to be reminded, it was Joshua Lassiter who successfully diverted an assassination attempt on my life. I am well aware of who we are rescuing." He turned away from the Admiral. "Secretary Davenport, reach out through diplomatic channels," JD stated, then turned to Calvin. "I expect to be briefed in the Situation Room within the hour on our progress."

Calvin stood. "Gentlemen, Situation Room in ten."

Once Secretary Davenport and Admiral McGary closed the door, JD looked to Calvin. "Synopsis," JD said as he walked around to take the seat behind his desk.

"It's no secret Ashton is not a fan. However, he serves at the pleasure of the President."

"Ashton is going to follow orders. It's McGary I don't like or trust," James stated. "My concern is the growing number of top brass in the room that we can't trust."

"I can't change my history James." The President looked up. "I didn't serve my country in combat. I'm serving my country in the way that I can make a difference."

"You don't have to justify your lack of service to me or anyone else. Certainly not to the Admiral or the assholes that follow him. For some reason, they believe carrying a gun is the answer to every ill in the world. The hell with them," James shouted. "We go in and get Joshua. Apparently the Admiral has forgotten the fifth stanza of the Army Ranger creed, which states, 'I shall never leave a fallen comrade to fall into the hands of the enemy' quote, unquote. The dumb ass."

JD and Calvin stared at James. They had known the man for a number years now. They could count on one hand the number of times they had seen him pissed.

JD grinned. "Thank you for being pissed on my behalf."

James nodded his head. "You're welcome." The three men laughed. James stood. "You may want to give Al a call. The property Joshua was on belongs to his friend Alejandro Mateo."

"Name sounds familiar." JD lowered his head trying to remember how he knew the name. His head shot up. "He was the man who tipped Al on the McClintock assassination attempt during the campaign."

"He is also the head of the Mexican Cartel," Calvin added. "The request for assistance should not come from you or this office."

JD turned from Calvin. "Understood."

A few hours later, President Harrison walked into the private residence of the White House where he was promptly greeted by the sound of laughter coming from the family room. Regardless of what the day threw his way, those sounds always soothed his soul. He listened as his youngest girls, Brianna and Gabby laughed joyously at something his baby boy, William was doing.

"Do you have to make all that noise?"

JD grinned and lowered his head. *Ah yes, Jazzy,* he thought. *His eleven year-old daughter, who for some reason which was unclear to him, thought she was twenty.* JD loved his children. They were healthy and happy, more due to their mother than anything he'd ever done. He walked into the room and was bombarded with hugs.

"Daddy," they called out in unison.

JD kissed each of his girls, then reached down and picked up William. He kissed his son on the cheek, then took a seat on the sofa. Gabby climbed onto his free leg, as Brianna sat next to him. Jasmine, who they all called Jazzy, stood in front of him. "What have you been up to today?" JD asked.

They all began to talk at the same time. Miraculously, JD seemed to understand what each of them was saying.

"Wait, we can't all talk to Daddy at the same time," Jazzy said with her hands on her hips. "I'm the oldest. I will tell him."

"Tell me what, Jazzy?"

That made Jazzy smile, for she now had her father's full attention. The other children quieted down as Jazzy spoke. She flipped her hair over her shoulder, then began talking. "Well, Daddy, I think JC got in trouble at school. I don't know why, and when I tried to talk to him, he said I was too young and wouldn't understand. Daddy, I'm not that much younger than he is and I don't like it when he calls me young. Grandma Lena said, "I'm a maturing young woman.""

"Grandma Lena would say something like that," He tweaked her nose. "But you are my baby girl. I want you to stay that way for a little while longer," he kissed her on the forehead. The child's smile was as bright as her mother's. "Where's your mother?"

Jazzy's smile faded away. She hunched her shoulders. "I don't know. Probably somewhere with JC."

"She's in the kitchen, Daddy," Gabby offered, earning a frown from her big sister.

He sat the children down and stood.

"Daddy, you can't go yet." Jazzy grabbed his hand. "We haven't finished talking."

JD squeezed her hand. "We'll talk later. I need to talk to your mother first."

"Why? You can talk to me, Daddy. I'll listen."

"I know you will Jazzy, but this is something for Daddy and Mommy." He walked out of the room and away from the frowning child.

He found his wife, Tracy, in the kitchen, at the island stirring something. He walked up behind her, eased his arms around her waist, then kissed her neck. "Didn't Mrs. Gordon tell you to stay out of her kitchen?"

"Yes, and so did all the other cooks in this place, but I wanted to make this soup for you," she turned. "Taking a break?"

"I wanted to talk with you about something." He frowned as she spooned him a taste of the soup. "It needs a little sugar." His lips touched hers the moment he finished the sentence. "Mmm, that's much better." He smiled. Tracy looked up at him with sparkling brown eyes. They had been married fifteen years and he still wanted to make love to her every time he looked at her. "You are a beautiful first lady, did you know that?"

"Flattery will get you nowhere."

"It got me five children on our way to twelve."

"Ha, you must be having the other seven. I'm finished, buddy."

He pulled her close and kissed her on the neck. "Are you sure about that?"

She closed her eyes and inhaled, taking in the scent of him. "You make a compelling argument, Mr. President. However, as much as I would like to engage in the process of procreation, we are not having another child."

"Speaking of my children, what's going on with JC? Jazzy said he got into some kind of trouble at school."

Tracy exhaled, shaking her head. "JC did not get into trouble at school. Where did she get that?"

"I have no idea, that's your daughter."

"Oh no, you spoiled that one rotten."

He kissed her cheek and took the spoon from her to dig into the soup again. "That's because she looks so much like you." He tasted the soup, and smiled. "Just right."

Tracy took the spoon and hit him on the shoulder. "Stop eating out of the pot."

JD grimaced as if the hit hurt and grinned as he took off his blazer and sat at the table. "Have you spoken to Al today?"

"No." Tracy turned to look at him. His looked indicated that this was something more than just a casual inquiry into her brother's well-being. "Why?"

"Just wondering," he said as he lowered his head.

Tracy watched her husband for a moment, then turned back to the stove. "I'm going to call him later. Anything in particular you want to ask about?"

"Alejandro Mateo," JD replied. Tracy nodded, but asked no questions. "So what's happening with JC?"

Tracy looked out the door to ensure no agents were standing there, then inhaled. "He's worried about you."

"About me? Why?"

Tracy shrugged her shoulders, the same way Jazzy had moments ago. "I'm not sure. He mentioned something about traitors in your administration. I think you should talk to him."

"I don't want him to worry about that."

"I know." She turned to face her husband, who was looking a little dejected. "JC is an intuitive young man. He sits back watching and listening to everything. He may not say much, but he is always aware of things and people around him."

"Your brains and my good looks. I tell you, that son of ours is going to be something."

Tracy smiled. "Like his father."

JD stood. "No, JC is going to exceed everything I've ever done." He kissed her on the cheek. "I'm going to talk to him. I'll be right back."

Tracy watched as her six-foot-four, two hundred and twenty pound husband, grabbed his suit jacket and walked out of the room. *The man looks good coming and going.*

JD knocked, then walked into his son's room. Most fourteen-year-old boys would have clothes all over the floor, with video games keeping them company, JC's room looked more like a study hall. Books were neatly tucked away on shelves, a television was ensconced inside an insert in the wall, and the walls were covered with maps of the world. The video games were arranged alphabetically on the shelves. The gaming system was not on, but the television was on and tuned into World News.

JC, who was sitting at his desk reading, looked up when his father entered the room.

"Hey, son, you have a few minutes for your dad?"

"Anytime," the young boy replied as he closed his book. "Is everything okay?"

"Of course it is. Why do you ask?"

"I saw you standing at the window with your hands in your pockets and your head down last night. That's usually an indication that you are trying to work something out in your mind. Do you want to talk about it?"

JD wanted to smile, but he knew how serious JC was, and the truth of the matter was he enjoyed talking things through with his son. They talked regularly and it never ceased to amaze him just how insightful his son was. JD sat on the bed, kicked off his shoes, then sat back against the wall. "A friend is in trouble. I have to decide if we should help him or not."

JC pulled his chair up in front of his dad, rested his elbows on his legs then clasped his hands together. "You help your friend, Dad. A man has a few things he values above all else: his word, his wife, family, and his friends. Your friend is in need." He shrugged his shoulders as if nothing more needed to be said.

Inside JD was smiling, but he nodded to his son as if he was in deep thought. "You have a point." He sighed. "We're friends, right?"

"No, Dad." JC grinned. "You are not supposed to be my friend. You are my father, mentor, and role model." JC sat back. "But we're cool."

JD smiled displaying the identical dimple his son was showing. "I'm happy to hear that, son." He cleared his throat. "Since we're cool, would you tell me what happened in school today?"

JC stared at his father for a moment, then stood. He walked over to the window, put his hands in his pants pockets, then hung his head. The last thing he wanted to do was add to his father's worries. As the leader of the free world, not only did the people of the United States depend on him, every country expected him to keep peace amongst them. The things that happened to him in school, because of who his parents were, he should be able to handle. Today was a little different. This involved an adult. He knew he should not have disrespected the man, but there was no way he could allow what he said to go unchecked.

JD watched the play of emotions across his son's face. Whatever transpired concerned him deeply. JD stood, slipped back into his shoes, and walked over to the window next to JC. He put his hands in his pockets, then looked down at his son. "You know, what's going on in the world does not supersede what's happening with you. I am your father first. All other roles come after that."

JC, who now stood about five feet eleven inches and was still growing, put his hand on his dad's shoulder and a finger to his lips. He looked up at his dad with his serious brown eyes as he reached into his desk drawer to pull out what looked like a pen. He pushed the top and a green light began to flash, then turned solid.

"Son," a questioning JD began to speak, but JC, again put his finger up to his lips to silence his father as he continued to walk around the room.

"School was just school, Dad." As he walked back to his father, the light began to flash. JC frowned. He looked up at his father, who appeared to be as confused as he was. "You want to go shoot some hoops?" JC pointed to the green light then to his dad, then to his ear. "You will have to change your clothes."

The reality of what was happening hit JD like a ton of bricks. He took JC by the shoulder and pulled him from the room. "I think that's a good idea." He motioned to the Secret Service Agent outside the door to come inside. JC pulled away, gave a slight shake of his head then stared at his father. JD saw the look of concern in his son's eyes and immediately changed what he was about to say. The agent came into the foyer of the living quarters. "We're going to shoot some hoops. Would you secure the court?"

The agent nodded. "I'll have that taken care of ,Mr. President." He put his finger to his earpiece and began speaking as he walked from the room.

JD swiftly walked across the hallway into the master bedroom then stripped out of his suit. He slipped into a pair of sweats and a top as he picked up his cell to dial a number.

JC watched his father take steps to secure the room. JD placed the clothes he was wearing into a plastic bag. His father gave him a pair of sweats then held his hand out. JC knew he wanted the device. He gave the pen to his father and watched as he scanned the sweats he had put on. Once he was satisfied, he placed the bagged clothes inside the bathroom suite, turned the shower on then closed the door behind him.

Love was one thing when it came to family. Admiration was something different. JC not only loved his father, he admired his calmness under difficult situations.

"What is this? Where did you get it?"

JC pulled the sweat shirt over his head then looked at his father. "Mr. Joshua gave it to me. I use it regularly to check my room for listening devices."

"Why?"

"For reasons like this, Dad." The young man looked up at his father. "You are always talking to Mom about being too trusting. You're just as bad." JC shook his head then bent down to pick up his discarded clothes from the floor. "You are trusting people you shouldn't," JC said as he turned back to his father. Instead of tossing the clothes in a corner, as most young men his age would do, he placed them on the bed and began folding them.

The action reminded JD so much of Tracy he almost smiled, but the situation was too serious. JD placed his hand on his son's shoulder. "JC," JD inhaled, "look at me son. Tell me what happened in school today."

JC exhaled. "Dad, I think Vice-President McClintock is coming after your administration."

Of all the things JD expected, that was not one. It took him a moment to gather his thoughts. "Why would you be concerned with Vice-President McClintock?"

Before JC could answer, a knock sounded at the door. Brian Thompson, the head of JD's personal security detail, walked into the room. The two had been friends since high school. It was Brian who had taken a few bullets in his back to save JC when he was two-years-old. He was still taking JD and his family's protection personally.

Standing six-three, dressed in his signature black suit, white collar shirt with no tie, he closed the door behind him. "What's going on?" He looked from JD to JC.

JD handed the device to Brian. "According to this, there is a listening device in my clothes."

Brian looked from JD to JC, then back at the device in his hand. "Good work." He handed the device back to JC. "Where are they?"

JD hesitated for a moment then nodded. "In the bathroom." He looked at his son then Brian. "You know about this?" he asked as Brian walked into the bathroom.

"Sure," he replied when he walked back into the room. As if there was nothing to it, he pulled out his cell phone. "I need a clean sweep team in the residence." He disconnected the call, then put his cell phone away. He looked at JC. "What made you sweep the room?"

"I was about to tell Dad about school today. The information was sensitive, so I did what you and Mr. Joshua told me. Secure the discussion area."

Brian smiled as he nodded his head. "I'm going to make you an agent yet."

JD watched as the two talked. The idea of his son or any of his children being involved in security issues did not sit well with him. He started to say something, but Brian's next question stopped him.

"Did McClintock come?"

"No, his wife spoke to the class."

"Did she approach you?"

"No, but one of her advisors did, and I did not like him."

"What!" JD exclaimed. "What in the hell is going on here, Brian? Why is McClintock approaching any of my children? And why in the hell does it seem like you are aware of something I'm not."

"Because it's my job to protect you and your family," Brian replied. "As for McClintock, I'm attempting to determine that now."

"Okay. Everyone let's take it down a notch or two." JC looked from his Dad, who looked very angry, to Brian, who seemed to want answers. "Dad, Vice-President McClintock was scheduled to speak to our Government class today. Uncle Brian told me to be on guard in case he tried to get his agenda to you through me. As it turned out, he wasn't there, Mrs. McClintock came."

"Did she approach you?" A concerned JD asked.

"No, however, one of her advisors did and as I said before, I did not like him."

"Did you get a name?" JD asked, angry at the thought that anyone from his administration would dare approach any of his children.

JC replied, "His name was Holt."

"David Holt?" JD and Brian yelled out the question in unison

Chapter Two
Mexico

Roc stood on the cliff overlooking the property known to belong to Alejandro Mateo, the head of the Mexican drug cartel. Any move onto his property without prior consent could have repercussions on many levels. Looking at the handheld, the message was clear. Wait for orders to proceed. Holding patterns to wait for government approval always placed this type of operation in jeopardy. However, to Roc, an order was an order. It was not to be questioned. It was to be followed. The distance from the drop point to the location of the victim was minimal, less than a hundred yards away. There were no concerns about getting to the victim. It was the victim's weakening condition that made time their enemy. How long they would have to remain stationary depended upon the man known as the legendary Absolute.

The man's reputation preceded him even in her circle of inactive agents. When she received the call to rescue him, it was an honor. It spoke volumes of the White House's belief in her ability to bring one of the country's beloved agents home—alive. That was the order. As she watched the cabin, that was the only thing on her mind. Bringing Absolute home—alive.

According to her handler, the man's vitals were weakening by the minute. Meanwhile she waited for the order from the same White House that had assigned her this mission.

Pushing the frustration away, Roc surveyed the premises to determine the best point of entry. Using her handheld, she scanned for explosives. Anyone who knew anything about Absolute, knew his preferred method to kill was blowing people out of the hemisphere. The handheld began blinking. She had her answer. The entire house was surrounded with explosives. The two windows on the front and the door, all indicated some type of explosive was connected. Roc smiled, even injured, the man was thorough. With that in mind, Roc searched with her eyes for devices the handheld may not detect. Why did that thought cross her mind? Because it's exactly what she would have done under the circumstances. Her search discovered devices leading to the front porch. Roc exhaled, "All right, Absolute, make life difficult, why don't you."

Each step she took was measured, as Roc deactivated device after device. "Well darn Absolute how many of these little buggers did you have?" She reached the porch alive, but did not venture onto it, yet. She looked at her handheld. Still no go ahead order. "Okay, you have two minutes to give me the order before I go in," she said to the handheld.

Examining the area around the porch, Roc determined the best way to gain access to the cabin was right through the front door. The handheld beeped. *Proceed.* "About time," she mumbled while reaching down to twist the heel of her shoe. She retrieved a small plastic case and carefully removed a device no larger than a button on a blouse, from inside. She threw the device onto the porch and ducked behind a tree. As expected, the small explosive tore the porch to shreds, but did not penetrate the door. The noise from the explosion wasn't loud, but she looked cautiously around to ensure she was still alone.

After a few moments, Roc walked over the debris of the shredded porch and peeked through one of the windows. Nothing, she couldn't see anything. But then she was certain Absolute would not be close to the window, for she wouldn't be. She would be as far back in the house as possible. "Okay. Let's try this another way." From her jacket, Roc pulled out a rubber band type device, placed it around the knob of the door, then pointed her handheld towards it. She pushed a button. Roc ducked back against the building, counted to five and the device began to eat through the lock of the door. Soon the metal knob simply fell to the ground. An uneasy feeling hit Roc. There should be gunfire coming through that door or at least an explosion. There was nothing. No response from Absolute. That was not a good sign.

Roc took a quick peek through the hole left by the melting knob, then ducked back against the building. She had a sinking feeling about this. "Absolute," she called out. "Ned sent me. I prefer neither of us die at the hand of the other. With that said, I'm coming in. Please don't make me take you out."

Roc stepped into the doorway. The sight of the man known as Absolute was worse than expected.

"Okay now, Lord, can you give a brother a break? I know my mother told me to talk to you a little more often and lately I haven't. But hell, you know my heart and that is supposed to be enough. In case you

had some doubts, I'm telling you now, I've run out of options here. The clothes may be bullet proof, but it don't do a damn thing to keep me warm. Sorry about the curse word, but things are a little serious down here. Keeping things moving forward, I have to talk to you to keep my mind sharp, cause I don't mind telling you I'm losing it. I've been a good man, for the most part. Yeah, I killed a few people, but God, they were bad people and needed to die. But I've saved some people too, that should count for something. So, I'm just saying, if you have an angel up there with my name on their list you might want to send them on this way or Sally would do just fine."

Absolute paused for a moment contemplating his family. His mother was an angel. His parents, Joseph and Sally Lassiter, had twelve children. He was number two and the most daring. His father Joe said he was that way because he was always trying to live up to his big brother Samuel. With all his antics as a child, his parents never stifled him. No, they always encouraged him to explore and be adventurous, even after he almost burned the house down. He remembered his mother saying, I'm keeping you close to the church, cause you are headed straight to hell with all your mischief. Joshua was beginning to lose consciousness as he thought about his brother. Samuel was the closest thing to God in Joshua's estimation. He forced his eyes to open wide.

"Lord, things are getting serious down here. I have no idea what is taking Samuel so long, but could you hurry him along? I know he's looking for me. It's cold as hell down here." He laughed out loud. *"Hell isn't cold, Joshua."* Pain shot through him causing him to grimace. He closed his eyes, thinking about when he was ten years old and he caught a cold from running barefoot across a frozen pond because

he wanted to outdo Samuel. Of course, Samuel had on his boots, a coat and gloves at the time. But, no he had to do one better to show his invincible brother he was just as tough. The stunt put him out of commission for a month. His mother fed him hot soup, gave him cool baths, and rubbed his chest with vapor rub. Samuel would come in every night and sleep at the foot of his bed. To make sure his feet stayed warm. How he wished his mother was here right now. *"Lord, my mother is going to kill me if I die here. I don't ask for much, but please don't do that to my mother. I promised her grandchildren."*

For the first time in his life, he was losing his belief that he would survive. There wasn't an enemy he couldn't beat down. Bullets seemed to bounce off him, knives might cut, but they did not penetrate. But this enemy, the cold, was a force he couldn't blow up, or out smart. This was a force of nature that he could not beat. The human body was warm blooded. The cold was its enemy. This time he knew when he closed his eyes, it would be for the last time. When next they opened, he would be at the pearly gates giving his account of his life. Maybe then he would be sent to Hell. His last thought was, *at least it would be warm there.*

The blast from outside the door stole him from that peaceful blackness he had been fighting. It was an indication that someone had located him. Absolute pulled the last explosive from his pocket. If he was going to meet his maker on this day, it would be on his own terms and he was taking some bodies with him. Joshua fumbled inside his pocket with his bloody hand, trying to remove the device from its plastic casing but it dropped to the floor.

"Absolute."

He heard someone call his name. Ned came to his mind. Maybe, just maybe, Ned had sent Monique to him. His mind drifted back to the last time Monique had come to rescue him. What he thought was bliss, turned out to be one of the worst periods of his life. To this day, some three years later, he still thought of Akande. No, she was Queen Sofiat Ashro of Asmere. She married Prince Raheem Ashro of Emure to merge the two countries. The sound of the fizzle at the doorknob brought his thoughts back to the present. He knew the sound. He had used the same explosive many times to gain access to a locked structure. Someone was about to enter the cabin. Not sure if it was friend or foe, he blinked to clear his mind. He had to be ready. When he opened his eyes, he wondered if he had died during the blink for an angel was standing before him. His eyes closed thinking, *a woman?* He whispered,   "Lord,   why   hast   thou   forsaken me...again?"

Chapter Three
Mexico
Day One

Time was of the essence. Roc sent a message to Ned. *Absolute located. Critical. Must stabilize here.* The reason Roc was sent on this mission was rescue, not recovery. Recovering a body was not in the cards. Roc was determined to take Absolute back to the United States alive.

This was where Roc's medical expertise came in handy. Bending down next to the cot, which was soaked in blood, the first order of business was to stabilize his condition. It was clear from the amount of blood there were external injuries. Checking his vitals showed his heart rate was slow and his skin was cold to the touch. It was a good seventy-seven degrees outside, yet Absolute's body felt as if it was in a freezer. The amount of lost blood made it difficult to locate the injuries. Turning his body over, Roc groaned. "Goodness." Several wounds were in the man's back. Whoever did this stabbed him from behind, repeatedly with a sharp item. That was a coward's action. A lot more than applying pressure was needed for the wounds, they would need to be cleaned and closed, before she could move him.

Dropping the backpack to the floor, Roc searched the cabin for an area that could be sterilized and used for what she had to do.

The cabin consisted of one room separated into a kitchen, which was near the door, a living room in the center, and the bedroom area near the back. To the right was what looked to be a bathroom and a closet. Roc pulled her weapon then walked the cabin to ensure no one else was around. After checking the closet, Roc came back into the open room.

Moving swiftly, she walked to the kitchen sink to check for hot water. Roc was pleased to see the hot water running freely. Next the gas stove was checked and found to be in working condition. "Great." She smiled knowing she could clean the area. She cleared and wiped down the kitchen table. She pulled a sheet from her knapsack, removed the plastic packaging, unfolded it and placed it on top of the table. Next Roc donned a pair of surgical gloves, then proceeded to strip the bloody clothing from Absolute's body. Each piece was folded, covered with plastic wrapping and placed carefully inside the knapsack. Operatives' clothing at times carried technology within that could be dangerous if put in the wrong hands or if not handled properly. Once each piece was secure, it was time for the real work to begin.

Working briskly, but carefully, Roc cleansed his body, removing the dry blood to determine which wound was the most serious. Once that was determined a plan of action came to mind. Roc carried Absolute to the table. Being a part of the military, even women had to have the strength to carry their comrades if needed. At five-six, one hundred twenty pounds, Roc had carried men twice her weight. The problem with Absolute was his height. The man had long legs, but she managed. She placed him on his stomach, which allowed easy access to the wounds. His long legs hung over the end of the table, but there was nothing that could be done about that.

Roc unzipped the bottom of the sack to pull out a white box. Inside was a metal pole, which extended to stand on the floor. Next, from an insulated ice filled cooler, she retrieved two plastic medical pouches, one containing saline, the other Absolute's blood, drawn previously, just for such an occasion as this. Checking the date on the bag, Roc was pleased to see he had given the blood within the last thirty days and it had been treated to prevent clogging. She ran two IV lines into opposite arms. Blood to replace what had been lost, the saline to help with lost fluids. A device, similar to a clothespin, was placed on his finger, the other end was attached to the handheld, sending his vitals directly to Ned's computer as the procedure began.

Absolute's blood pressure was low, but that was to be expected. The fluids would eventually bring that under control. His heart rate was rapid and needed to be stabilized, but time did not allow. The blood loss had to be stopped.

Assessing the wounds, there were three open gashes, one dangerously close to a kidney. Roc could not swear by it, but it did not appear the kidney was punctured, maybe just bruised. Attention had to go there first. The two other wounds were deep, but not life threatening. Plan in place, Roc administered a sedative, settled in and began singing, *The Battle Is Not Yours*, by Yolanda Adams, then went to work doing exactly what was expected of her, saving the man's life.

Finally, his mother was there. He knew she would come. Joshua could feel her hands lovingly, washing his body. *Ouch, she could be a little more careful around the wounds, that hurt. She may be angry because I got my church suit dirty.* "Mom, I'm sorry for getting my suit dirty. I'll pray that God will keep me out of the mud from now on. *When did his mom get so strong? Oh, it's Sammy. Sammy's here. Now he knew everything was going to be all right. He was in good hands. Sammy and Mom were there with him.* His body began to relax with that comforting thought. *As he drifted off, allowing the darkness to capture him, he remembered there was something he had to tell Sammy.* "Sammy, NS, White House, don't trust." *Now he could rest. Hmm, he never knew his mom had such a beautiful voice.*

His mind was swallowed back into darkness.

For a little more than an hour, Roc worked to stabilize his vitals. Afterwards, she closed Absolute's wounds. She placed pressure dressing on them, then gauze wrapping to secure the dressing around his mid-section. She stood back evaluating her work. Satisfied, she removed the gloves, and washed her hands. Now that Absolute was stabilized Absolute she felt good about his prognosis. Securing their location was next on the agenda.

Covering Absolute's body with another sterile sheet from the backpack and a blanket from the closet for warmth, Roc stepped outside for some fresh air and to secure the premises. It wasn't ideal, but they would have to stay put at least until dark before an attempt could be made to move Absolute. Arrangements had to be made to get him home. There was no way the original plan to drive him across the border would work. The drive alone could kill him, especially with questions surrounding the kidney wound. He needed to be flown out with medical equipment on board. Absolute's words came to mind, *NS, White House, don't trust.* He also said he was praying to God to keep his clothes clean. She had no idea what that was about, however, when an operative made a statement, even while under anesthesia, Roc knew the information could be vital to the mission. Therefore another route had to be taken to get him home.

Roc repaired the door, then proceeded to secure the immediate area surrounding the building. A trip back to the jeep, to gather supplies for a short stay, gave her the chance to set a few detectors in place just in case anyone attempted to venture towards the cabin. When she walked back into the cabin, she glanced at Absolute. His skin color was returning, his breathing wasn't as labored as before and his vitals, while still not where they should be, were stabilizing. Roc decided to work on an exit strategy. Taking a seat next to the table, where the patient was expected to be under for at least three hours, the first message went to Ned. *Patient remains critical, but stabilizing. Changing exit strategy. Will keep under wraps.*

An immediate reply came back. *Negative. WH request update.* "Okay." She frowned, then looked over at Absolute. His face was turned towards her. She touched his forehead. He was warm to the touch, no longer cold. That was good, his temperature was adjusting. She continued to stare down at him, he had a strong profile, but it was hard to see his face for it was covered with a mustache and beard, but he had the longest eyelashes, lying against chocolate brown skin. Staring at his face, there was something childlike about him. That was not the case with his body. She frowned. "Where did that thought come from? Hmmm."

She cleared her mind and turned back to the message. Not one to disobey orders, a message was returned. *Affirmative*. After the plan was set, Roc set up a second exit strategy. She wasn't ready to dismiss Absolute's words. Besides, one can never have too many escape plans. The man indicated there might be a trust issue at the White House. Since Roc did not know much about this administration, what Absolute said would take precedence. A backup plan needed to be in place in case the man was right. After all, if one dies, they both die. Another message was sent, but not through Ned. *Need escape route from Mexico.*

Chapter Four
Richmond, VA

Sally Lassiter knew something was wrong when she opened her eyes. She did not know what or who, but she knew one of her children was in trouble. Her husband, Joe, had just fallen asleep after working the midnight shift at his night job. She did not want to wake him with her concerns, so she kissed him on the cheek then climbed out of bed. Before her feet hit the floor a long arm wrapped around her waist pulling her back into the bed snugly against his body. A knowing smile formed on her face as she welcomed the warmth and comfort of her husband's arm.

The moment her body touched his, Joe could feel the tension. He tucked her securely under him, gently kissed her lips, then stared down into the eyes of the woman who brought a daily ray of sunshine into his life. "Which one of my gems or gents has you worried?"

She chuckled low as she rubbed his broad shoulder. "You know me too well, Joseph Lassiter." She sighed. "I'm not sure which one it is. I'll have to do my usual roll call."

"Well." He yawned as he rolled onto his back, pulling her 5'4 frame on top of his 6'11 body. "Process of elimination." He gently rubbed her back. "I spoke to Mathew, Luke, Adam, and Jade yesterday."

"Talked to Timothy, Ruby, and Opal." Sally stretched out. "Diamond and Zack are okay."

"Sammy came by the job and had lunch with me last night. That leaves Pearl, and Joshua." They were both quiet at the last name mentioned.

"Did Samuel mention Joshua?" Sally asked.

"No."

"I talked to Jade and Pearl, last night, their teenage daughter, Sapphire spoke from the doorway as she entered the room. Her parents looked up as she walked right over and climbed into bed with them as if it was the most natural thing to do. Joe, lovingly wrapped Phire into his arms. "It's Joshua," she said as she snuggled next to her daddy.

Joe looked at Sally as she slid to his side. "That's your child."

Sally grinned. "Be happy the rest of the children aren't here."

"Daddy, are you going to call Mr. JD and make him bring Joshua home?" She looked at him with the most serious eyes and clearly expected him to do exactly what she asked.

Joe looked to his right at his wife, then to the left at his baby girl and laughed. "Phire," he spoke in a 'have you lost your mind' tone. "No, I'm not calling the President to tell him to do anything."

Phire looked over her father's chest to her mother. "Mommy, you call then. I know you are not afraid of him. And you tell him we need Joshua home. And make sure you let him know we are still upset with him."

Joe and Sally lay there listening to their youngest child vent about her displeasure with the President.

They halfway agreed with what she was saying, but could not believe she expected them to call the man.

"Joshua has been gone for too long. I'm in my senior year of high school now and I need him." Sally could see the tears beginning to form in Phire's eyes. The young girl was just as her name suggested, full of fire, but she loved her brothers fiercely and would do anything to keep them safe.

Joe held his daughter to him and kissed her forehead. "Joshua is going to be just fine."

"No, he's not, Daddy. Something is very wrong." She threw the sheet back. "If you're not going to call the White House, I'm calling Pearl." She jumped out of bed. "I know she is not afraid of Mr. JD."

She stomped towards the door. As she reached it, she slowed her steps then turned back to her parents. "You're not going to stop me?"

Both shook their heads. "No."

A confused look covered Phire's face. Then it dawned on her. "You two are getting ready to do the nasty, aren't you?" She put her hands on her hips and shook her head at them. "While I'm in the house? Don't you know I'm an impressionable child?"

"If you don't close that door, you're going to be a child with a sore behind," Joe declared.

"Tsk Tsk, you should both be ashamed. Doing the nasty at your age. My friends would be appalled, I tell you, appalled." She ducked when the pillow came flying across the room at her. She closed the door giggling, then peeped her head back in. "You missed."

Joe and Sally laughed with her. Once the door was closed and they knew she was not within hearing distance, they both got out of bed.

"You call Samuel. I'll call Lucy." Sally put on her robe. "Someone is going to tell me where my son is before this day is out."

Quantico, Virginia

There weren't many things that ex-CIA operatives could do once they retired that would match the excitement of life in the field. Lucy Russell had been fortunate. During her last year in the field, she'd met and worked closely with Joshua Lassiter, a patriotic young man who believed in God, his family and his country. One day he asked her what was she going to do with all that technical knowledge she possessed. She replied, share it with her dogs. He said he had a better idea. He needed a computer lab and a technician who did not have to answer to the government, hence bypassing delays in action. His one requirement was that she use only top of the line technology. What techie would turn that down? He brought her to his house and said, "Welcome home." That was five years ago, yet, she was still there with no plans of leaving him or The Cave.

In that timeframe, he had built an impenetrable home and she had built The Cave, a command center to rival the Pentagon. Lucy always thought Joshua must have had a Batman cave when he was young and wanted his own bat crave. It was in The Cave at the command console where she watched Joshua's vitals run across the monitor. Yes, she'd tapped into Ned's computer system without his knowledge. Hell, she could do that, after all, she taught him everything he knew about technology, just not everything she knew.

Lucy had never met Roc, but she knew the woman's reputation before she quit the agency. Roc was the best medical operative in the business. Lucy knew Joshua was in good hands and would be home soon in need of medical care. Lucy was making arrangements when the encrypted message came through.

The question of why, crossed her mind, but she learned long ago to do, not question. She glanced up at the vitals. They were improving, but why had Roc contacted an outside entity for extraction when she had just confirmed Ned's extraction plan? Something was off, however, she had to believe if Roc made the request, there was a reason. There were agents who worked within the confines of rules and regulations of the government. Then there were agents who understood that every now and then, one had to work around those rules and regulations to protect the United States from itself. This involved Joshua's life. The latter of the two was needed. This was not the time to be asking a million and one questions as the government has a tendency to do before making a decision. Lucy picked up the secure telephone and punched in a code, then hung up. Two minutes later the telephone rang three times. Lucy sent a message from a handheld. *Medical extraction needed for Absolute.* A second later a message came back. *Details?*

Lucy smiled, no questions asked. She sent the info and was waiting for confirmation when the house phone rang. "Hello."

"Hello, Lucy, have you heard from my son?"

Damn, the woman had an internal radar system when it came to her children. "Hello, Sally. Have I heard from him?" Lucy looked at the vitals again. "No," Lucy frowned as she slid back from the desk. "I haven't heard from him."

"Hmm, well, here's the thing, Lucy. I'm very concerned about him. I can't explain why this time is different, but I feel like....like he needs me. He needs his mother."

Lucy looked at the monitor showing Joshua's vitals. They had moved a little, but not enough for her to tell his mother, her son was fine. The desperation in Sally's voice forced Lucy to respond. "A child could always use their mother around. I'm certain he'll be home in a day or two."

There was a short intake of breath on the other end of the phone. "All right, Lucy. If I don't hear from him in a day or two, you will see me."

Lucy hung up the phone and sighed. "I have no doubt about that." She shook her head and began putting things in place to get Joshua home when she noticed, another intercept was placed on Ned's computer. "What the..." Not trusting the computer, she sent a message using her handheld. "Bogie in your system."

Chapter Five
Washington, D.C.

Mr. Johnson, Secretary Davenport is here to see you."

Calvin looked up from the work on his desk. "Send him in, Jane."

"Yes, Sir." Jane, Calvin's secretary, opened the door, then stepped back. "Mr. Secretary, he can see you now." Jane closed the door after the Royce stepped in.

"Mr. Secretary," Calvin stood and shook Royce's hand. "What do we have?"

"He has been located. We are ready to bring him home."

Calvin sat back relieved. "The President will be happy to hear that. What's his condition?"

"Critical, according to his handler. He is getting medical attention to stabilize him for the trip home. We have a medical team available on the plane."

"Who is handling the military end of the operation?"

"General Ashton."

Calvin frowned. "Jane." He waited.

"Yes Sir."

"I believe General Ashton is in the Sit Room. Have him to report here immediately."

"Yes, Sir." Jane retreated.

"Concerns?" Royce asked.

Nodding, Calvin replied, "From time to time the General believes his opinion is more important than that of The President's. He delays certain orders at will. I want to ensure he understands this is not one of those times."

"Ashton believes he is more powerful then he actually is. Be careful dealing with him."

"You've dealt with him before?" Calvin asked.

Royce nodded as he stood. "He's more bark than bite. He'll try you because you have no military background. Put him in his place once. That should rein him in for a minute." He extended his hand to Calvin. "I'll keep you abreast of the mission."

"I appreciate that." Calvin returned the handshake, just as General Ashton burst into the room. "Don't you ever summon me when I'm in the middle of a mission."

Royce smirked as he sent a knowing look Calvin's way. "You never disappoint, Ashton," he stated as he nodded to Calvin and left the room.

Calvin looked up at the angry expression on the General with the buzz cut from hell. That would give anyone a reason to be an ass all the time. At the moment Calvin did not have time for him or his asinine ways. "Have a seat, General."

"I don't have time for this, Johnson. Some of us have real work to do. My day does not consist of pushing paper around."

Calvin rounded his desk, took his seat, then cut the General off. "My time is at a premium, General. What's the status on the Lassiter mission?"

"Who are you to question me on a status?"

Calvin shook his head, picked up a pen and began to do paperwork. "The one who is going to have your stripes if you don't answer my question." Calvin paused and looked up. "Right now." He looked back down, and began writing again. "Status?"

The General looked as if he was ready to explode, but knew the Chief of Staff had the power to do just what he'd stated. "A medical plane has been deployed to the area. We expect touch down at nineteen hundred hours." Calvin looked up at him. "Sir," the man seethed.

Calvin put down his pen and sighed. "General. I'm not clear on the hostility. Would you be kind enough to take a moment to enlighten me?"

"May I speak freely, Sir?"

Calvin nodded. "I don't see how I could stop you."

"You and your boy in the Oval Office know nothing about protecting this country. I've served in the United States military for close to thirty years now. And I have to take orders from a boy who is too young to even shine my shoes." He angrily pointed to the Oval Office, which was through the connecting door to Calvin's office.

Calvin stood, as he spoke calmly to the General. "You're a military man, so I'm going to assume you understand the chain of command. In your thirty years of service have you liked everyone who has held the office next door?"

"No Sir, I have not," came the indignant reply.

Calvin nodded as he walked around to the front of the desk. "Have you openly disrespected them as you have this President? And please speak honestly."

"I don't recall," the General replied hesitantly.

"You don't recall?" Calvin asked standing toe to toe with the man. "Do you recall running for President of The United States?"

"No Sir." The General narrowed his eyes.

Calvin pointed to the Oval Office. "That *boy* did. Seventy-five percent of the citizens of this country voted that *boy* into office. That *boy* probably has more battle scars than you will ever have. When you are elected into an office, then you have earned the right to disrespect anyone you like. However, as long as you serve in *this* United States military, you will answer every damn question I ask of you. Every time I summon you, you will appear. And you will never...refer to the President of the United States as *that boy*. If you do so, in person, in public, in the damn bathroom under your shower, I will strip you and have you court marshaled. Are we clear, General?"

The General stood sharply at attention. "Yes, Sir, we are."

Calvin turned his back, then returned to his chair, picked up his pen and began working again. "I expect an update every hour until Operative Lassiter is back in his mother's arms, safe and alive. You are dismissed."

The General walked out of the room, then dialed a number on his cell phone. "Get that plane in the air—now." He hung up the phone then looked over his shoulder at the closed door to the office he'd just exited. If looks could kill, the Chief of Staff's office would have exploded.

Mexico

Roc checked the message again. The one from Ned indicated the plane would be at the drop site at nineteen hundred hours. The second message indicated a Black Hawk would land at the designated spot at eighteen hundred hours. It was taking a chance, but the safest route, to Roc, was with the Black Hawk. She wasn't sure what the situation was with the White House and Absolute, but she was positive the person in the Black Hawk would get the man home. She sent one more message to the man in the administration whom she knew she could trust. *Absolute secure. WH?*

Preparing to depart, Roc reached to touch Absolute's forehead to get a gauge on his temperature. His hand sprung up grabbing Roc's wrist as his eyes opened. Troubled, confused eyes looked back. Then, they softened as if something private was revealed to him. "Angel." He smiled then closed his eyes as his hand dropped back to the table.

Roc had been called many things in this line of work, *angel* had never been one of them. The handheld beeped. It was a message from Ned. *Security breach. Get Out.*

In less than five minutes, Roc had dressed Absolute in black sweats, stuffed his clothes in the sack, and was walking out of the back with him across her shoulders. The man's legs were so long, it created a balance problem, but Roc was trained for this. They were going to meet that chopper and get out of Mexico alive.

The dark of night covered their movements. The night vision goggles provided a clear view through the trees, leading in the opposite direction of the jeep. After walking five hundred feet from the structure, Roc stopped, placing Absolute on the ground against a tree trunk. There were two things Roc did not do. Run was number one. When you run with the enemy behind you, they will eventually catch you. Roc's motto was why run when you can kill.

Ned's message indicated their position had been compromised. Roc needed to know by whom. Who was the enemy? Knowing the answer to that question would determine the next step. It did not take long for the answer to appear. At the sound of engines, Roc stooped down next to Absolute's body and watched as the cabin was surrounded. Not a hundred feet from where they were, a jeep with four men inside stopped. The driver stepped out, looked around then pointed, giving instructions to the other men. While three of the men were clearly of Mexican descent, the leader, was not. He was an American. The men pulled weapons from the back of the jeep and headed towards the cabin. Now what was an American doing leading a group of Mexican assassins? Their weapons of choice made that distinction clear. They came to that cabin to kill. To Roc's way of thinking, there was only one course of action. The handheld beeped as one of the men reached the perimeter markers put in place earlier. Roc nodded. "Take a few more steps and your behind is mine."

There were now three beeps on the monitor indicating three members of the team were within 100 feet of the cabin. One was about to reach the front door and would soon be inside. Once they entered, game over. They would know Absolute was no longer there. Capturing one to determine how they found his location would be ideal. However, Absolute's life was at stake. The question would have to be answered later.

Roc positioned Absolute back over her shoulder, checked the handheld, then pushed a button. Roc began the countdown as they moved towards their pickup site. When the handheld beeped a second time, Roc picked up speed.

BOOM! The sound of the explosion ricocheted through the air. Roc continued to move through the brush, to the top of the ravine where their transportation would be waiting on the landing strip above. The additional two hundred pounds made it difficult to climb the steep hill, but not impossible. Once the ground leveled off, there were only a few feet to the strip. The problem was, it was an open few feet. If someone were on their trail, they would be clear targets. Couldn't worry about that, the order was to bring Absolute home. Roc had to get to the top to accomplish that. Whatever they encountered once there would be handled.

"All right, Absolute," Roc stated as the landing strip came into view. "This is where it gets a little tricky." Looking around Roc noticed a small aircraft with the American flag on the wing was already on the strip. "The good guys are here," Roc said right before a bullet sailed in their direction, striking the tree trunk next to them. Roc ducked back into the bush. "I may be wrong on that."

Whoever took the shot had night vision wear. There was no way they could have been seen by the naked eye. Roc typed a quick message as they moved swiftly down the strip, being sure to stay out of sight. *Under attack.* Roc stopped, remembering the message from Ned. The message was deleted. "Looks like we're on our own, Absolute. The good guys are misbehaving. That's not right," Roc said as the area was scanned for a safe spot. Roc adjusted Absolute, then moved behind a large tree trunk and sent a message to her backup. *Under attack. ETA?* Before another step was taken a message came back. ETA- *Two minutes.*

Roc messaged back, *Expect fire.*

Lock coordinates.

Roc pushed a button on the handheld. *Done. Stealth mode.*

Roc looked up. The density of the trees would not allow for a clear evacuation. They had to go to open ground. A sound came from behind them. Then another sound came from the left. The bad guys were trying to surround them. They had to move. Roc sent one last message, *Track,* pocketed the handheld then moved forward.

The strategic move would be to cover the perimeter of the landing strip, cutting off their escape route. Roc was not going to that area. They were going to a less dense area within the woods that would allow a ladder to drop from above. The handheld beeped. Roc took that as an indication their transportation was in place. Looking around, a few feet away there was a slight opening. The area looked as if campers were recently there. Roc took up a position next to a tree looking up for any sign of their transport. Nothing. Then gunfire rang out. Taking a protective stance with Absolute on her shoulder and gun in hand, Roc scanned the area. The shots were not in their direction. "What the...?" Rapid gunfire continued. Roc heard a whoosh sound and looked in the direction of the opening. A rope ladder was hanging. Looking up, there was the transport in midair. Not thinking twice, Roc holstered her weapon, ran and grabbed the ladder. As soon as Roc's foot hit the bottom step, the chopper pulled up. Roc climbed up as quickly as the extra weight would allow, praying they would clear the trees. By the third step, shots were coming in their direction. Suddenly the weight of Absolute's body was pulled away, giving Roc the freedom to move quickly up the ladder. The gunfire was directed at them now. That was too much. Roc pulled a button from the knapsack, bit the plastic covering and dropped it below. "Pull up," Roc yelled. The ladder burst full speed across the top of trees, smacking Roc's body against branches, just as the small device exploded below. Boom!

"Give me your hand," a familiar voice demanded.

Roc looked up to see none other than Sly Dawson, the man who'd mentored them. Reaching up Roc grabbed the extended arm and was pulled securely onto the floor of the chopper.

"Get us the hell out of here," Sly ordered then looked down at Roc who was still on the floor of the chopper. "I see I'm still getting you and Absolute out of hot spots." Sly grinned.

"What in the hell took you so long?"

"Patience was never your forte."

"Not when people are shooting at me, no." Roc stood, then walked over to the bunk where Absolute lay still. Roc checked his vitals. His pressure was a little high, but that was to be expected after what they just went through. Taking a seat, Roc gave Sly a murderous look. "Who's shooting at us and why?"

"The who, is the good old US of A. Why, is the question we need answered before we put Absolute in harm's way." Sly took a seat across from Roc. "What do you know about his mission?" he asked as he nodded towards Absolute.

"Nothing. Ned may have an answer or two."

"He's been silent since the initial contact."

Roc sat up. "Silent? Ned?"

"Not a sound since I confirmed the transportation plans."

Roc thought for a moment, looked over at Absolute, then back to Sly. "He stays with me until I'm satisfied he can take care of himself." Roc pulled out the handheld and pushed a button. No message was sent. Just notification they were going dark. No communication with anyone, until it was clear who was friend and who was foe. "Who's flying?"

"Melissa Sue. A friend of a friend," Sly replied. "Who knows you are here?"

"Mateo."

"Alejandro?"

"Yes."

"How do you know him?"

"A friend of a friend."

The two stared at each other. Trust was a dangerous trait to have in their line of work. Sly mentored several operatives, including Absolute and Roc. He taught them to give only the information needed to complete a mission and to limit the number of people you trust.

"We're about to have company," the voice of the woman piloting the chopper yelled back.

Roc stood. "I am tired of this. What's on board?"

Sly reached behind the seat and pulled out a missile launcher.

Roc smiled. "Never travel light when you can carry power." Taking the launcher, then lying flat on the floor of the chopper, Roc yelled out, "Open the back door."

The back door slowly opened. As soon as the opening was wide enough, the swoosh sound of the missile launch echoed throughout the interior of the chopper. Moments later the chopper following them exploded in mid-air.

Roc sat up, placing the launcher back in its secured location. "Take us home."

Sly watched as the door slowly closed. He tilted his head towards Roc. "You think someone may notice a United States military chopper exploding over Texas?"

Roc never acknowledged the question. "Take me to Atlanta. He's with me until I know why the country he puts his life on the line for is trying to take him out."

Chapter Six
Atlanta, GA
Day Two

The pain pierced through him like a bolt of lightning, waking him from what seemed like a long sleep. His eyes shot open. Years in covert operations taught him to put pain out of his mind and deal with the safety of his surroundings. The sounds from the monitor caused him to look to his right, then down at his hand. He snatched the clip from his finger, threw the covers back and stood. His knees buckled beneath him. Hands grabbed him from behind and eased his body back into the bed.

"Not sure where you thought you were headed, but this bed is going to be your best friend for the next day or two."

Absolute felt the covers being placed back over his body. Once he was back on his back the pain began to subside. The chopper going down, the message to Ned all flashed through his mind. The voices approaching the crash site, being strung up, the knife slicing into his back, the blood dripping, the cold of the warehouse wall, came to mind. The man coming back, taking him for dead, cutting him down. Killing the man with his bare hands, running through the woods, finding the cabin, setting the explosives, all flashed like a movie across his mind. No memory came after that. He cleared his mind and was lost to the darkness again.

What seemed like hours later, he slowly opened his eyes. *Take a minute. Assess your situation.* Drapes, dresser, television on the wall, beeping. He looked to his right, a hospital monitor showing his vitals. It wasn't a hospital, the bed was too comfortable. Looking to his left there was an open door, yellow walls, a chair near the door, white carpet. He closed his eyes again, music was playing, someone was singing in another room. He inhaled, a scent hit his nostrils. A nice soothing scent lingered in the air. Light footsteps and the voice were approaching the room. He opened his eyes again. Standing in the doorway was the angel, singing. He attempted to get up again, he wasn't ready to meet his maker.

A small, but firm hand held him down. "Take it easy, Absolute. I know you have a number of questions, as do I. However, you have a number of stitches in your back. I know because I put them there. Some of my best work, so I need you to be still."

Absolute tried to move again.

The single small hand held him down again. "I will strap you in if I have to. I don't want to, but I will."

Absolute looked up, surprised by the strength of the hold. "You're real," he said more to himself than to her. "I thought you were an angel."

"Sorry, I'm quite real. I'm too stubborn to let you meet your maker today." The woman smiled.

He stared, at her, smiling at him. The wonderful scent from before was more prominent now. It was her scent. He could not remember a perfume fragrance that smelled so smooth. Large, expressive, brown eyes, encased in cocoa brown skin looked back at him. There was no makeup, yet her skin looked flawless as she leaned over tucking him back into bed. It felt like Sally taking care of him when he was young. The woman looked nothing like his mother, it was just the way she covered him with such care. No, this woman was not his mother for his body was having a reaction to her touch. He basked in the comfort she was providing as he wondered who was this woman with thick kissable lips. Those lips reminded him of another pair of lips that were also kissable. He frowned.

Roc noticed the change in his demeanor the moment the frown appeared. Having no idea what was going through his mind, she continued. "Are you in pain?"

"No," he replied even with pain ripping through his back. Never let the enemy know your weakness.

"Okay." The woman stepped back then stared down at him. "We appear to be in a bit of trouble with our government." She raised an eyebrow. "You have any idea why?"

"Who are you?"

"Roc."

He was about to turn away when the answer registered. Recognition hit him immediately. He turned back and stared at her. "Recovery Operative Commander?"

"I see your brain is intact." She smiled.

"But, you're a woman."

"As is half of the world's population. Is there a point."

Agitated, he attempted again to sit up. "They sent you to get me? A woman?"

"You have a problem with women?"

"I have a mother and six sisters. No, I don't have a problem with women. I have a problem with you. Get Ned on the phone."

Calmly filling the needle to give him another dose of pain medication, Roc smiled down at the man, who seemed agitated by her presence now. "How can you have a problem with me? You don't know me."

"I know enough about you. Get Ned or get Sally and I'll contact Ned myself."

Roc was stunned by the bitterness of the man's reaction. Oh, she had been up against men before, questioning her abilities when she was named Captain of the recovery team. It was rare she was held in such contempt, once she had rescued them. "Don't know who Sally is but Ned went dark about twenty hours ago."

The statement captured his attention and he stopped struggling to get up. "Ned went dark?"

She nodded then bent to give him a shot. "He did. Right after I reported on your location."

Absolute sat up then. "Don't put me under." He lay back down then exhaled, willing his mind to take over the pain. He reached around. "Where are my clothes?"

"If you don't want me to put you under, sit still."

He stilled then watched as she walked over to the dresser. Approximately five-six, Absolute estimated. Nice breasts, small waist, and round hips. Thirty-six, twenty-four, thirty-six: yes, nice. He closed his eyes to the thoughts going through his mind. He was not going down that road again.

Roc pulled a plastic bag from the dresser. "This is what you were wearing when I found you in the cabin."

Absolute took the bag, opened it and pulled his suit blazer out. Reaching inside he pulled out the letter from the inside pocket. He sat back relieved. "I need to speak to the President."

"I'm not sure that's a good idea."

"Why not?"

"The reason you are here, in a safe house, instead of in your home is because US forces attempted to shoot us out of the air, twice."

"What happened?"

"I retaliated."

"You took out a United States aircraft?"

She shrugged. "They shot at us, what was I supposed to do, welcome them to my bed?"

The thought of this woman taking out a military aircraft almost made him smile. But then reality set in. the United States of America, the country he had put his life on the line for many times over the last fifteen years, was attempting to kill him. Hadn't they taken enough from him?

"Where am I?"

"Atlanta."

"Georgia?"

"Is there another Atlanta?" she asked raising an eyebrow.

He threw the covers aside again, sat on the side of the bed, but did not attempt to stand. "I need to get to Virginia. Get me a secure line."

"No can do until I know why our government is trying to kill you."

"It's not our government." He shook his head, "At least not the loyal members of our government."

"The government is the government. There is the United States military, which in someway you and I are a part of. There's the good guys and the bad guys. Which are you?"

He stared at the woman. "You are ROC, you trained under Sly Dawson the same as I. What do you think I am?"

"That's the only reason you are still alive. Sly vouched for you. Like him, we have no idea what you have been involved in for the last three years. You've gone rogue. How do we know you haven't been compromised?"

Did she just question his loyalty to the United States? Who in the hell was she to question his loyalty to his country?

The expression on his face was easy to read. "I realize, even injured, you are a dangerous man. But don't let the little body fool you. Jump, and I will take you out. Now I ask again. Why is the United States military trying to kill you?"

She stood just out of reach, as any sensibly trained agent would. Her stance indicated she could react to any action on his part, quickly and decisively. She wasn't young, like Monique. There was a maturity about her. But damn if she wasn't pretty. "Sly trained you?"

Roc nodded. "He did. So you know it's not going to be easy for you to take me down. Notice I said down, not out." She looked him up and down, "In your current state, it wouldn't even be a fight."

"Hmm, cocky are we?"

"Is there any other way under Sly?"

Absolute grinned, then shook his head. "No," he exhaled. "I need to make that call."

"No." She was adamant. "I don't want anyone to know you are alive or where you are until I'm clear on who is the enemy."

He attempted to stand, but did not quite make it. "This is a matter of National Security," Absolute stated as he began to feel himself sway.

"What's in the letter?"

Absolute looked at the letter then back at her. "The President's eyes only."

"Then you have a problem. Until you prove to me it's not President Harrison who ordered that transport to fire at us, we are not contacting him. Think of someone else."

Absolute understood where she was coming from. He would demand the same thing if he were in her shoes. But she didn't know JD Harrison, he did. However, whoever tried to take them out was still looking for him. That he was sure of. What he was not certain about was, whether the VP's office or the VP himself was involved in this situation which to him, fell into the area of treason against the United States. Like she said, he could not swear the President did not send Gary to sell the weapons in the first place. We have been known to supply the enemy with weapons before. It just did not seem like something the JD, he knew, would do. But he had to be certain.

"Fair enough. Contact Samuel Lassiter."

She hesitated. "Hurricane?"

"Yes, you know him?"

Roc pulled out her handheld as she nodded. "About as well as a wife would know a husband."

The statement made Absolute frown. He watched as the woman dialed a number. "You'll need a code to speak with him."

"It took you long enough to answer," the woman said with a warm smile as she listened to the reply. "Goldie locks?"

How did she know the code, Absolute wondered. "Is that Samuel? Let me speak with him."

The woman ignored him as she listened to a reply then she disconnected the call.

"He'll be here in about an hour." Roc walked over. "I'm putting you back into bed. I realize you were gathering your strength while we were talking. But believe this. I will take you down, shoot you up with drugs and you will be out before your head hits the pillow."

"You're a bad bitch if you think you can do all of that."

"I am bad, what I'm not is anyone's bitch." She gathered his legs and placed them back into the bed. "You rest for that hour."

He allowed her to have her way, this time, for she was right. He needed to gather his strength. She reached for the letter and he grabbed her wrist. "This stays with me." He released her then placed the letter under his pillow. Her shoulder length hair, splayed across his face from the closeness. It was as smooth as silk. Akande crossed his mind. Her hair wasn't processed, but it was as soft as cotton. He shook the thought away. "How do you know Samuel?"

"We work together," she replied as she stood.

"How do you know Hurricane?"

Not trusting her with more information than she needed he replied, "We work together from time to time."

"It seems we've found our first common ground. We both trust Hurricane."

Roc sat at her kitchen table with a glass of wine. The national news was on the television, but her mind was on the man downstairs. There was something familiar about him, but she knew for a fact she had never worked with the operative known as Absolute before. And why did he become angry at the thought of her being a woman? What was that all about? She kicked her shoes off and put them in the chair next to her. The truth was her body reacted to him.

When she undressed him in the cabin, her mind was focused on finding his injuries. She was strictly in medical mode. Washing his body down, once she was home, was an entirely different matter. The man had the body of a warrior, in every sense of the word. Muscles ripped his arms, his abs, and good lord, the thighs. The man had powerful legs. As tough as she was, there was no way she could ignore the sexual member of his body. Even in the limp status it was long, thick and tempting.

She released the air building up in her. It had been a long time since she had been with anyone. It was by choice, but maybe that was the reason this man was affecting her. There was something about him that reminded her of someone else. She just couldn't put her finger on what. Shaking the thought from her mind, Roc began to think of the situation they were now in. Secretary Davenport was her contact in Washington. It was because of her relationship with him that she took this assignment in the first place. She had resigned from the agency five years ago because she wanted to settle down, get married, and have babies. The things normal women did. Roc, however, was anything, but normal. She was raised in foster care and learned early how to take care of herself. During high school she joined the ROTC and found it was a way to pay for college. She received an ROTC scholarship, which allowed her to get a degree in nursing. She excelled in the program, served her base eight-year stint in the Army, which gave her time to attend medical school. Choosing research over clinical she received a doctorate in medical research. She was able to apply those skills when recruited by the CIA to handle the recovery of injured agents. That led to her being trained by Sly Dawson on how to bring agents home safely. Her brains and beauty allowed her to infiltrate areas and situations that men could not. It only took her a few years to demonstrate that her ability to supply medical assistance and recovery skills, was superior to others. She was named Captain of the recovery unit, gaining the name of Roc along the way.

Roc never revealed her real identity to anyone, nor did she ever let her close associates or her one true friend know what she did for a living. They all believed she was a professor at one of the colleges in the area. However, those in the agency or connected with the agency knew and admired her. They were all stunned when she stepped away from the agency at such a young age. At thirty, Roc wanted a chance at having a family. At thirty-five, she had only met one man she would consider doing that with. Unfortunately, that man was someone she did missions with therefore making him unattainable at the time. Now, that same man was happily married with children. Leaving her to search the world for the man to father her children. No takers so far.

Roc reached over to pick up the remote when she saw an image of President Harrison on the screen. Now, that's a fine specimen of a man and of course he was taken. She pushed the volume on the remote to hear what was being said.

Something was amiss in Washington. The broadcast was showing President Harrison being bombarded with questions surrounding Attorney General Roberts. According to the reports, Attorney General Gavin Roberts was being accused of misrepresenting information regarding weapons found on U.S. soil. Attorney General Roberts claimed to have no knowledge of the weapons, however, documentation showed a trail leading to the Attorney General's office.

"President Harrison, are you protecting your friend Attorney General Roberts from prosecution?"

"President Harrison, were the weapons found in Texas a part of a shipment sold to our enemies, by our government?"

"President Harrison, did our own weapons bring down one of our aircraft killing several military personnel?"

The President stopped then turned to the group of reporters who were shouting out questions to him. "The information is coming in on the weapons found in Texas. I would caution all, including the Republican delegation, on the course of action taken until we know all the facts. I am curious as to how the delegation can be calling for hearings on the Attorney General's actions, when the information was only received less than an hour ago. We live in a democracy which gives everyone the right to a free trial when accused. Nothing I have seen thus far points to any wrongdoing by the Attorney General or anyone from his office. More will come from my office once all the facts have been determined."

The President turned to walk away, when another reporter yelled out, "Mr. President, wasn't Roberts the Attorney General of Virginia when then Police Chief Wilbert Munford was gunned down in his home? At one time you suspected Roberts in that deal. Did you not, Mr. President?"

It was clear the question rattled the President. However, his response showed no indication. "Until all the facts are reviewed, Attorney General Roberts has my full support." He turned and walked into the entrance of the White House.

"Only a hand full of people know the facts of the deal," a voice said from behind her.

Roc smiled as she sat her glass on the table, and pulled her legs from the chair they were in. She turned and smiled at the six-six, two hundred-twenty pound

Samuel Lassiter as he leisurely leaned against the doorframe of her kitchen door. "Hurricane, you are a sight for sore eyes."

He walked towards her with a swagger not matched by many and his arms opened. Roc walked right into them as if it was the most natural thing in the world. He gently kissed her lips. "You look good enough to eat."

She leaned back looking up at him. "You sound surprised."

"You called me out of the blue. It's been what, ten years? I know how reckless you used to be. I figured I'd find you tied up with gasoline poured around you and a man with a match about to send you to the depths of hell."

She stepped back and grinned. "Does that sound like something I would get involved in?"

Samuel folded his arms across his chest. "No, you're right. That sounds a little too calm for you."

The two smiled at the memory of him saving her from the situation and a few others better left in the past. "How's the wife and girls?"

Samuel's face lit up. "Beautiful and happy."

"The family life suits you." Roc smiled. "You look good."

"What about you, Roc? Anyone special yet?"

"No." She put her hands on her hips and looked down at his feet. "They would have big shoes to fill."

Samuel tilted his head. "Roc, you know my rule. I never cross the line with anyone I work with. Doesn't mean I wasn't tempted once or twice."

Roc smiled. "That's a good thing for a girl to know Samuel." She waved him off. "I got past your rejection when I was twenty-five. I called you for another reason." She frowned. "Now that I think about it, this operative reminds me of you a little. Not quite as handsome, with all the hair on his face. But, now that I think about it, there is something about him that resembles that quiet strength of yours."

"Operative? What's his name?"

"Absolute."

Samuel tensed and grabbed her. "Where is he?"

Stunned, she pulled away. "In one of the recovery rooms."

Samuel anxiously turned and hit the button on the keypad next to the refrigerator. The wall in the hallway opened and Samuel quickly descended the staircase that came into view.

"Samuel," Roc called out as she hit the button on the panel inside the opening to close it behind them. She followed him down to the recovery room located in her basement, which was not detectable to the normal eye.

"Joshua?" Samuel called out as he pushed open several doors.

"He's in number 3," Roc called out as she ran to catch up with him.

"Joshua," Samuel exhaled when he reached the open door. He stopped at the sight of his brother on the bed, then ran into the room and grabbed Joshua by the shoulders. "Joshua."

"Hey, hey, careful, Sammy. That hurts like hell."

"Joshua." Samuel was so overjoyed he couldn't say anything else. It had been three years since he'd seen his little brother. Oh, he had seen him on monitors when he was handling a mission, but not in person to touch him. JD told him of Joshua's situation and the steps they were taking to get him home, but he wasn't given any details.

He looked over at Roc who walked into the room behind him and watched. "This is my brother." He walked over to Roc, hugged her, picking her up off the floor, kissed her then sat her back down. "You brought my brother home." He went back to Joshua, towering over him. In a demanding voice he said, "Call your mother right now." He pulled out a cell phone.

"She's giving you hell, huh?" Joshua grinned.

Samuel looked down at him. "You may wish you were dead once she gets a hold of you."

"Samuel." Roc walked over to him then took the telephone. "You can't do that."

Samuel grabbed at the phone. "Oh hell, yes we can."

Roc stepped away. "No, we can't."

Anger flared through Samuel as he reached to take the phone, but quickly found himself on the floor with Roc's heel at his throat.

"Whoa," Joshua yelled as he looked up at Roc, then back down to Samuel on the floor.

"Listen to me, Samuel."

Samuel looked up at Roc. The fact that she took him down was no surprise, he knew her skills, for his life had depended on them a time or two. The reason for it was what confused him. "What in the hell is going on, Roc?"

Roc stepped back, extended her hand, then pulled Samuel up. "The US government is trying to take him out. They take him, they take me and now you. You have a wife and children. I plan to have a boatload of children myself one day. I have to live to accomplish that."

Joshua began to laugh, then grabbed his side. "Oh man, that hurts."

"Then stop laughing." Samuel scowled.

"Man, I've never seen you taken down like that," he continued to laugh.

"One of you better start talking," Samuel growled.

Chapter Seven
Atlanta, GA

Roc led up a chair for Samuel to take a seat. She then pulled another for herself as the two sat next to Absolute, whose actual name, she now knew, is Joshua Lassiter, Samuel's little brother. This world was too freaking small.

Joshua sat up as much as he could. The fact that Samuel was in the same room as he gave him the strength he needed to begin the healing process. He hated the thought of being at the mercy of someone he did not know, even if she was sent by the White House. He was now comforted knowing, if anything were to happen, Samuel had his back.

"Jonas Gary."

Samuel stared at Joshua, as he repeated the name. "Gary, police Chief Munford case?"

Joshua nodded. "The weapons were being brought in by Gary and controlled by Munford, back when JD was Attorney General."

"I remember." Samuel nodded. Gavin was Governor.

"I ran into him in Mexico in the middle of an arms deal." Joshua sat up. "When they completed the deal, I decided to take a look around their warehouse. Sammy, there was an arsenal that made me blush. All assault weapons, even launchers. There was no way I could let those weapons come into the United States."

"How do you know they were destined for here?"

"Gary indicated the weapons were for an operation in the U.S. You know I couldn't let that stand," Joshua said as he tried to sit up. Roc started towards him. Samuel stopped her by gently grabbing her hand. Joshua noted the movement, then continued. "I decided to search the office." He gave up trying to sit up in the bed, frustration clear on his face. "When I searched the office there were pictures of Gary with Admiral McGary and the VP mounted on the wall. Those men are advisors to POTUS. We know JD, he trusts people he shouldn't. Sometimes it works out, then there are times like this." He shook his head. "I know he would never be associated with Gary." He reached under his pillow. "I also found this." He handed the letter to Samuel.

Samuel read the letter. "This is a pardon for any actions taken against the United States." Samuel looked up startled. "Why would Gary need a pardon?"

Joshua shook his head. "That's the question we need to ask POTUS."

"Whatever it's for, someone in our government does not want interference," Roc stated as Samuel passed the letter to her. Joshua saw the action and frowned. "I'll have it authenticated." She stood to leave, but stopped when Joshua spoke.

"That doesn't leave my sight."

Samuel looked from Joshua to Roc. "It's safe in Roc's hands."

"It may be for you, it's not for me. I don't know her."

"I do." Samuel nodded to Roc for her to continue.

Roc hesitated, then gave the letter back to Joshua. She understood his concern. "I'll bring the equipment in here. You two talk." She left to gather the equipment.

Samuel turned to Joshua. "We have a problem here?"

"You know her?"

"Very well."

"I don't," Joshua exclaimed. "That's a problem."

"She brought you home Joshua. I'm willing to bet she saved your life a time or two in the process."

"Until I know what in the hell is going on, this stays with me." He put the letter back under the pillow.

Samuel studied his brother. He looked terrible. His hair was in an uncombed Afro. Facial hair covered his once handsome features and he was pale, which was saying something, for his brother was a dark chocolate brother who wore nothing but suits, stayed clean-shaven and never had a hair out of place. The decisions of the last President had taken a toll on him. As close as they were, even Samuel had not been able to penetrate Joshua's shield after the Akande situation. Since that time, Joshua would kill on a whim. He even blew up an island on U.S. soil, with good reason, but still. He knew Joshua better than any person on this earth with the exception of their mother, Sally. He was hurting, physically and mentally. At the moment his pride was at stake. For now, he would let Joshua have his way. Samuel sat back in his chair after assessing his brother. "You look like crap."

"I feel like crap. I need to get to the Cave."

"Roc is not going to let you out of her sight until she knows you can take care of yourself."

"I don't give a damn about Roc or whoever she is. I need to find out why there was a stockpile of weapons headed to the United States. And where in the hell is Ned and Monique?"

"I don't know what's happening with Ned. Monique is in Ashmere. What do you mean by was?" Samuel raised an eyebrow.

Joshua grinned. "BOOM! Took them out. "

"Then what happened in Texas?"

Joshua shook his head. "What are you talking about?"

"The President was on the air when I arrived. Something about weapons being found in Texas that have a connection to the Attorney General."

"Gavin Roberts?"

"The one and only," Samuel replied with a snicker.

"I don't know who gives the man the hardest time, you or Brian Thompson." Joshua sat up. "I destroyed a warehouse full of weapons. Could there have been more?"

Roc walked back in the room with a computer. She placed it on the dresser, then picked up the remote control. "You better take a look at this."

They all looked up at the monitor on the wall, as the news reporter spoke.

"In breaking news, the Republican Senate has called an emergency session regarding the weapons found in Texas earlier today. According to the leadership, indictments will be issued ordering the Attorney General and members of his staff to appear to answer questions regarding the weapons found and the death of military personnel. According to sources, the indictments could go as far up as the White House, including the Oval Office."

Joshua looked at Samuel. "They're going after JD's administration. Think about it. Who is the next in line if JD goes down?"

"How would going after Roberts impact the President?" Roc asked. "At the most, it may be an embarrassment on the administration, but it shouldn't take down the Presidency."

"JD is not going to allow them to take Gavin down." Joshua sat up groaning. "He is going to stand by him to the end. That's just the way the man operates. If JD does that, the Senate is going to try to indict him. What would that do for his Presidency?"

Samuel looked at Joshua. "You think that letter from the VP may be the evidence needed to stop this from snowballing into a conspiracy?"

"It's hard to say Sammy. First we need to determine if there is a conspiracy." Joshua pushed the cover aside. "Is Roberts involved in any way, is the next question."

Samuel rubbed his hands over his face. "It wouldn't be the first time he dabbled on the wrong side of the law."

Joshua gingerly stood. "I think your judgment may be a little tainted because of your wife's involvement with the man." He looked at Roc. "I need my clothes."

"Exactly where do you think you are going?" she huffed.

"Home."

"In twenty-four hours."

"No, now. My President needs me."

Laredo, TX

In a bunker near the Texas-Mexico border another meeting was taking place.

"Any word on Lassiter?"

"None, since the chopper was shot down."

Admiral McGary slammed his fist against the wall. "Find him and kill him. The chopper did not just disappear. Get the FAA involved if you have to. Tell them it's a matter of National Security. Look at all the footage. Find out who was piloting that chopper and bring them to me. I am not going to be the one left holding the bag on this operation."

Jonas was in a back room leaning against the wall as McGary gave orders to his men. He waited until all of them were gone before he made an appearance. "Years ago, there was a man as desperate as you who wanted to take Harrison down. He was unsuccessful. You haven't shown me anything to indicate the outcome to this is going to be any different."

"This plan is years in the making. We are going to bring him down, if not him, his administration," McGary stated with an air of confidence.

"Yeah, heard it before." Jonas stated. "Let me tell you what is not going to happen. If this goes wrong, I will not go down with you. You and the man pulling the strings will die before that happens. Keep that in mind as an incentive to find Lassiter."

"Don't you threaten me!"

"As Harrison would say, my word is bond." Jonas opened the door to leave then looked back at the Admiral. "Tick, tick, times a wasting." He laughed and left the building.

Inside his SUV, Jonas pulled out a secure cell phone. "Any word on your end regarding Lassiter?

"Nothing," the voice replied.

"Are you certain he has the document from the VP's office?"

"The safe was underground, and fireproof. When I pulled the box the pardon was gone. Yes, I'm sure he has it."

"That's not good for you, my man."

"Let your man know, I go down, he goes down too."

Arlington, VA

A cynical smile crossed David Holt's face. "I suggest you get a backup. Things are progressing as planned on this end. Check your national news." The call was disconnected. David turned to the woman next to him in bed, then smacked her on her naked behind. "It's time for you to talk to your husband."

Eleanor McClintock was a beauty. She represented the cream of the crop of grand ladies from Texas. As the wife of the Vice-President, she wielded a great amount of power and influence. Just not enough to satisfy her. Her husband had never been enough to satisfy her in bed, or in life as a whole. However, he was the Vice-President of the United States, in part from work she did lying on her back, or other positions. The woman was talented in many areas when it came to getting what she wanted from men in powerful positions. Early in their marriage, she used the bottle to get past the boredom of being married to Jerry McClintock. Then she turned to men, even his father, Senator Jeremiah McClintock, until he resigned from office after the scandal surrounding the assassination attempt on JD Harrison when he ran for President. That scandal led to the death of the Vice President Elect. As fate would have it, Harrison was a man who believed in uniting the country and had the misfortune of nominating her husband, Jerry McClintock to replace the Vice-President. For some reason, he thought having a Democrat and a Republican running the country would show the world that the two parties could work together. Her husband, as foolish as it may sound, agreed with the man. She, on the other hand, remained quiet through the process and bid her time to make a few adjustments to the plan. To Eleanor, in the whole scheme of things, the country would be better off once her plans came to fruition.

"What do you need him to say, darling?" she asked as she draped her creamy leg over David's thighs.

"A statement condemning the situation in Texas, while encouraging the people of the country to believe in President Harrison. Feed them the usual, 'I support the President' crap."

She kissed his neck. "You write up a statement. I'll see to it that he gets it and reads it verbatim." She climbed on top of him, pushing her long blonde hair away from her face. "Now, what are you going to do to feed me?"

David grinned, twisted his fist in her hair, pulling until she was flat on her back. "You like it rough, don't you?"

"You know I do. Give it to me hard and fast."

David did exactly what she asked and enjoyed inflicting as much pain as possible.

Washington, DC

"All hell seems to be breaking loose around us, Calvin," JD stated as he walked through the door of the Oval Office from the garden. "What do we have on the military craft shot down in Texas?"

Calvin walked into the office from his connecting door. James came in behind him, along with Secretary Davenport and General Ashton. "It was one of the carriers sent to assist with the rescue of Joshua Lassiter."

"What are you saying, Calvin? Joshua shot down one of our planes?" JD asked.

"We're not certain what occurred," Secretary Davenport explained.

"It's not the one we deployed, Sir," General Ashton stated. "When our plane arrived, the airstrip was vacant. No signs of Lassiter or Roc in the area. We checked extensively."

"Who deployed the other plane?"

"We don't know," the General replied. "We can confirm it was one of ours. The men on board were active duty military personnel."

"I will never believe Joshua shot down one of our planes." JD yelled. "Get recon on that airstrip. I want to see with my own eyes what took place."

"Yes, Sir," General Ashton saluted, then left the room.

"Talk to me Calvin, what in the hell is happening? How did Gavin's name get caught up in this?"

"It started with a reporter's speculations, and it has snowballed from there," Calvin replied.

"This is moving too fast. In less than twenty-four hours, not only does the public know it was a military aircraft that was shot down. They have connected it to weapons found in the area," James stated.

"Not just weapons, Mr. President, weapons of mass destruction on U.S. soil." Calvin, shook his head. "This seems like a well planned game of shoot the rabbit, with all of the weapons pointed at the White House."

"Where is Admiral McGary? Why isn't he on this?"

"Unavailable?"

"What the hell do you mean, unavailable?" James frowned.

"His office indicated he was unavailable, that's why Ashton was here."

"Find him now," JD demanded. "Calvin, I want to know who all the players are. Who contacted the media, who implicated Gavin and who initiated the talks on the Hill."

"You got it." Calvin walked out of the room.

"And get Gavin in here," an angry JD yelled.

James was about to follow when JD called him back. "James, hold back for a minute."

"Sure." He walked back and stopped in front of JD's desk. "What do you need?"

JD hesitated, then put his hands in his pockets and turned towards the window. He lowered his head in thought. "I didn't want to be the one to tell you this, but here it goes." He turned to face James. "David Holt is out of prison and in the area."

Anyone who did not know James Brooks, would have missed the vein pumping vigorously in the man's neck. Very little rattled the man. He handled difficult situations with the ease of a man confident in who he was and what his life was about. The only time the man had lost his cool was when David Holt attempted to rape his wife and JD's sister, Ashley. The cool, calm, reserved James Brooks disappeared and was replaced by a man with murder in the forefront of his mind.

"When was he released?" James asked in what appeared to be a question of mere curiosity, but JD knew better.

"I don't know. What I can tell you is that he is an advisor in Eleanor McClintock's office. I can also tell you he approached JC at school."

A surprised James stared at JD in disbelief. "Is JC okay?"

"Yes, Brian is handling things on my end."

"The VP's wife?" James asked as JD nodded. "Does she know that he is a felon? Why in the hell would they have a felon in their camp?"

"I have a better question," JD stated. "Why would they have a political advisor in their camp?"

James closed his eyes and shook his head. "JD, I hate to say this. But many people warned you against putting a Republican in the VP spot. You gave him the experience to run against you."

"I have not decided if I'm going to run again."

"You're kidding." James almost grinned. "You have more things you want to do for this country. You may not have told Tracy, but you are running again. If McClintock does not bring your administration down, first." James stopped and thought for a moment. "Could that be what he is trying to do? " James leaned against the desk. "Think about it JD. The Republicans have been calling you soft on defense. What better way to convince the public of that than an attack on American soil?"

JD shook his head. "As desperate as McClintock is to have this seat, not even he would stoop that low."

"Maybe not, but people around him certainly would."

JD stared at James for a long few moments. "Check into it, James. If McClintock's name comes up don't tell me, handle it."

"Will do, Mr. President." James started to walk out of the office.

"James." The man stopped and turned back to JD. "Stay away from Holt."

James did not acknowledge the statement. He simply walked out of the room.

Outside the Oval Office, James pulled out his cell and dialed a number. "Douglas, our mutual friend has surfaced here in D.C."

Vice-President Jerry McClintock was blessed and cursed with good genes. He's what one would look at as the all American boy. Tall, blonde, blue eyed, attractive son of an ex-US Senator, grandson to the now deceased, ex-Governor of Texas. To the world he was a blessed man, to Jerry he felt trapped.

Jerry's father and grandfather had been involved in a plot to kill the then newly elected President Harrison. During the attack the Vice-President Elect was killed. The President-Elect believed in Jerry despite the Democratic Party's objections. He selected Jerry as his new Vice-President. Members of the Republican Party believed Jerry should exploit that trust. Even his wife and father have attempted to influence his decision on crucial legislation which if not passed could hurt the Harrison administration. Jerry's thoughts were different. His loyalty was with the United States of America. He wanted the country to unite, just as Harrison intended when he gave him the opportunity to serve his country in a way few ever had. His performance during his term as Vice-President, would determine if he would get the opportunity to serve this country on an even higher level. There wasn't much anyone could say or do to convince him to jeopardize that.

"Mr. Vice-President, James Brooks, the President's advisor is here."

Jerry looked up from his desk. "Show him in," He rose extending his hand as James walked in. "Good Morning James. How the heck are you?"

The two men shook hands. "Good morning, Mr. Vice-President. I'm doing well. Yourself?"

"Doing well." Jerry pointed to the chairs in the corner of his office. "Have a seat. How may I help the President today?"

James took a seat. "A situation has come to our attention that you may be able to clear up for us."

"Of course," he replied with his southern drawl. "What do you need?"

"There is a political advisor in your camp. The President was wondering if it was your intention to run in the next election?"

Jerry laughed. "James we are politicians. We are always planning to run for election somewhere."

James smiled, nodding. "True." He sat up. "I'll be more direct. Do you plan to run for President in the next election?"

"We are only in the first half of this administration. I don't think anyone has made a decision regarding the next campaign. Has the President declared his intent?"

"No," James replied.

"Why is the President concerned at this point?"

"The political advisor I mentioned is someone we are very familiar with. He's a felon who was prosecuted by our Chief of Staff Johnson a few years back for the attempted rape of my wife. I'm certain you can see our concern with your involvement with this man on several levels."

"If I remember correctly..." Jerry sat up. "The President's brother-in-law is an ex-felon. Everyone deserves a chance to redeem himself, wouldn't you agree, James?"

"I do agree, Jerry," James smirked. "The President's brother-in-law does not work on his campaign and is not in the President's camp in anyway. However, the question is still on the table."

"You are certain he's in my camp?" he asked, concerned with the implication and the possible public backlash. "What's his name?"

"David Holt."

Jerry frowned thinking. He shook his head. "I don't recall anyone by that name, James."

"This man was with your wife when she visited the President's son's school on yesterday." James sat up. "I'm certain you can imagine the President's concern when this man approached his son. I don't have to remind you or your staff how protective the President is when it comes to his children. Especially, since this man has a past we are all familiar with."

Jerry stood, walked to the door. "Mary," he called out. "Would you give me a list of my wife's staff?"

A young blonde came to the doorway. "Yes, Sir," she replied.

"We should have an answer in a moment." He sat back down. "Why did this man approach the child?"

"We are attempting to determine that now."

"Mr. Vice-President."

"Yes, Mary."

"Here's the list."

Jerry nodded. "Thank you Mary." He turned to James once the woman was gone. "He is listed as a volunteer. He is not a paid staffer. I'll place a call to my wife regarding him."

"No." James stood. "We will handle this. Jerry I would be remiss not to mention that you never answered the question about running for President." Jerry started to speak, but James put up his hand to stop him. "You are an ambitious man. JD is not. He just," James shrugged his shoulder, "is. It doesn't take effort for him. It's the one thing I admire about him. There's one more trait he has I wish I possessed. It's his uncanny ability to trust and believe in people. He expects the best of people." He glared at Jerry. "I on the other hand, don't. I anticipate and plan accordingly. Have a good day, Mr. Vice-President."

Jerry knew a dangerous man when he saw one. James Brooks was not a man to cross. He'd made it very clear, he was not happy. He was used to his wife getting caught up in things. This was one time he certainly hoped she knew what she was doing. James Brooks was not the kind of man you wanted as an enemy.

Ten minutes later James was in the foyer of the Second Lady of the United States' office. "Mr. Brooks." Eleanor extended her hand. "My, my, you are a handsome devil. We don't often get visits from White House Staff. May I offer you a cup of tea, coffee, or something a little stronger?"

"This isn't a social call, Mrs. McClintock."

"It isn't. Well, what other kind of call is there, darling," She touched her pearls as she spoke.

"Business," James replied. "David Holt is working in your office. I'd like to have a word with him."

"Whatever for?" she asked.

"Business," James replied.

"That's rather vague, Sir." She raised an eyebrow. "Would you care to be a little more specific?"

"No. Is he available?"

"That was rather brash, darling." She turned to the woman at the receptionist desk. "Would you ask David to step out here please?" She turned back to James. "Is this personal business or are you here on behalf of the President?"

"Mr. Holt stepped out," the receptionist said as she returned to her desk.

"Oh." Eleanor turned back to James and smiled. "Well, I could have sworn he was in. Would you care to leave a message for him?"

"No," James smirked. "I believe the message was received. You have a good day." James walked out of the office confident that David Holt received his message loud and clear.

Eleanor returned to her office to find David sitting at her desk. "Why do you suppose the President's Political Advisor is looking for you?"

David shrugged his shoulder. "Maybe he wants to hire me."

"That's funny. Darling. I have the distinct impression the man wants to kill you." She walked over to him. "Tell me you are not into anything that will prevent Jerry from becoming the next president."

Chapter Eight
Washington, D.C.

Attorney General Gavin Roberts and his wife, Carolyn, sat in the Roosevelt Room of the White House just a few doors from the Oval Office, livid. Well, Carolyn was, Gavin sat quietly while he watched his wife pace back and forth cursing the administration for even allowing this to happen. Gavin knew it for exactly what it was, a political ploy to disgrace JD's presidency. He was just as certain JD, or at the very least James and Calvin, were also aware. "Carolyn, calm down," he suggested. He knew trying to tell his wife to do anything would set her off. Today, he had too many pressing issues to deal with.

"I will not calm down, when they are disgracing your name and mine right along with it. I should call Daddy. He knows how to handle those idiots on the Hill."

Gavin smiled. "Darling, we are a part of those idiots."

Carolyn, with her stylish A-line dress, heels and pearls, turned toward him with her hands on her hips. "This is not a funny situation, Gavin. They are trying to remove you from office."

"No, they are not. They are trying to remove all of us from office. Which is what the opposing party is supposed to do."

"Not by telling lies."

Gavin took her hand, and pulled her to sit beside him. "Let's be very clear. So far, they have not told a lie, Carolyn."

"But the implication, Gavin, could ruin you."

"You sound genuinely concerned." He smiled.

She sat back and frowned, "Of course I'm concerned. Whatever affects you touches me."

Gavin smiled and kissed her. "Now, that sounds like the Carolyn I love."

She smiled, then began to straighten his tie. "Stop trying to make me feel better."

"Listen, there was a time when you wanted to be the First Lady next to JD. It's good to know I have your full support now."

"That was a long time ago. Now, I will fight him tooth and nail if he doesn't defend you from this ridiculous plot."

The door opened. "Gavin." Calvin extended his hand. "Good to see you. Sorry it's under these circumstances." He then turned to Carolyn. "Carolyn, you look angry." He smiled.

"I am angry, Calvin, and I'm going to let JD know that."

"I'm sure you will, however, that will have to wait. He wants to see Gavin alone."

"What? No, I'm going in with you," she snarled.

Calvin tilted his head towards the door. "I think that agent there would beg to differ." He turned to Gavin. "Shall we go?"

Gavin kissed Carolyn on the cheek. "Stay put," he warned. "I don't want to have to bail you out tonight."

"I'm calling Tracy," she said more to Calvin, than Gavin.

"You do that." Calvin smiled and closed the door behind him.

"Gavin, this isn't going to be pretty. He's pissed."

"With good reason," Gavin replied as Calvin opened the door to the Oval Office. "Mr. President." Gavin stepped inside and extended his hand to JD who was sitting behind the desk.

JD stood, walked around to the front and shook Gavin's hand. "Gavin, have a seat." JD sat in the lone chair at the top of the oval carpet while Calvin sat to his left on a sofa, facing another where Gavin sat. "Who knew the facts in the Munford case and how deeply involved were you with him at that time?"

"I was as much of an enemy to Munford then, as you were. Unfortunately, during the time you investigated that case, I was included in that investigation. That's what the reporter has."

"How does that connect to the weapons in Texas?" Calvin asked.

"I have no idea. I can tell you, I have nothing to do with what's going on in Texas."

JD sat forward. "We know that, Gavin. And know you have my support on this. However, I can't help but feel as if we are missing something. There is something to connect the two events." He looked to Calvin. "All three of us were involved in the Munford case. I figure if the three of us talk it through we may figure out what the House Republicans think they have. Calvin, you were the lead investigator. What do you remember about the case?"

A knock sounded at the door. "Mr. President," Mrs. Langston, his secretary, spoke from the doorway. "Mr. Thompson is here to see you."

"Please send him in."

Gavin, Calvin and JD stood to greet Brian.

Brian shook each hand, with the exception of Gavin's. He simply nodded. "Gavin."

He unbuttoned his suit jacket and sat next to Calvin. "What are we talking about?"

"The Munford case," Calvin replied. Pain raced across Brian's face, then disappeared just as quickly.

JD knew that was a painful memory for Brian. He was shot four times in the back, trying to rescue JC from Munford's attack. "A reporter asked a question about that case, specifically, about our suspicions of Gavin, at the time."

"How would a reporter know about that?" Brian asked. "It wasn't public knowledge. Although I've always had my doubts." He glanced at Gavin with a raised eyebrow.

"That's the question," Calvin stated. "Who had access to that information?"

"Who was involved in the investigation?" Gavin glared towards Brian.

"You're still alive. Clearly, it wasn't me," Brian replied sitting forward and glaring directly at Gavin.

"Okay," JD cut in, knowing there was no love lost between the two men. "Calvin, how many people were in the room during the investigation?"

"Rossie and myself were the only two who handled anything connected with Gavin." I spoke with Rossie earlier today. None of his files have been touched. He checked them himself."

"If it was no one from the inside," Gavin spoke, "who else would have knowledge of the situation?"

"What about the people working with Munford?" Calvin asked. "There was another man involved."

JD sat forward as he remembered the night Munford was killed. He was there, in Munford's home, pointing a gun at the man, wanting desperately to kill him for having Brian shot. Samuel and Joshua Lassiter were there too. Joshua was talking him out of pulling the trigger when shots rained through the window. "Jonas Gary," JD and Calvin said the name at the same time.

"He got away," Calvin said.

"Where is he now?" Brian asked.

"We never found him. It wouldn't have mattered if we did, we had no evidence against him."

"How would he know about the investigation on me?" Gavin asked. "He wasn't a part of your office," he said to Calvin. "Therefore he wouldn't have been privy to that information."

"He's right." Calvin shook his head. "Only Rossie and myself knew all the details. Most of which we never even shared with you, JD."

"Did you talk with Jackie about the case?" Brian asked then looked at JD. "Or did you talk to Tracy?" He then looked at Gavin, "Or Carolyn?"

"No, I never took the office home to Jackie," Calvin replied.

"I would never put Tracy in danger that way," JD said. "Now, I talk to her about everything."

They all turned to Gavin. "If I remember correctly, things were very interesting between you and Carolyn back then." Brian raised an eyebrow. "Is it possible you talked to her and she may have shared the information with one of her bed partners?"

Gavin, now angry over the insult Brian had just slung at his wife, stood. "I will not dignify that with a response." He turned to JD who had stood. "Let me know when you find the leak. You can reach me in the office or at home with my wife." He emphasized the word wife as he looked at Brian. He shook JD's hand. "Mr. President, Calvin." He nodded to Brian, then left the room.

JD and Calvin just stared at Brian.

"What?"

"Why did you go there?"

"We all know how Carolyn was back then and so does he. She was sleeping with anything and everything that had a stick, including," he looked at JD, "David Holt."

"David Holt," Calvin questioned. "What does he have to do with this?"

JD walked back around to his desk as he answered. "He approached JC at school."

"I thought he was in jail. Hell, I put him there myself."

"He's out," Brian replied as he pulled out his electronic pad. "According to our records, he was released on probation two months ago."

"Does James know?" Calvin asked.

JD nodded. "I advised him to stay away from the man."

"Did you give that same advice to Douglas?" Brian smirked.

"No." JD looked up at Brian concerned. "Give him a heads up. And keep Holt away from my son."

David stood on the side of the basketball court as he watched young boys shooting hoops. They looked pretty good. One or two looked like they had some skills. However, he wasn't interested in the basketball game. No, he was there to see one person, to render payback to the whole damn lot of them. He looked around trying to pick out the Secret Service agents he knew were there. The last thing he needed was to have a run in with one at this point in the game. No, his mission was a simple one today, get into the mind of JC Harrison, the President's son. He knew he had gotten to him at the school. He wondered if he told his father or better yet, his mother, about their little chat. Yep, the kid was their weakness. First born to the Harrison's was his target. Because of James Brooks' visit, Eleanor had become a little skittish. The boy was going to be his contingency plan if things did not go as anticipated with McClintock.

David continued to survey the area, looking from one person to the next. He nodded knowingly, each time he recognized an agent. Branding his mind with their images. As he continued to survey the area, he noticed there were a number of agents around. He wondered why so many? The child of a President would have two maybe three agents on him. So far he had recognized at least five agents.

"Excuse me," a young girl's voice rang out. "You're blocking our view."

David turned and almost jumped out of his skin. A slim young girl, who looked to be the spitting image of someone he knew, stood behind him.

"We are watching the game and you are standing in front of the guys."

David smiled and bowed slightly. "My apologies ladies." He all but licked his lips at his good fortune. "Who might you be?"

Jasmine blushed at the handsome man with the dimples. "I'm Jazzy, this is my cousin, Jada."

"You know we are not supposed to talk to strangers, Jazzy," Jada warned.

David nodded. "She's right." He put his hands in his pockets to keep from rubbing them together. He could not believe his good luck. "I'm not really a stranger. I know your parents...all of them, I think. Let me see." he pointed to Jasmine. "You must be

Tracy's daughter." Then he looked at Jada and smiled, trying hard not to over play his hand by allowing his mouth to water. "You can only be Ashley's daughter." He managed not to smirk.

"If you know our parents, why did you ask who we were?" Jazzy asked.

"You're as smart as you are pretty."

Jazzy blushed again. "Thank you. I know."

"Let's go Jazzy." Jada pulled at her cousin's arm. "We can sit on the other bench."

"Jazzy," JC called from the court. He threw the ball to his friend then walked swiftly towards where the girls stood.

David watched as several agents attempted to detain JC, while others approached him. Two agents,gathered the girls behind them.

"Just talking, gentlemen," David held his hands up. "Just talking."

"Jazzy and Jada, go to the car, now."

"I don't want to go to the car," Jazzy pouted.

JC looked up at two of the agents. "Take them to the car, now."

"What's going on, JC?" His friends from the court started towards him.

"Nothing, I'm good. I'll be back in a minute. Calvin, you take the ball out." The boys hesitated to make sure their friend was okay, then most of them turned back to the game. The one named Elliott stood behind JC and watched.

JC looked up at the remaining two agents. "Will you give me a minute, please?" The agents stepped away, but kept their eyes on him.

JC took a step closer to David. They were matched in height, though David had a little more weight on him. "I don't know your game, Mr. Holt.

What I do know is you are going to stay away from my sister."

"But she is so cute," David smirked.

"You're an adult, she's eleven years old. Come near her again, and you will have me to deal with."

"You're just like your father," David laughed.

"In some ways. In others I take more after my Uncle Al Day. You know the name."

David knew the name and the reputation. "We shall meet again, young Mr. Harrison." David turned, whistling as he walked away. "Have a good day gentlemen." He saluted as he walked by the agents.

"What was that about?" Elliott asked JC.

JC never took his eyes off the man until he was in his car. "Nothing, just an old friend of my parents." Which was what his father had told him, in addition to stay away from him.

"He didn't look like a friend."

JC laughed at Elliott. "You are just like Uncle Brian, always looking for a fight."

"Yeah, and you are just like your dad, not taking people as a threat. You shouldn't have even been talking to that man."

JC looked over his shoulder to the vehicle David now sat in. "No, he needs to know I'm not afraid of him."

"Are you going to tell your parents about him?"

"No. They have enough to deal with."

Elliott watched his friend walk back to the court. He looked over at the vehicle the man was in. Elliott pulled out his phone and sent a text message with the license plate number to his father.

A new plan began to formulate in David's mind as he walked away. At first he only planned to mess with JC's mind a little. Tell him the truth about his mother. Since James Brooks invaded his territory, his game plan had to be altered. Why not have a little fun at his expense? Tracy and Ashley's daughters would put the icing on the cake. He snickered to himself. *Yes, this new plan is going to be bittersweet.* The one-two punch, was coming. Payback for Ashley accusing him of rape when he was in college, and messing up his professional football career, and last but not least, for that damn meddling, Tracy. As for James Brooks, well, after spending the last ten years of his life in prison this was the perfect way, to make them all pay.

David sat in his car, pulled up the Internet and began to do a little research into the database of the Secret Service department. There was a blog post that only agents had access to. It's amazing how small details could become dangerous. The inquiry revealed a bit of information regarding the Harrison children that David could definitely use. It seems that Jasmine, they called her Jazzy, *that's so cute* he thought, had a way of manipulating her Secret Service agents. To combat that problem, the Harrisons decided to switch off agents weekly. *Hmm, how convenient,* was his last thought as he pulled away.

Gavin waited until he and Carolyn were in the car before he spoke. "Interesting conversation took place in the Oval Office."

"All I want to know, is JD going to have your back?"

"I'm certain he will."

"Did he say that?"

"Yes, he did."

Carolyn exhaled. "That's good to hear. Now all we have to do is squash this hearing crap. I spoke with Tracy to ensure JD holds up his end."

Gavin watched out the window as the vehicle drove from the White House to his office. It was hard reliving those days when his wife couldn't keep her legs closed. She wasn't, technically, his wife at that time, but in his heart Carolyn Roth was his wife. He'd loved her from the first moment he saw her with JD Harrison. Looking back, damn if she wasn't right. She said that JD was going to be Governor of Virginia and probably President one day. And here we are, President Jeffrey Harrison. Back then he was jealous of JD. He had it all. The women, the politicians, even the people in the streets loved him. Most of all, he had Carolyn. Then Tracy came along. She was their savior, his and JD's. From the moment Tracy came on the scene, JD began to disregard Carolyn and that gave him a way in. He knew the only reason she was with him was because of his political ambitions. Carolyn wanted to be First Lady of Virginia. To have that she had to marry him, for JD was no longer an option. He knew her reasons and accepted them. He thought those days were behind him. He was wrong. Now he had to deal with another memory, David Holt.

"Carolyn."

"Yes, darling?"

"Did you ever discuss the Munford case with David Holt when you were sleeping with him?"

Chapter Nine
Atlanta, GA

The trip to Joshua's home in Quantico, Virginia did not go as smoothly as they all had hoped. Ned was still dark. That concerned everyone. However, they did not have the time to figure out what was happening with Ned. When he was able to contact them, he would. Which meant they had to use other means to acquire transportation without giving the government any indication of their location. Roc had personnel she'd used a time or two whenever she had to travel under the radar. Joshua did not feel comfortable with that.

"I don't trust people I don't know. I don't know you therefore your people are out."

"Understandable," Roc calmly replied to the illogical thinking of the man. If she or her people were the ones who wanted him dead, he would be dead. "The alternative would be we remain here until you are able to travel on your own."

"Are you deaf, woman? No," Joshua yelled. "I need to leave here, now."

His raised voice may have affected others, but Roc did not flinch. One of her most valuable assets was her ability to keep her cool.

Samuel was another story. "Joshua, we don't talk to women like that. Especially one, who by the looks of things, just saved your life. Where is my fun loving little brother?"

"He grew up, Sammy. Became a part of the real world."

"In the real world my brothers, all of them, were taught manners. We do not raise our voice at women. We treat women the same way we treat our mother. And I know damn well you would not raise your voice at her."

Joshua turned on Samuel. "Who are you, her keeper?"

"No, but I am your brother." Samuel took a step towards Joshua, "and will become your keeper if you don't settle down."

"Samuel," Roc stepped between them, touching his chest and looked up into his eyes. "It's okay. I can handle this. Why don't you go upstairs, prepare us a decent meal before we hit the road."

Samuel looked down at her. She always had a special way of looking at a man to get him to do whatever she wanted. Roc never raised her voice, or said a cruel word. She didn't have to. He nodded, stared at Joshua, then left the room.

Joshua watched the two then remembered her statement. *They knew each other as well as a wife knows a husband.* He smirked.

"I think your brother is very happy to see you alive. When was the last time you spoke to him?"

Joshua frowned at her. "Who are you now, the family counselor?"

Roc ignored his dig. She opened a dresser drawer and pulled out black sweat pants and a top. "I'll help you get dressed while we decide what's the best way to get you home." She walked over to the bed where he sat on the side. "Would you like something for the pain before I try to move you?"

"No. I don't want anything from you." He snatched the clothes from her hand. "I can dress myself."

Roc took one step back. She learned a long time ago, not to approach a wounded animal. Joshua was injured in more ways than physical, she could see that now. According to Samuel, they had a very close family. Why did it seem Joshua was on the outskirts of that? To help with the healing process, she needed to know. "You realize, your connections will be on a government watch list. Trying to use any of them could cause..." Joshua dropped his pajama pants to the floor revealing his naked body, stopping her mid-sentence, "-problems."

Joshua grinned at her reaction to his physical appearance. "Impressive, isn't it."

Roc looked up to his face. Despite the arrogant statement, she knew his knees were about to buckle. Her first instinct was to let it happen after that remark. However, the medic in her would not allow him to cause further injury to himself. She put her hand around his waist, and used the other to pick up the sweat pants. Try as she might, she could not ignore the part of his anatomy that was now lodged between her breasts. "Lean over my back," she said in the calmest voice she could manage.

"I can do this," he said with less conviction than before.

Roc never acknowledged his statement. She bent down low enough for him to raise a leg into the pants, and then the other. She pulled the pants up over his butt, covering his private parts. Unfortunately, her memory was very good. The sight of him would not be leaving her soon. She checked to ensure the bandage around his waist was tight, then sat him back on the bed. "Let's get your shirt on."

He reached to take the shirt, but she pulled it away. "We're going to put one arm in at a time." She placed one arm in, then the other and pulled the sweatshirt down over his head. She heard him grunt at the action. "It's going to be a minute before you can lift that arm. Let's get you a pair of shoes. What size are you?"

"Twelve," he stated as the pain throbbed in his back.

Men and their pride, Roc shook her head. "I'll be right back."

Joshua lay back on the bed. He couldn't understand why he was angry with her, but he was. The fact that they sent the woman he lost the commander slot to, ate away at him. The fact that his back hurt like hell, ate away at him and to make matters worse, Sammy was seeing him at his weakest. That ate away at him. He could take any other member of his family seeing him this way, but not Sammy.

Roc walked back into the room and knew he was in pain. She placed the shoes next to the bed, prepared a needle for him and did not ask if he needed something for pain. She cleaned an area on his arm, then inserted the needle into a vein. She walked to the door and turned out the light.

"Thank you." The deep somber voice of Joshua was barely above a whisper.

"You're welcome," she replied then walked out of the room.

Upstairs she secured the area and walked into the kitchen.

"Is he asleep?" Samuel asked from the stove where he was in his element. Cooking was one of his favorite pastimes.

"Probably." She picked up one of the pot tops from the stove and inhaled the scent, then smiled. "I gave him a heavy dose of morphine." She put the top back then picked up another. Samuel hit her with the wooden spoon in his hand. "Ouch."

"Stay out until I'm finished."

"Do you do that to your wife?"

"No, I don't have to. Cynthia is content to stay in her seat until I serve her dinner. Unlike you, who has no patience when it comes to food."

"Hey, I like to eat, what can I say," she replied as she sat at the table. "So, Absolute is your brother? Is covert operations the family business?"

Samuel smiled. "No. I joined the Seals and Joshua went CIA. My sister Pearl is Press Secretary to President Harrison. That's about where government service ends." He dipped a spoon in the pot of Alfredo sauce, blew on it and held it to her mouth. "Taste."

She did. "Mmm, you haven't lost your touch." She wiped her mouth as he turned back to the pot. "What's his story?"

"What do you mean?" Samuel asked as he placed chicken breasts in the oven.

"He's hurting. Not just from his wounds. There's something else." She watched as Samuel picked up the hand towel after washing his hands and turned to her. "You know, to help him heal properly I need to know all the facts." She tilted her head. "His behavior reminds me of you when I rescued you from Iraq. You were suffering from a lot more than your physical injuries. Is it the same for him?"

Samuel exhaled, placed the hand towel back on the rack. He reached into the refrigerator. "I see you've changed to Merlot." He pulled out a bottle of wine, then reached up to the wine rack and pulled down two glasses. He sat at the table, then poured a glass for her and one for himself. They saluted each other, savored the taste, then looked at each other. Samuel sat the glass on the table. "What happened to Joshua was worse. Are you familiar with the Emure-Asmere assignment?"

She nodded. "Somewhat. A few years ago there was a coup attempt to take over Asmere. The true Queen was found and married a Prince from the bordering country of Emure to secure the area."

Samuel nodded. "That's right. What the general public doesn't know is Joshua was the person who found the Queen of Asmere. They fell in love with each other before her true identity was discovered. If you remember, there was a bit of unrest happening in the region and the United States decided the solution to stabilizing that area was to unite Asmere and Emure. The woman Joshua fell in love with is now married to another man at the United States' urging. That happened about three years ago. This is the first time I've seen my brother in person since. We kept tabs on him when we could. But, as you know when an operative is on a case, his whereabouts are confidential. Joshua has taken every assignment that came his way and some other operatives would not have touched."

"Okay, he hates me because I'm a woman?"

"No, he hates you because you are Roc and he is not."

Roc frowned. "What?"

Samuel smiled. "You beat him out of the position."

"No." She grinned. "Really?"

"Yeah."

"Does he have a medical background?"

"No, but that didn't matter. Joshua is one of the best trackers in the United States arsenal of operatives. If you are alive, he can and will find you."

"Then what?" Roc asked. "He would not be able to administer any medical assistance when needed."

Samuel smiled. "You don't get it." He chuckled,."You never did. Men do not dislike you because you're a woman. They dislike you because you are a beautiful woman who is as capable, or more so, than they are. They feel inferior to you. What makes it worse is you have this nonchalant attitude about it. You really ought to be more sympathetic to a man's pride."

Roc stared at him for a long moment, then fell out laughing. "You are full of it, Samuel Lassiter."

Samuel laughed with her as he took a drink. "It really is good to see you Roc."

"You too Samuel." The two held each other's gaze, thinking about moments of life and death they'd shared. "I've thought about you a lot over the years. Going from man to man comparing each one of them to you." She shook her head. "Never found him."

"He's out there, Roc. Hell he better be. You gave up the agency for him."

Roc smiled. "Yeah. Well, any ideas how we are going to get your brother home?"

"Use your contacts."

"He's going to be upset."

"Yes, he will, but he will be home and safe. Therefore, I don't give a damn."

To get Joshua to the airport, Roc decided to contact Sly. Thinking since they were both mentored by Sly, he would be the best bet to keep the man happy. Wrong. They figured the airports would be on alert for anyone fitting Joshua's description. So they had to go private. Sly had access to a plane owned by a music executive. The first hurdle was getting Joshua to the plane without anyone spotting him.

After they had dinner and cleaned the kitchen, Roc picked up the bag she'd packed and was walking out of the door.

"Where are you going?" Joshua asked as his brother held him up next to the black SUV in her garage.

"With you."

"Like hell you are."

"Okay." Roc threw her bag into the back seat of the vehicle. "If you can stop me from getting into the car, I won't go."

Samuel laughed as Roc climbed into the third row of the vehicle, then patted the second row seat. "I left the comfortable one for you."

All Joshua could do was watch her, for he barely had the strength to stand up much less stop anyone from doing anything.

Samuel helped Joshua get in the backseat, then climbed into the driver's seat. He adjusted the rearview mirror and looked at his brother. "I suggest you cut your hair and shave before your mother sees you like that."

Roc sat up. "I can help you with that if you like."

"If I need your help, I'll ask for it." Joshua got as comfortable as he could in the seat.

The ride to the airport would take longer than normal. Samuel wanted to make sure they were not being followed. The radio was playing, *Guess Who I Saw Today*, a smooth jazzy number by Chanté Moore. Roc began singing. Samuel, who knew about her voice, smiled in the rearview mirror, settled in for the drive and the entertainment. Joshua listened to the smooth voice, surprised. That was the voice he heard when he was out of it. The sound soothed him then and was doing the same now. He closed his eyes and allowed her voice to play like a lullaby. He had almost fallen asleep when it angered him that her voice could sooth him to that point.

"Let the woman learn in silence with all subjection."
1Timothy, Chapter 2: Verse 11.

"Make a joyful noise to the Lord, all the earth! Serve the Lord with gladness! Come into his presence with singing!"
Psalm 100 Chapter 1 Verse 1 and 2.

She sang louder.
Joshua couldn't help it, he smiled. A woman in her line of work who could quote scripture. "Hmm." He closed his eyes and allowed her to sing him right into a peaceful sleep.
When they arrived at the airport, Samuel drove into the private hangar and waited for the doors to close. He helped Joshua up the steps of the plane, sat him on a sofa in what looked more like a living room, dining room combination, than the inside of a plane. He looked around taking in the decor. Across from the sofa, which was long enough to accommodate Joshua's six-four height and more, was tan leather seating for four more and a table with a place setting for four. Further down the aisle were additional seating areas and tables. The plane could easily carry twenty people without anyone sitting in the same area. The decor was impressive even to the three new occupants, who were no strangers to luxury. Roc

checked Joshua's vitals as Samuel settled into one of the seats at the table.

Joshua looked at Samuel and did not like the idea of him seeming weak by lying on the sofa. "I'll sit in one of the chairs," he said to Roc.

"I think you will feel better lying rather than sitting up. Your body would gain more strength in a resting position."

"I don't recall asking you," he replied.

Roc stepped back. In the calmest voice she could manage, she replied, "All right. If you can get up, you can sit in the chair."

It took him a few attempts, but he was going to show her his strength was returning. Fighting through the pain, Joshua stood, then took one step and stopped. He took another and stopped. Roc was doing all she could not to laugh at the arrogant man who apparently would go through pain to have his way. Finally reaching the seat, he slowly sat in the chair near the aisle.

Samuel glanced at Roc with a questioning look as she sat across from him. He then looked at Joshua. The discomfort was clear on his face. "Now is not the time for you to feel you have to prove anything to anyone, Joshua. I know who you are and your capabilities. You are my brother who has had my back more times than I can count. Even in your current state, I will take you over any man to cover me."

"I'm good, Sammy," Joshua exclaimed. "Give me a minute to adjust to sitting here." Before he was able to lay his head back, Roc had pulled her weapon and jumped in front of him as someone stepped onto the plane. Joshua had heard the sound, as had Samuel, but neither reacted with as much speed as Roc. Her body literally covered his in a fashion that any weapon, bullet or knife would have to go through her before it touched him. As the person revealed himself, she eased off of Joshua then stood, holstering her weapon.

"How many times do I have to tell you not to sneak up on me?"

"Checking your skills." Sly smiled as he emerged from the shadows.

Samuel still had his weapon pointed at the man dressed in a suit, gator shoes and a hat that looked as if it came straight from the set of the movie, Super Fly.

"He's good," Roc said to Samuel.

Joshua looked up as Sly came into view, closed his eyes and shook his head. It was bad enough that he had to have Samuel seeing him at his weakest point, now he had to endure Sly, of all people. The one man, other than Samuel he looked up to. "Sammy, shoot me now...just shoot me."

Samuel never took his eyes off Sly, "Say the word Joshua."

Joshua exhaled, grimacing in pain as he lifted his arm to pull Sammy's down. "Don't shoot him, Sammy."

Samuel eased his weapon down but did not holster it. He remained standing next to his brother as the man sat across from him.

"Sammy, you know Sly." The two men assessed each other, giving a curt nod.

Suddenly the air was thick with tension. Roc wasn't sure why, but it was clear there was an issue for Samuel. "We appreciate the ride to Virginia, but we weren't expecting any other passengers. What are you doing here, Sly?"

Sly was a cautious man. He never took his eye off of a man with a weapon. "Melissa Sue is missing," he said glaring at Samuel.

"Who?" Roc asked.

"Al Day's pilot?" Joshua asked. Sly nodded. Joshua sat forward with a grimace. "When?"

"Last contact was five hours ago." Sly stated. "Give me something to go on Absolute. Who could have taken her and why?"

"What's her disappearance have to do with Joshua?" Samuel asked.

"She's also the pilot who brought you home," Sly replied to Joshua instead of Samuel.

"Coincidence?" Roc asked.

"I don't believe in coincidences," Samuel and Joshua said.

"What's happening here, Absolute?" Sly asked.

"Not clear at this time," Joshua replied as Samuel put a hand on his brother's shoulder cautioning him.

"Something on your mind, Lassiter," Sly asked as his eyes moved to look at Samuel. "You seem tense."

"Not tense, Sly," Samuel replied as he held the man's glare. "Cautious when you are around."

There was definitely bad blood between the two, Roc thought as she looked from one to the other. She knew both well. Neither would be easy to take down if it came to that. However, the possibility of that occurring was something she wanted to avoid, for she was certain one of them would not survive.

"I ran across a weapons deal in Mexico. Took the weapons out, but not before they locked a missile on me."

"Was Mateo in on the deal?"

"No." Joshua shook his head. "I'm not sure Mateo knew it was going down on his property."

"What else do you have?"

"The man making the deal was Jonas Gary."

"His last location," Sly asked.

"Mexico," Joshua replied.

"Is he the person who did this to you?"

"Not important."

"It is to me," Sly and Samuel said at the same time. The two eyed each other.

Now, it was becoming clear to her. The two men were jealous of each other. They both wanted Joshua's admiration. Roc contained her grin. Watching men operate could be so entertaining.

Joshua looked from one to the other. "If the pissing contest is over, will one of you reach out to Al. You know how he is about his people. Melissa Sue has been with him for a while. She's like family."

Samuel nodded, as he pulled out his cell phone. "There is something to be said about protecting one's family." He stared at Sly as he made the comment.

"Who is Al?" Roc asked, silently agreeing with Joshua about the pissing contest taking place.

"The one person who could take down this government, if he so chooses," Sly replied.

Roc raised an eyebrow. "That connected?"

"On both sides of the law," Sly replied.

Joshua looked at Sly. "Where was the last place she was seen?"

"Laredo," Sly replied.

"Then we are going to Laredo."

Roc shook her head. "That's not going to happen." She looked at Samuel and Sly. "I can't tell you guys what to do, but him," she nodded towards Joshua, "he's going to Virginia."

Joshua's eyes narrowed, not only because she was trying to dictate his life, but because she was making him out to be a weakling in front of Sly, his mentor and Samuel, his big brother. Both of whom he had been trying to live up to. "Laredo," he exclaimed.

"Virginia," she replied as she stood, then walked over to the aisle. "Sly, on your way out, tell the pilot we are ready to take off." She reached into the bag she had placed next to the sofa, then looked at Samuel. "You might want to catch your brother."

Samuel shook his head as a warning.

"I don't need Sammy..." Joshua's voice trailed off as the sedative. Roc inserted into a vein in his neck took effect.

As asked, Samuel caught Joshua before he slumped to the floor, and placed him on the sofa. Sly stood shaking his head at Roc. "You are going to catch hell from him for doing that."

"Probably, but he is in no condition to track anyone. He has an agent he was mentoring."

Samuel nodded. "Monique."

"I suggest you call Monique." She pointed to Joshua. "That man is going home."

Ned sat in the safe house gathering as much information as he could through his computer system. The message from Lucy was fresh in his mind as he closely monitored his movements. Something was off. The slight movement in his keyboard was the first indication that someone had infiltrated his system. Next there was a flash of light that was no more than a millisecond long, but it was there. He immediately took precautionary steps to protect his agents' information. He locked down the system, GPS locators and all personal information. He had gone dark twenty-four hours earlier. He was given an order that was not beneficial to the United States. He was ordered to give coordinates on two of his agents, Joshua and Roc. The four agents', under his command, lives depended on him. There was no way he would put any one of them in jeopardy. However, he was an agency man. Didn't always agree with what his authorities asked of him, but he never once disobeyed an order. Rather than doing so now, he went dark. No communications coming in or going out. He knew anything coming from his IPS number would be picked up. As all good handlers know, you never allow anyone to know all of your options.

Standing, taking one last look around, he knew what had to be done. Closing his black case, he opened the door, stepped out, took one last look around the room he had operated from for over ten years, then closed the door behind him. He didn't walk to his vehicle, at least not the one he used regularly. No, he walked out the back door of the apartment complex, across the alley, into another building, then walked out of the front door. Across the street from the Chinese restaurant, Ned unlocked the door to a 1969 Mustang convertible, then pulled off. He drove until he was a good ten miles out of the city, pulled over then opened his case. Taking a small remote from inside, he opened his car door, stepped out, turned back facing the city then pushed a button on the remote. An explosion rocketed through the air, but little of the sound reached Ned, for he had gotten back into his car and pulled off.

Chapter Ten
Quantico, Va

Getting Joshua from the plane to his home in Quantico, Virginia was going to be difficult without help. Samuel did not want to interfere with Roc's mission, however, he knew people who could make this journey a little less stressful. "Roc, what's your plan to get Joshua from the airport to his home without being seen?"

"I called a friend. Transportation will be waiting for us at the airport."

"Can your friend disable the cameras in the private air terminals?"

"No, but we can." She held up her handheld device, then placed it back on her belt.

Samuel nodded, satisfied with her plan. "I have a friend who not only has access, but can get us through traffic."

Roc tilted her head to the side. "I don't trust unknown factors."

"But you do trust me." Samuel held her stare.

Roc looked towards Joshua. "I know he's your brother, but at the moment, he is also my mission. That trumps brother."

Samuel nodded, "Understood."

"Anything happens to him, I take you out. Are we clear?"

Samuel knew she meant what she was saying. He pulled out his cell. "I need transportation and firepower. What do you have available?"

The private plane landed at Reagan International about thirty minutes later. The hangar doors were up, allowing them to pull in. Once the plane's tail cleared the entrance, the doors closed behind it.

Samuel looked out the window, surveying the area to ensure there were no unwanted guests, and then he saw the familiar face. "We're good," he said as he looked at Roc.

"That remains to be seen." Roc had her weapon in hand, ready to fire at the first sign of trouble.

The door opened and the steps were lowered. Samuel had Joshua over his shoulder, as Roc descended the steps first. "Name and rank," she called out as she pointed her weapon at the male standing inside the hangar.

"You going to let her shoot me?" The man smiled up at Samuel.

Samuel shrugged, as if Joshua was not on his shoulder. "Him, you can shoot, her, no."

Roc looked at Samuel, then turned in the direction he nodded to see a female dressed in black pants, turtleneck, boots and a black blazer, step from the opposite side of the plane. She reached behind her and pulled another weapon, pointing it at the woman.

"Roc, no," Samuel called out as he took a couple steps down. He knew Roc did not ask questions. She took out whomever she perceived as a threat.

"I don't like this."

"Magna, lower your weapon," Samuel yelled.

Magna Rivera never took her eyes off of the woman with the gun aimed at her. "Right after she drops hers."

"Not going to happen," Roc stated.

"Now Magna." Samuel demanded.

Magna watched as Samuel walked between the two women.

"Women." Brian grinned.

The two women turned and glared at him. Brian threw his hands up. "I have two at home. Love them dearly."

"Then don't make comments that might get you killed," Roc stated as she holstered her weapon.

"What in the hell is going on, Samuel?" Brian asked as Samuel placed Joshua in the back of the SUV parked near the door.

"That's what we have to find out." He turned to Roc. "Brian Thompson, Magna Rivera, meet Roc. Joshua's protection is her mission and she takes it very seriously."

Roc nodded. "I will feel a lot better when we are in a secure location."

Samuel nodded. "Let's get the pilot out of here and on his way."

Roc took a position next to the SUV where Joshua was on the backseat. Using her handheld, she pushed a button to scramble the signal on the camera. She did not want the plane tracked. The doors opened and the plane began taxiing out of the hangar. They all watched as the plane taxied down the runway and went airborne.

"He going to be okay?" Brian nodded towards the SUV

"Roc is going make sure he is, even if it kills him."

Brian lifted a brow, glanced at the woman, then looked back at Samuel. "He's giving her a hard time?"

"You can say that," Samuel smirked. "Like I said, Roc will whip him back into shape whether he wants it or not. I know, she did it for me." Samuel hesitated. "The President is in trouble. Someone is coming after his administration."

"What do you have?"

"Do you remember the name Jonas Gary?"

Brian thought for a minute.

"The Munford case," Magna spoke from behind them.

"That's right." Samuel nodded.

"What's he got to do with the President?" Brian asked.

"Nothing concrete. Can you get a secure call between Joshua and the President without White House tracking?"

Brian stared at Samuel perplexed. "I can work that out."

"Good." Samuel patted Brian on the shoulder, as he walked off. "The sooner he can make that call, the better."

Satisfied the plane had departed safely, Brian turned to Samuel. "The vehicle is fully loaded." He handed the keys over to Samuel. Hit the red button on the console and instructions on its use will be read to you."

"Appreciate it."

"You want an escort to Quantico?"

"We're good." Samuel climbed into the vehicle. "Make that call happen."

Brian and Magna watched as the vehicle pulled out. "Wasn't Gary into weapons trafficking back then?" Magna asked.

Brian nodded. "Yes, he was." He stared at Magna over the top of the vehicle they were about to enter. "That's the second time today that Munford has come up." He looked away for a minute then tapped the top of the vehicle. "Get a location on Gary. Let's see what he's been up to the last few years."

"You got it, Boss."

The ride from Reagan National to Quantico was less than an hour's drive if they took Interstate 95. Under the circumstances, Samuel felt it was best to take Route 1, which was longer and more of a rural area. If anything were to hop off on 95, there was no escape. Using Route 1, would give them a number of options. Samuel wasn't one to anticipate impending doom, however, he had worked as a Seal long enough to prepare for the worst.

"Brian Thompson wouldn't happen to be the President's personal security guard, would he?"

"That he would be."

Frustrated, Roc shook her head. "Samuel," she sighed. "What part of I don't trust people do you not get? It was a United States chopper that tried to take your brother out."

"That may be. But I would bet my life on it, that JD is not aware of that?"

"Are you willing to bet your brother's life on that. Because that's what you just did."

"Look, Roc, I understand you don't know JD like we do. In this, you will have to trust my judgment." He exhaled. "Do you think for one minute I would do anything to put my brother's life in jeopardy, or yours for that matter? You know me better than that."

Roc knew Samuel would not jeopardize any of them, but for some reason her nerves were on edge. The closer they got to their destination, the more an intense sense of danger thickened around them. "Does anyone else know we are here?"

"Not from me." Samuel looked over at her. "Why?"

Looking out the window in all directions, Roc shook her head. "I don't know Samuel, something just doesn't feel right."

Samuel looked in the rearview window. There weren't many cars on the road. None that had been with them long, for he had been randomly checking to make sure they were not being followed. He pushed the red button on the console that Brian had mentioned. "Let's see what we're carrying."

"Good evening," the console spoke. "Who do I have the pleasure of serving today?"

Roc and Samuel glanced at each other. "Samuel Lassiter."

"Please hold while I do a voice analysis to verify your identity."

"What the hell?" Samuel grinned.

"May I call you Samuel or do you prefer Sammy?"

"Samuel is fine."

"I can't seem to locate you in our data base, Samuel. Have you used our technology before?"

"It's hard to say since I have no idea what technology your are referring to. Why in the hell am I talking to a car?"

"No need to be insulting, Samuel. I am not a car. I am the state of the art in automobile designs."

Roc laughed. "Samuel, I think you hurt her feelings."

"You have someone with you?" the console replied. "Please identify yourself."

"Hello, Genevieve."

Roc turned to see Joshua sitting up.

"Joshua, how wonderful to hear your voice."

"Genevieve, Samuel is my brother. Please do not eject him from your warm embrace."

"Your verification is all I need. Please proceed with your request."

Roc gave Joshua an open mouthed stare. "You talk vehicle."

"Automobile," Joshua replied. "State of the art automobile. Watch. Genevieve, please search the surrounding automobiles for any unusual chatter."

"Anything for you, Joshua," the console replied. A click occurred, as the lights on the dashboard began to flicker.

"Force fields are in place. You have two bogies tracking you, one from above, the other two vehicles behind you."

Everyone became alert. "What are they tracking?"

The console lights bounced as if a mind was thinking. "GPS located in the passenger in the backseat."

Roc turned to Joshua. "You have a tracking system implant. That's how I located you in Mexico."

"The only people with access are CIA personnel." Joshua glared at her through the dark interior.

"Where is it located?" Roc asked as she climbed into the backseat with him.

"You really don't want to know."

The light on the console began to flash again. "A vehicle to your left is approaching at an increasing speed. Shall I take evasive action?"

"Yes," Samuel replied. The vehicle lurched forward as Genevieve took control of the gas pedal and steering wheel. "Please secure your seat belts."

"A little damnit late Genevieve," Joshua groaned.

"Weapons locked to fire, shall I prepare to retaliate?"

"Hell yes," Samuel replied. "Can she control this vehicle, Joshua?" Samuel asked as he pulled his weapon.

"Yes. Open the weapon tray, Genevieve." The ceiling of the vehicle opened revealing a selection of automatic weapons. Joshua pulled out an Uzi.

"What the hell?" Roc smiled. "Where is the GPS located, Joshua?"

"In his left thigh, near his groin," Genevieve replied.

"Oh," Roc replied. "Since you located it, can you deactivate it?"

"No, however, I do have scramble capabilities. Would you like for me to implement the scrambler?"

"Yes," they all yelled.

"Scramble sequence activated. Another vehicle is approaching from the right," Genevieve announced.

Roc pulled a weapon down. "I want some of this action. Do we have to wait for them to fire at us?"

"Hell no," Joshua yelled, as the vehicle's speed increased. "Genevieve, take the next right."

"Affirmative," Genevieve replied. "They have been firing. My anti-shields are up. The ammunition is bouncing off as it should."

Roc looked at Joshua and grinned. They both rolled down the window and began firing at will. Samuel shook his head thinking they were acting like children at Christmas with a new toy. Genevieve took a sharp right as instructed, throwing Joshua against the door.

"Ouch, damnit. Take it easy Genevieve."

"Missile locked from above."

"Haul ass, Genevieve, haul ass," Samuel yelled. "Can you counteract?"

"Counteraction initiated." The vehicle shook. Then they heard a whistle sound. Occupants in the vehicle stopped and watched.

"BOOM!"

Samuel looked on as Roc and Joshua sat back watching the explosion in awe. "Hell, if a car can do all of this why do we need an army?"

Genevieve fired two more shots taking out the vehicles trailing them, then came to a complete stop. "I am not a car. I am a state of the art automobile. One more insult and I will eject you."

"My apologies, Genevieve."

Samuel and Roc stepped out of the vehicle to assess the damage. They looked at each other. There was none. Joshua opened the door to get out of the vehicle, but had the door promptly closed back on him, then blocked by Roc.

There were fires and destruction all around them. "We need to get out of the area," Samuel stated. "This place is going to be crawling with local, state and federal authorities in a minute."

"And they are going to be pissed," Roc added as they entered Genevieve. "You okay back there?"

Joshua was in excruciating pain, but there was no way he was going to tell her that. "Alive," he replied frowning. "Take us home, Genevieve."

Genevieve roared her engine, as Samuel just held the keys in his hand. "I've got to get me one of these."

Joshua smiled. "A nice toy, isn't she?"

Fifteen minutes later, they were a mile away from Joshua's home. Samuel had regained control of the vehicle. Roc was in the passenger seat, and Joshua was in the back, wishing he had accepted the pain meds offered earlier. Any movement would send sharp pains through his back.

Roc looked over her shoulder. "His coloring is changing. We have to get him settled."

"I'm good," Joshua said feeling as if his guts were about to spill onto the floor of Genevieve.

"No, you are not. Genevieve, are you equipped with medical screening capabilities?" Roc asked.

"Affirmative."

"Not needed," Joshua groaned in agony. "I said I'm good."

"Give me vitals on Joshua. He's seated in the back."

"Joshua's body features are in my data bank. When he is in our automobiles, we become one."

Roc stared at the console, then looked up at Samuel. All Samuel could do was shrug his shoulders. "He has a way with females."

"Medical attention needed immediately. Pressure dropping rapidly. Directions to closest medical facility loaded."

"Negative, Genevieve." Joshua closed his eyes as he moaned. "Go stealth mode. Take me home."

All of the lights in the vehicle dimmed, the engine quieted to a non-detectable level and began to move forward.

"Heat sensors show two occupants in a vehicle on the side of the road ahead," Genevieve advised.

"Are we able to pass them undetected?" Samuel asked.

"Negative."

"What's the problem?" Roc asked.

"The entrance to Joshua's home is down the road ahead," Samuel replied. "We need to make a turn, right in front of them, to get to the entrance."

Roc looked around. The area seemed to be deserted, with the exception of one or two houses down the dimly lit road.

"Are they males or females inside the vehicle?" Roc asked.

"Males," Genevieve responded.

Roc reached up and then removed the band which held her hair in a ponytail. She ran her fingers through her hair, spreading it over her shoulders. "Pull back, Genevieve." The automobile moved back into the shadows. "Give me a name of one of the residents on this street." Genevieve's monitors came to life.

"Ian Holmes, house number 2652."

"Thank you, Genevieve." Roc stepped out of the vehicle, bent over to tuck her jeans inside her boots, zipped her black leather jacket. She pulled out her phone, put the earphones in, then began walking down the street.

"You may want to watch this, little brother." Samuel smiled.

Joshua opened his eyes to see the back of Roc as she walked down the street. "Damn."

Samuel grinned. "Yes, damn is right."

Joshua watched the movement of Roc's behind in those jeans as she moved closer to the vehicle. He may be in pain, but the sight of her in those jeans made part of his anatomy come to life. He watched as she walked past the vehicle, stopped, looked around, then pulled the earphones from her ears. They dropped to the ground. She slowly bent over to pick them up. He groaned.

Samuel looked at him through the rearview mirror. That was the little brother he knew. "Something to behold, isn't she?"

"You two seem chummy."

"We're more than chummy, Joshua. We have a connection. Just like you do with any partner."

A man got out of the passenger seat of the parked vehicle and was talking to her. Roc flung her hair over her shoulder, then smiled at the man. Joshua's gut clinched. She was beautiful. The passenger door opened and the other man stepped out. Joshua started to move but was engulfed in pain.

"No." Samuel grinned. "Watch."

Joshua watched as Roc turned to the other man with the same disarming smile. She pointed to a house as if explaining what she was doing there, then suddenly punched one man in the nose with the palm of her hand, sending him to the ground. Kicked the other in the groin, then in the face, knocking him out. She had taken them both out in less than a minute.

"Beautiful."

"Thank you, Joshua," Genevieve responded.

Samuel laughed, started Genevieve, drove down and parked next to the vehicle. Roc had picked one man up and placed him back inside the car. Samuel placed the other man in the driver's seat. They both got back into Genevieve then pulled off.

"Did you enjoy putting yourself in danger?"

Roc looked over her shoulder at Joshua, then sideways at Samuel. "I did enjoy that little action. It's been a while. But I was in no danger from two men in a car."

"They were men," Joshua seethed.

"And your point?" Roc questioned.

Samuel watched Joshua through the rearview mirror wondering what was his problem. He knew none of his brothers had any concerns about their sisters being able to defend themselves against anyone, especially men. There was something else in play when it came to Roc, he just had to figure out what. He turned onto a gravel road, then stopped at what appeared to be trees at the end of the road.

"Genevieve signal." Joshua groaned from the back seat. Genevieve flashed her lights to the Lord's prayer. The trees parted. They drove in and waited.

Genevieve was scanning the area. The single level, four bedroom, three bath home, was nestled away on four acres of land in Quantico, Virginia, only forty-five minutes from Richmond or Washington, D.C. Views of the river could be seen from many of the rooms in the home. The place had a calming effect on his family when they came to visit. In addition to providing comfort for his eleven brothers and sisters, with its calming water views, the house contained a twenty-seat state of the art theater room, and an indoor heated pool, plus his one-hundred and twenty pound Chow/Rottweiler mix and lovable pooch, Commando. However, like Commando, the home and its surrounding grounds were a danger zone for unwanted visitors. Anyone approaching could be detected from miles away. The house, located outside of the subdivision, had one road leading into the property. The road was lined with sensors, which could detect the number of people in a vehicle or on foot. Some of those sensors had triggers, which would eliminate unwanted visitors without Joshua ever stepping foot outside. The land was covered with trees and blocked the view of the house from the subdivision. There were land mines strategically placed throughout. The extreme security measures were only activated at times of danger. This was one of those times.

"The area is clear," Genevieve advised.

Roc sat back as Samuel drove the vehicle forward and stopped. The trees behind them closed, and lights appeared, lining the corridor as they moved forward. It looked as if they were driving through a tunnel.

"My sensors have been shutdown," Genevieve advised.

"Thank you, Genevieve," Samuel replied before he could stop himself from talking to the automobile.

"You are welcome, Samuel, brother to Joshua."

Samuel shook his head as Roc surveyed the area and what was happening. Above she could see cameras in the ceiling watching as they drove through. About two miles in, Samuel stopped again, waited as the white wall in front of them slid open. Before them appeared a garage, with several vehicles, and a woman standing at a door, with a huge dog beside her. Samuel drove through and parked. The wall closed.

"Where in the hell are we?"

"We are amongst friends," Genevieve replied.

"Yes, Genevieve. We are home," Joshua replied, then passed out.

Chapter Eleven
Quantico, VA
Day Three

Joshua awakened the next day, knowing exactly where he was but having very little memory of how he arrived there. It didn't matter, it felt good to be in his own bed. The pain in his back wasn't throbbing as it had the previous day. He smiled, that to him was a good indication that he would be up and back in action in another day or two. Hell, with Lucy taking care of him, there was no doubt in his mind, he was ready to start moving around again. Pushing the comforter aside, he put his legs over the side of the bed, attempted to stand and fell flat on his face.

Roc was on the sofa in the sitting room connected to Joshua's bedroom. Lucy offered her a room down the hallway, but she declined. She needed to be close to him to ensure he didn't do anything stupid, like trying to get out of bed too fast. When she heard the thump, she threw the throw aside, and walked into his room to find him on the floor turning onto his back moaning. Commando ran by her, straight to Joshua's side. He turned back and looked at her.

"I got him boy." She rubbed Commando behind his ear as he licked Joshua's face. "Good morning," Roc said as she bent over where he lay on the floor.

"Well, his coloring looks better, doesn't it, boy." She patted Commando and he licked her hand. "Let me help him up." She reached down, but he pushed her away.

"I can get up on my own."

She kneeled down beside him. "Yes, you can, in time, if you take it slow."

Commando watched as Joshua attempted to sit up. He whined then barked at Roc. She sighed at Commando, then looked at Joshua. "Would you like my help?"

"Don't you get it? I don't want anything from you. Just leave me the hell alone."

"I can't do that yet, Joshua. Move aside, Commando." Commando pulled the comforter on the bed back with his teeth.

"No bed for him, boy. We're going to get him to bathe, then moving around today." Roc reached down and picked Joshua up, being careful not to touch certain areas on his back. She put him over her shoulders then took him to the bathroom.

At the time, Joshua was too shocked by her strength to complain. "Where the hell are you taking me?"

"To your tub," Roc replied. "You are going to start doing those things that will make you feel like you again. Besides, your Jacuzzi will help with your muscle soreness."

"What?"

She sat him on the edge of the tub. "I spoke with Lucy at length last night. She showed me pictures of you. To my surprise, you know what I found out? You are not a bad looking brother." Commando stood in the doorway watching. She turned on the faucet to begin filling the tub. "I mean, you could give Sammy a run for his money."

"Hell, I know that," Joshua replied, as he willed his mind not to accept the pain.

"Arrogant too, I see."

"Where is Sammy?"

"Samuel went home to his wife. Then he is going to bring your mother here."

"What?"

She turned to him as she grabbed a towel and washcloth from the closet located inside the huge bathroom. "He wanted to ensure she arrived without being detected. He also had to return Genevieve to Mr. Thompson."

"Genevieve is not the name of the automobile, it is the computerized system inside. I have her in all of mine. Why is he bringing Sally here?"

"I take it she was designed by a man?" she asked as she walked back to him with the items in her hands.

"Sally?" He snatched the towel and washcloth out of her hand.

"No, Genevieve."

Commando lay near the door and watched the two go back and forth.

"Ned designed her. I named her."

"Figures," she said as she walked out of the room. "He feels you need to see her."

"Genevieve?"

"No." She walked back into the room. "Your mother."

"No."

"No, what?" Roc stopped in front of him.

"I don't want to see anyone."

"Why? I'm certain your family and friends are concerned about you."

"I can take care of myself. I don't need friends and I damn sure don't need you. I'm home now. Consider your job done."

Commando's head came up at the sound of Joshua's voice rising. He whimpered and tilted his head.

She turned the water off. "You are upsetting Commando." She turned to the dog. "He's okay boy." She turned back to Joshua. "Please don't raise your voice around him again."

Joshua looked over at Commando and could have sworn he smiled. Commando put his head back on his paw and continued to watch the battle between them.

Roc sighed. "I can't leave you just yet, Joshua." She put her hands on her hips. "Are you ready for your bath?" She watched as his eyes seared through her. For a moment, on the highway, she had a glimpse of the playful Joshua she'd heard so much about the night before. She knew the man was still in there. She just had to find a way to pull him out. Her job was not to just recover agents, it was to restore them to themselves. Usually, after a day or two, her patients tended to come around. This man was proving to be more of a challenge. She needed him to not be this way. Between his mahogany skin tone, the bold, cocoa brown eyes, the killer body, even in a hurt state, he was more of a turn on than she could manage. For her own sanity, she needed to get him well, so she could get the hell out of Dodge.

"Okay, I'll make a deal with you. As soon as you can take care of yourself, physically, I'm out of here. I give you my word. My word is my bond."

"That's a man's motto," he seethed. "As much as you try, you are not a man."

She smiled. "You noticed." She sighed, then looked at Commando. "He knows I'm not a man."

Commando barked.

Joshua rolled his eyes. "That's my dog. Don't try to seduce him."

"I'm not seducing your dog or anyone else." She noticed he was having trouble raising his arm. "Here, let's get you undressed." She reached out to move the towel from his lap to help him stand. "Time to get you in the tub."

"I don't need your help." He yanked the towel from her with a little more force than he should have. The quickness of his movement did not give her time to react. She let go of the towel, causing him to fall backwards into the tub.

The water splashed in her face and all around her feet, soaking her from head to toe. Roc gasped at the impact, and froze. Commando jumped up and began barking. Lucy came running into the room. She looked around, saw the water on the floor and Joshua submerged in the tub, with his pajamas still on and the towel covering his face.

"What in the hell did you do, Roc?"

Joshua was splashing more water as he tried to sit up. Roc gave Lucy a 'don't try me' look. She stepped inside the tub and pulled him up.

The sight was hilarious, and Lucy did all she could not to laugh, but it came bubbling out of her anyway.

Roc turned and gave her a murderous look.

"Come on, boy," Lucy said to Commando. "We're going to leave the children in here to play."

Roc turned back to Joshua and could see the pain on his face. His body was tense and he was mentally willing the pain away. She had been there before. She sighed. "Well, that wasn't the way I intended for you to get into the tub, but since you are here, lets get that bath out of the way." She pushed the wet hair out of her face, and knelt beside him.

Joshua sighed with relief, once the pain began to subside. The tub was set on low, pulsating. Other than his vehicles, it was one of the most luxurious items he owned. It was made from European marble, and encased in dark wood, which allowed for heating. Its extra-long length accommodated his long legs and it was wide enough for him to stretch his arms out to either side. At that moment, all he wanted to do was yank her ass down into the water so he could drown her. He could sense her laughing at him.

"Get the hell out." He did not want her, his mother or anyone seeing him weak. He was the protector, the one everyone should turn to when they needed help. Who in the hell could he help right now? No one, not a damn soul. He couldn't even help himself.

Roc felt his pain. Not just from his back, but from his pride as well. She walked over to the vanity, opened the drawer, searched around, closed it then opened another. She pulled out a pair of scissors.

"Joshua," she spoke softly to him as she sat on the side of the tub cutting away the bandaging. "Trust me, this will pass. Your strength will return and you will be the agent you once were." She sat the scissors aside and picked up the washcloth, lathered it with the body wash and began washing his chest. "Your injuries are bad, however, you will recover from them. Give it a day or two and you will see." She began singing, *This Too Shall Pass*, by Yolanda Adams, and continued to wash him.

Lucy stood outside the door listening for a while. She smiled at Commando. "He's in good hands. She won't let him walk over her. I like her. What do you think?"

Commando walked back over to the bathroom door and looked inside. He began wagging his tail, then turned and walked back to Lucy. He licked her hand and the two walked out of the suite.

Joshua didn't have the strength to fight her. The gentle motion of her hands, and the soothing tone of her voice began to ease the pain away. She pulled him towards her and began to wash his back. It felt as if an angel from heaven was caring for him. Massaging each wound, until it was only sore, not throbbing. Then she laid him back and began to wash each arm, gently, massaging the muscles until they were so relaxed they simply fell to the side, back into the water. She then began to wash his thighs. Every vein in his body began to vibrate, bouncing as if they were about to pop out of his skin. Akande came to his mind, and the pain returned, but it wasn't alone. Anger accompanied the pain.

He reached down and grabbed Roc's wrist. "Get out," he seethed.

Roc wasn't sure what caused the change. One minute his body was relaxing. The next minute, she felt his muscles begin to tighten. Before she could react, he had grabbed her. However, his strength in his current state was no match for hers.

"Joshua, I want you to think about where my hand is." She moved her other hand, which was very close to his manhood. "Please release me." She wrapped her hand around him as she stared into his eyes.

He almost leaped from the tub at her touch, causing him to loosen his grip on her other hand.

She removed her hand from him and stood. "You soak for a few and I'll be back to dry you off."

Joshua watched as she walked out of the room. There was no way he could let her stay around. He closed his eyes. God help him. He was beginning to like her. There was no way he was going to open his heart to another woman. With her looks, gentle touch and soothing voice, he could feel her slipping inside. That, he would not allow to happen.

Fighting the pain, he pulled himself up, to sit on the side of the tub. The towel she had left was soaking wet. He pulled it from the water, wrung it out then placed it on the floor under his feet. Putting most of his weight against the tub, he pushed himself up to a standing position. His back throbbed in protest, but he stood, gave himself a minute then took small steps to the closet. He pulled out a towel to dry himself as best he could, then took one of the robes out and put it on. He leaned against the closet, willing the pain to stop.

Roc walked back into the room to find him standing in the closet doorway. He needed her. There was no way she could see him in pain and not help. She wrapped her arms around his waist, then put his arm over her shoulder. "Lean on me," she said. She felt him hesitate, then he complied.

"I don't want you here," he said as he took a step.

"I know, Joshua. I know." She helped him back to the bed. She pulled out a clean pair of pajamas but he waved her off.

"I don't sleep in those." He dropped the robe to the floor, eased back on the bed, then turned onto his stomach.

Damn, she wished he would stop doing that. She closed her eyes, and regained her equilibrium enough to complete her task. Roc rubbed her hands together to warm them, then took a bottle of baby oil from her pocket. She poured some into her hands and tried to determine where to start. Every part of his body was tempting to touch. However, that wasn't her purpose. The task was to massage him with oil and relax him to a point where he would sleep without medication. Today needed to be a turning point for him.

She decided to start with his feet. She nodded. Yes, that was the place to start. There was nothing sexual about the feet. The man had big feet, with long toes.

She started singing *There's A Stranger In My House* by Tamia, to keep her focus on the task at hand.

She was proud when she completed massaging them and was confident her reaction to his naked body could be controlled. Next she massaged his calves. They were solid, nothing but muscle. Then she did the back of his thighs. She was beginning to see a pattern with this man's body. All of it was muscle, not an ounce of fat anywhere. And they were thick, the thighs, that is. They were thick, and had the nerve to pulsate under her touch. By the time she finished singing she had reached his back, her voice reaching high levels as she massaged his firm behind, his back, and his arms. She turned him over and to her surprise he did not fight her. She could feel him watching her beneath his lowered lashes as she put oil on his arms, then his chest. Yes, she was more than half way through when she reached his manhood. Not one to tempt fate, she decided to leave that part of his anatomy to his own hands and went down to his thighs. She did everything in her power to keep her eyes away from the rise of his temple as she worked the front of his thighs. Her inner lips vibrated with every touch. Why was she able to block this out with every other patient she'd done this for, including Samuel, but with Joshua her body was not listening to her command? She forced herself to quickly complete the task. Never once did she look into his eyes for she knew what she would find. His body gave him away as did hers. She closed the bottle and put it back into her pocket. She turned him back onto his stomach and re-bandaged the injured areas on his back. She pulled the comforter over him, then turned to walk from the room. As she reached the door, she heard him speak.

"Thank you."

She nodded, then continued on. Reaching the sofa, she sat down and sighed. *How in the hell am I going to make it through this mission? It is my job to care for him, but Lord, this is just a little too much for you to ask of your child. I know you said you would not give me more than I could handle. But Lord, this man is...he is more than I can handle.* She looked up to the ceiling. *How in the hell am I supposed to not see what the man is packing? You know it's been a minute and you send this to me.* She sighed. *I need a break.* She went to the room Lucy had given her, and jumped into the shower.

The aroma hit her before she walked into the kitchen. "Don't stand back there wondering. Come on in here and get some breakfast."

Roc walked into the kitchen smiling. "You knew I was there."

"Before you hit the hallway." Lucy smiled. "I can't take the credit. Commando's tail started wagging."

Roc reached down and rubbed Commando behind the ear. "Hey boy." She tilted her head. "You can go to him." Commando stood. "Don't let him out of bed." He barked and went on his way.

"He likes you." Lucy put a cup of coffee in front of her.

"Coffee?"

"No caffeine?" Lucy asked. Roc nodded. "Not a problem. Joshua doesn't do the coffee thing either."

"Have a seat." Lucy removed the cup and poured the coffee out, replacing it with a cup of hot water and a tea bag. "So, you are the person that beat him out of the job."

"I guess so." Roc shrugged as she accepted the cup.

"He's not taking that too well, is he?"

"No, he's not."

"He will just have to get past it then, won't he?" Lucy placed a plate of hash brown potatoes, scrambled eggs, bacon and toast in front of Roc. "You're not one of those people who doesn't eat meat, are you?"

"No, ma'am. I'm a carnivore for life." Roc smiled. "Thank you."

"Then we can hang." Lucy sat across from the woman and studied her for a minute. "What's your story, Roc?"

"What do you mean?"

"Why did you leave the agency? What are you, thirty?"

"Thank you," Roc said as she sat her cup down. "Thirty-five," she shrugged. "I was ready to settle down, have a family. Never found the right man."

"Is that a fact? Hmm, I hung around until I was in my fifties." Lucy began to eat. "Took a year off when I had my baby girl. Missed it. I thought I would go crazy with the normal life."

Roc shook her head. "Not me. I love my life."

"Just missing the man and a family?" Lucy asked.

Roc shrugged. "My life is full. It could be enhanced a bit, but I'm patient. As Samuel says, it will happen when it happens."

"You knew Samuel before this?"

Roc looked down as if the food was suddenly the only thing in the world. "Yes, we've worked together before."

"Hmm, he's the one that got away, huh?"

"No, not really, no." Roc protested a little too much. "This is good."

Lucy laughed. "Just plain old bacon and eggs, but, if you say so." A moment of silence filled the room. "He looks bad."

Roc reached over and touched Lucy's hand. "He is going to be fine. Joshua has a special force within him, he just has to tap into it again." Roc continued to eat. "I'm not sure what caused him to go rogue, but if it was the Akande situation, time will heal that, when he allows it. Then he will see that it was a lesson to prepare him for what is coming to him. God works in that way."

Lucy watched and listened as the woman talked. She didn't look her age, but the wisdom was there. She seemed to be a loner, and definitely a fighter. It was clear she knew very little about Joshua. The real Joshua had yet to emerge. *Lord help her when that happens. She's not going to stand a chance.*

A buzz sounded. Roc looked around with her hand on her weapon. "What's that?"

Lucy stood. "No need for alarm. Someone is trying to reach out. I have to go down to the Cave to see what's happening."

"The Cave?" The curiosity was clear in her eyes. "Joshua mentioned the Cave. May I accompany you?"

Lucy smiled. "Sure, come on. I'll be happy to show off my creation."

The two walked toward the back of the house, past Joshua's bedroom. The double doors at the end of the hallway opened as they walked by the sensors.

"Wow," Roc exclaimed as she looked around at the monitors, each flashing with a different scene than the other. There were rows of monitors on the wall directly in front of her. Three rows, ten monitors deep. "Is that Israel?"

"Yes." Lucy smiled.

"Iran, Germany, South Africa, Somalia." She pointed at the monitors then stopped. Is that the White House on the center screen?"

Lucy looked closer. "Yes, ma'am. We keep our eyes on everything around here."

"I see." She looked around at the equipment. "Can you hear the conversations?"

"If we want to," Lucy replied as she pushed a button. "What's up, Spicy?"

"Did Absolute make it home?"

"Yes, he's here."

"How is he?"

"Not good, but mending," Lucy replied.

"Let him know as soon as I handle this situation for Sly, I will be there."

"Where are you?"

"Right outside of Laredo in a little town called La Presa. They are holding Melissa Sue."

"Is she alive?"

"Barely," Spicy replied, "but I'm bringing her home. Any word on Ned?"

"Negative," Lucy replied.

"Strange." There was silence. "Got to go. I'll check in later." With that she was gone.

"So, that's Monique." Roc brushed her hair back. "Well, she's a beautiful and young woman."

"That she is," Lucy replied. "She is going to be as good as my Joshua when it's all said and done." The buzz sounded again. Lucy pushed a button to switch to another screen. The tunnel came into view. "Samuel is back with Sally. Things are about to get real."

Chapter Twelve
Quantico, VA

"What do you mean he's not the same? He's your brother."

"Yes, Mother, he is. However, Joshua has been through some things most men have a difficult time dealing with under normal circumstances." Samuel explained. "The one area of his life Joshua has never had difficulty with is women. This thing with Akande messed him up a little bit. He became self-destructive." He continued to drive as he talked.

Sally sat next to him, excited to see her son. Oh, she listened, but for three years she had been worried about Joshua and all he endured because of some woman she had never met. Didn't he know that was a sign? Didn't he know if God meant for him to be with that woman they would be together today? If she was not someone you could bring home to your family, she was not the woman for him. She realized Joshua was hurt, but that was no reason for him to turn his back on his family or God. She knew God was going to forgive him, because that's His job, to forgive. However, her job as a mother was to guide him in the right direction. She didn't know what that direction was for Joshua, but she was sure she would recognize it when she found it. After all, she now had two children happily married. Her middle daughter, Diamond, was married to Zachary, a man who worships the ground she walks on and there was her Sammy. She looked over at him and smiled as he continued to talk. He was married to Cynthia. Truth be told, she could not stand Cynthia's mother, however, Sally loved Cynthia as if she were her own child.

"Mother, are you listening to me?"

She patted Samuel on the hand. "Of course I am, Sammy. You are explaining how much Joshua has changed since that woman hurt him. I heard every word you said. In my heart, I know a change is about to come for Joshua. I don't know why I feel that way, but I do. I trust and believe God has put this chain of events in place to help Joshua heal." She looked out of the window. "Why are we stopping here?"

Samuel played the tune on his stereo system while the lights on his vehicle flashed to the rhythm.

"Samuel, what is going on here?" Sally asked as the trees opened. "We're going to see Joshua."

"Why didn't you just drive up to his house?"

"Until Joshua is well and can fend for himself, we don't want anyone to know he's home."

"Are his injuries bad?"

"He has the best medic taking care of him. A few days and he will be back on his feet."

"I knew Joshua needed me. He needs his mother."

Before Sally could get out of the car good, Commando came running out to her. He jumped up, licking her and wagging his tail, then he began barking. Sally reached into her pocket and pulled out a treat. He jumped down and bowed his head. "You're welcome, Commando. Where's Joshua?"

Commando ran back to the door, passed Lucy then stopped to make sure Sally was following.

"Well, it looks like he's happy to see you." Lucy smiled. "Come on in let's talk."

"Mom, I'm going to leave you here while I check out a few things," Samuel said as he got back into the car. "I'll see you later."

Sally waved, then followed Lucy into the house. They walked into the kitchen where Roc was sitting at the table drinking a hot cup of tea.

"Roc, this is Sally Lassiter, Joshua's mother. Sally ,this is Roc, she was the one who brought Joshua home. She's also been caring for him as much as he will allow."

Roc extended her hand. "Good morning Mrs. Lassiter." She smiled.

"Hello, how is my son?"

"Have a seat Sally." Lucy said as she placed a cup of tea in front of her.

Sally looked around the kitchen, then back to Lucy. "Thank you." She took a drink. "Tell me about Joshua."

"Well, he's not our carefree boy we are used to seeing." Lucy took a sip of her tea. "He's hurting, physically and emotionally."

"Let's talk physical first."

Roc nodded. "I'll take that. He received multiple stab wounds in the back. One came dangerously close to his kidney. That's the wound giving us the most trouble. The first twenty-four hours were the most critical. Unfortunately, we had to move him and the journey was not easy. Now we need him to stay still just long enough to let his wounds heal. If he does that, then he will be as good as before."

"Then he stays in bed a few days until he heals." Sally shrugged her shoulders thinking it's a simple solution.

"That would be ideal." Roc stated. "However, the reason Joshua was injured is causing some controversy for the White House."

"Who cares at this point? Joshua needs to heal and that's what he is going to do."

"It's not that simple, Mrs. Lassiter. Joshua's duty is to protect his country. He takes his duty very seriously, as do I. My job is to get him back into action as soon as possible."

"Then you are not the right person to be caring for him. Your job should be to ensure his health and well-being. Are you a doctor?"

"Yes ma'am. I'm also an agent for this government as is Joshua. Please know, my first loyalty is to my country. As such, I've been ordered by my President to get Joshua to his full strength and back into his mother's arms. It is Joshua's wish to assist the administration in this situation." Roc stood. "Let me be very clear, what Joshua wants, Joshua is going to get. Excuse me." She walked from the room.

Sally watched as the woman walked out of the kitchen. Lucy began to laugh. Sally soon joined her. "I guess she told me."

"I guess she did."

The two women stared at each other. Sally put her elbow on the table, placing her chin in the palm of her hand. "Tell me about her."

"Glad you asked, cause you know I checked." Commando put his head down and covered his eyes with his paw and groaned.

Lucy looked over at the dog. "Oh shut up."

Ten minutes later Sally walked into Joshua's bedroom suite to find Roc sitting on the sofa reading from her tablet with sports center on the television. She looked up and began to stand when Sally entered the room

"No, please don't get up." Sally smiled. "Is he asleep?"

"Yes ma'am. But I believe a visit from you will be worth waking him up." Roc pointed to the room. "Please go on in."

Sally walked to the open doorway, then stopped. "Roc, I owe you an apology. I questioned your loyalty to your patient without cause. Please accept my apology."

Roc smiled. "Apology accepted. Have a good visit with Joshua."

Standing in the doorway, Sally admired the burgundy and gold, she and the girls had decorated Joshua's room in. It was fit for a king. To them Joshua was a king. Tears filled her eyes as she walked closer to the bed. The realization that it was indeed Joshua grew stronger with each step. She stopped before touching him, to thank God for sending Roc to bring her child home. Yes, he was a thirty-five year old grown man, but he was still one of her babies. And this one had lost his way. That's why she'd kept him prayed up over the last few years. She knew at some point God was going to step in and take over. Her prayer was answered, for there was her son, asleep in his own bed. Instead of waking him, she pulled up a chair beside the bed, took his hand and prayed.

Joshua felt it the moment she touched his hand, peace. Then he heard her voice, praying, thanking God for his deliverance. He listened as the words tried to ease his spirit, but it couldn't pierce through. As much as he wanted her words to touch his heart, he just wasn't ready. His hand closed around hers.

"Joshua," Sally spoke softly in case he wasn't fully awake.

He turned his head on the pillow and looked into the teary eyes of his mother. "Hi, Mommy."

Sally exhaled tears, that she wiped away as she stood. She kissed her son on the cheek. "Hello, my son." She gathered her son in her arms and held him. The tears flowed, dropping onto his bare shoulders. With each drop, she could feel his hold tighten around her. Feel the pain, the hurt, the confusion he was going through. Three years of needing his mother's embrace came through as the tears flowed.

Joshua spoke first. "My grief is beyond healing: my heart is broken." *Jeremiah 8:18*

"The Lord is my strength and my shield, my heart trusted in him and I am helped. *Psalms 28:7*.

"You must believe, Joshua." Sally held her son until his hold lessened, then she sat on the side of the bed as he turned away from her.

"Believe that is the one thing I cannot do. The Lord has forsaken me twice. First with Akande and now, with this." He smirked. "And you ask me to believe." He turned away pulling the cover back over him. "You shouldn't be here, Mother."

"This is exactly where I need to be at this moment," Sally touched his shoulder. "Look at me Joshua."

"Go away, Mother."

Sally's shoulders began to slump, at being rejected by her son. She was his mother and he was shutting her out. It hurt, especially from this child. Of her twelve children, this was the one she worried about the most. He was so carefree, filled with life and had this craving for danger. This man lying before her was only a shell of her son. Sally closed her eyes and said a prayer, asking for strength. A moment later she opened her eyes, lifted her shoulders and spoke with a deadly calm. "I said look at me this instant, Joshua Theodore Lassiter, and don't make me say it again."

Joshua turned to look at his mother. Yes, he was a grown man, with only a few things in life that he feared. The little woman sitting on his bed was one.

"Sit up." Sally now stood over him. "I realize this is your home. But the one thing you will not do, is disrespect me. You say the Lord has forsaken you yet I'm looking at you and see you are very much alive. Who exactly do you think saved your behind? You? I think not. Who gave you the strength to escape after you were captured or whatever happened to you? How many times have you tested Him by putting your life in danger? He has brought you back to us every single time. Don't you dare lie there talking about God has forsaken you. You better be happy He is a forgiving God, for you have truly tested His grace and now you are testing my patience and understanding."

Roc walked through the door balancing a tray weighed down with food. "I thought you two would like to have lunch together. Lucy has made a pot of vegetable soup that smells like heaven."

Before she could sit the tray on the dresser, Joshua bellowed, "Just leave it and get out!"

The rude reply caught Sally by surprise. Never had she heard Joshua speak to a woman in such a disrespectful way. "Joshua," she began to scold him.

"Stay out of this, Mother," he snapped never taking his eyes off of Roc.

Roc never showed any emotion. She nodded. "As you wish your highness," she gave him a full bow then turned and walked out of the room.

Sally couldn't help but laugh as she watched her son struggle not to laugh at the woman he was watching leave. "So she gets a rise out of you, huh?

That's no reason for you to treat her like crap. I've never heard you bark at a woman like that."

"Maybe if I had barked sooner I wouldn't have gotten bit."

"You can't hold Roc responsible for your choice."

"What choice?" He raised his voice. "The choice was made for me."

"What choice, Joshua?" Sally yelled back. She was tired of everyone tiptoeing around the topic. "Akande. What were you going to do? Leave the United States to be the kind of husband she needs? She needs a King. Someone who will be there to help her build her an army to protect her country, someone who would be there to plan strategies day in and day out on how to rebuild and restore her country. She needed a King. You are not a King, Joshua, you are a King maker. They are called Presidents. Go back to your Bible. Joshua was the strength and support beside Moses. He was there to help Moses carry out God's will. He was not Moses."

"She could have made a different choice. She could have chosen me," Joshua yelled.

"Oh stop it," Sally snapped. "And did what? Sit around here waiting for you to come home from whatever assignment you were on for months at a time while she watched her people suffer? Would you have given up your country as easily as you asked her to? No, you would not have and you still won't, because you are a patriot to the United States just as she is to Asmere." Sally sighed as she began to calm herself. She looked at her son and could see the anger fighting with reason. "Joshua." She reached out and took his hand. Tears streamed down her face as his pain radiated through their touch. "God gave us free will. You made the choice to allow this woman into your heart even when you knew something wasn't right. She was your choice, not God's. You shouldn't be angry with Akande, Roc or God. You should be thankful he protected you from a far greater heartbreak." Joshua looked up at her as if wondering what could have been worse. As if reading his mind, Sally continued. " She could have left here carrying your child. There is no heartbreak worse than wondering if your child is well, is he hurt, is he safe, is he being treated as a human. You could be wondering all those things. But God's mercy saved you from marrying the wrong person and the heartbreak of wondering about a child. He did not do all of that on a wasted life. If that was so, when Roc found you, you would have been dead." She wiped the tears from her cheek, stood, picked up the tray and placed it on either side of his legs. "You need to rebuild your strength if you plan on getting out of that bed anytime soon." She went to reach for the top on the food.

Joshua brought her hand to his mouth and kissed it. "I never meant for you to worry. I know it only felt like God deserted me, but I knew better. I continue to talk to Him. I'm just not sure my faith is as strong as it once was."

Sally shook the napkin out and placed it on his bare chest as she thought of the right words. "The book of *Joshua, Chapter 1, Verse 5*: There shall not any man be able to stand before thee all the days of thy life: as I was with Moses, I shall be with thee. I will not fail thee or forsake thee."

She waited.

"The book of *Joshua, Chapter 1: Verse 9*: Have not I commanded thee? Be strong and of good courage; be not afraid, neither be thou dismayed, for the Lord thy God is with thee whithersoever thou goest."

Chapter Thirteen
Quantico, VA

A few hours had passed since Sally's visit ended. Roc decided to check on Joshua after his mother's visit. Things seemed to have gotten a little heated there for a moment, but later the two had settled down. She wondered why they were at odds with each other. According to Lucy, they were very close. If there was anyone who could bring Joshua out of this funk, it was Sally. After the little she'd heard, Roc wasn't so sure of that.

She rounded the corner and stopped dead in her tracks. He was standing at the dresser, naked from head to toe. The bandaging did not distract from his broad back, the masculine shape of his butt or the powerful grooves of his thighs. All that glory wasn't what caught her off guard. He had shaved, cut his hair low and this profile was that of a different man, one she had never seen before.

He pulled a pair of sweats from the drawer and nearly keeled over when he tried to step into them. Clearing her mind of her appraisal of his tantalizing appearance, Roc went into medical mode.

"What exactly do you think you are doing?"

He turned to face her and she almost wished she had kept her mouth shut. But then she would have missed the full glory of him, and she was certain, this man's body was meant to be seen, for it was just that magnificent. She had seen many men in her career, in all stages of dress, but this man...this man, looked like a Greek god with dimples. If she was having problems breathing she prayed it didn't show, for the look in his eyes showed he knew exactly the effect he was having on her.

Joshua saw the appreciation for his body in her eyes and could not stop his body from responding to her appreciative stare. As he explained to his mother, he did not want to be vulnerable to this woman in any way. He moved quickly through the pain to pull his pants up just to be stopped at his arousal which was not cooperating with him. He turned away and continued dressing. "Did you need something?"

Did she need something? Was that a trick question? She had to stop herself from answering honestly. Thank you, she said as he began to struggle pulling the shirt over his head. She immediately stepped forward to help. "A button down shirt would be easier for you for the next few days. Do you have any?"

Joshua looked at her wondering why she asked such a ridiculous question. "Do I have any dress shirts?"

The dimples from the grin blocked her thoughts for a moment. She lowered her eyes to block out their effect. "Yes, dress shirts," she mumbled realizing looking at his naked chest wasn't helping matters either.

"I think I have one or two." He walked over to a set of double doors on the other side of the room that she hadn't noticed and pushed them open.

She stepped from behind him and gasped. There was a men's store inside the closet. No it wasn't a closet. "This is a freaking store." She looked up at him,."There is a store inside your closet."

Joshua walked by her towards a wall on the left with nothing but shirts. They were arranged by colors, first solids, then stripes, polos, jerseys, t-shirts. On the right were suits. A wall with nothing but suits lined up on a rack that had the nerve to rotate. Directly ahead was a mahogany dresser, with drawers on each side. She couldn't resist. She pulled one drawer open, watches, hundreds of watches. Another drawer, cuff links, hundreds of cuff links. She turned around in the floor in awe. Coming full circle, on the wall in front of her were shoes. Hundreds of pairs of shoes. She walked around the corner to see where he had disappeared to when he pulled the shirt down. Roc stopped dead in her tracks, there was a dressing room with ceiling to floor mirrors on every wall. He discarded the sweats, put on a pair of dark slacks, and was buttoning a long sleeved, crisp, white shirt. He hit a button and the wall slid open to reveal a vertical rack of ties. They moved slowly down until he hit the button again and took one out. She watched all three views of him through the mirrors as he put the tie on and knotted it with precision.

Joshua watched her watching him. Damn if that didn't turn him on. He saw when she looked down at herself, knew she was thinking she was under dressed in her sweater, jeans and boots. To him she looked exactly like what she was, an angel. He looked away and continued to dress. That was the reason he had to finish this mission and get her out of his house. She was becoming too much of a temptation. Yes, he could simply have her and be done with it as he had in the past. But, since Akande, being with other women did not have the same appeal. He had tried. For a full year he tried non-stop. But each night when he closed his eyes, it was Akande who appeared. So he gave up. For the last two years, he had not touched or wanted to touch another woman. Looking back up at her, he knew Roc was different. He took his suit jacket off the hanger and turned towards her.

Roc was stunned by the difference in the man, as he put his suit jacket on. This was the one she had heard so much about over the years. This was the suave, sexy super agent that she thought only existed in the minds of the people who talked about him. She caught the grimace when he put his arms in the sleeves, as she drooled over the man. He walked right up to her, then put those baby browns directly on her.

"Thank you for bringing me home," he said. Then he smiled.

Damn if she wasn't dripping in her panties from that smile. They stood there for the longest moment just staring into each other's eyes. His drifted from her eyes to her lips. Was he going to kiss her? Her lips parted to speak but nothing came out.

"Joshua." Neither of them moved at the sound of Lucy's voice. "Joshua. The White House is on the line."

Joshua looked up, then walked by Roc. It took her a moment to breathe, then she turned and followed him. He walked to the wall in his bedroom and the wall seemed to just open right into the Cave.

Roc looked at Lucy questioning. "How?"

"Biometric eye scanner in the picture."

Roc nodded. "I've been out of the business for awhile."

Joshua gingerly sat, then pushed a button on the console. "Absolute here."

"Good evening, Joshua. It's good to see you."

"Hello, Mrs. Langston. You are as beautiful as always."

"Miss you." She smiled fondly at him. "Please hold for the President."

A few seconds later, the President appeared. Commando seemed to stand at attention at Joshua's side. "I can't say how good it is to see you, Joshua."

"Same here, Mr. President."

"How are you?"

"Battered, not beaten."

JD nodded and smiled. "I'm happy to see you. Have you spoken to your mother?"

"Yes, Sir, earlier today."

"Good, is she still cursing me out?"

"Yes, Sir. A little happier now that she put eyes on me."

"I serve at the pleasure of the Lassiters." He sat forward in his private office in the residence. "Hearing wild stories on this end," JD said. "My military is telling me you are killing our own people."

"Been dodging bullets..."

"And U.S. missiles on this end," Roc added.

JD looked at Joshua and grinned. "Can you ever go anywhere and not bring a woman back?"

Joshua grinned. "You sent this one to me."

JD sat back. "Roc is with you?"

"Yes Sir, she is and a little pissed by the change of events."

"Talk to me."

"Who's in the room, Sir?"

JD looked around. "People I trust."

"Mr. President, there are people you trust who are not worthy. I ask again, who's in the room?"

JD frowned. "Brian, James, Calvin and Samuel."

"All the Presidents men." Joshua grinned. It felt good to see all of them with JD. "We have a situation, Mr. President. I believe members of your administration are plotting to bring down your Presidency."

JD sat up and looked at the men around the room. "Hold on, Joshua, I'm switching monitors." He clicked a button and Joshua appeared on the big screen mounted on the wall. "Please continue."

"I have a document with a pardon for one Jonas Gary for all past and future actions taken against the United States."

JD took a seat next to Calvin. "We've been hearing that name in connection with what's happening with the House Republicans and the Attorney General."

Joshua looked behind him at Roc.

Roc took the seat next to him. "Sir, I was the one who took out the plane over Laredo. The Attorney General had nothing to do with it."

James sat forward. "You are admitting that you shot down a United States Military aircraft, killing ten men?"

"Yes, Sir and I will do it again if put in the same circumstances."

The men looked at each other. "Roc, this is Chief of Staff, Calvin Johnson. Give us the chain of events," Calvin requested.

"While delivering a message in Mexico, I came upon a weapons sale with a man named Jonas Gary. I investigated the man for weapons trafficking a few years back. I'm sure you remember the case. The men mentioned that the weapons' destination was the United States. Seeing they were assault weapons, I decided to explore and found a warehouse with hundreds of crates of weapons from assault rifles to missiles. Further investigation revealed several photographs of Vice President McClintock, and the Secretary of Defense. The pardon is signed by the same two individuals." The men sat forward. "My sentiments exactly."

"Tell me you have that document, Joshua," JD asked.

"I do. I secured the document, then attempted to destroy the weapons before they could be transported here. Unfortunately, somehow they detected I was there. Locked one of their land to air missiles on my chopper and brought me down."

"That's where I pick up Sir," Roc began. "At eight hundred hours three days ago I received a message from Ned, our CIA handler, stating Secretary Davenport requested my assistance in the recovery of an Operative in Mexico who was also in need of medical attention. Based on information from Ned, I arrived at a cabin in Mexico at thirteen hundred hours on day two. Upon my arrival, the Operative was stabilized, but in critical condition. During the process the Operative stated, and I quote *NS, WH, Don't Trust.* I interpreted that to mean that there was a national security issue, the White House should not be trusted. Since I do not know you, Sir, that meant you and anyone surrounding you. At eighteen hundred hours I received a secure message from Ned, the location had been compromised. I then made arrangements to exit Mexico through two channels, prepared my patient and moved out. Upon reaching the designated destination, we were fired upon from the United States plane that I thought was sent as pickup. I proceeded to my backup transportation at which time we were again fired upon. Once on board, we received a report of a missile activation. Using a land to air missile, I took out the threat. It was them or us. I chose them."

The men in the Oval Office sat back glancing at each other. Calvin was the first to speak. "Joshua, during your investigation did you come across any information connecting the Attorney General to weapons trafficking?"

"No."

"Any connection to illegal activity at all?"

"No, stupidity, yes, but nothing illegal."

JD grinned, then became serious. "It's been suggested that the events of the past 24 hours have been an attempt to manipulate the American public into believing the AG is connected to the weapons found in Texas. That this is all connected to a conspiracy to take down my administration. Do you concur with that suggestion?"

"I do."

"Do you believe the document you have will curtail this attempt?"

"No, Sir, it has not been authenticated. On its own, this document only shows a questionable relationship between the three parties. The public may ask why would a man like Gary need a pardon for actions against the U.S., or why would parties connected to the White House give such a pardon?"

"At that point," James chimed in, "the Vice-President could say you ordered him to give such a pardon."

"We know that's not true and so will the public." JD stood angrily.

"It would be your word against his," Calvin added.

JD stood by the window with his head down and hands in his pockets. "Either they take down my administration by connecting Gavin to the weapons or by connecting me to Gary." He turned and looked at them. "I don't like either option."

"Beat them at their own game," Brian suggested. "We know that Gary is involved, I have men on him as we speak. Let's see how deep this conspiracy goes."

"Conspiracy?" JD scowled.

"Yes, Mr. President, this is a conspiracy," Roc added. "Your military has been given orders that countermanded yours, that's a conspiracy of two entities of government. The military that is controlled by the Secretary of Defense and The Vice-President's Office." James added, "Both conspiring against the President's Office."

"Mr. President, if I may," Joshua began. "Allow me to follow the lead on Gary."

"No, Joshua, we just got you home. You are not ready," Samuel objected.

"He would be the best person," James stated. He put up his hand. "Hear me out Samuel. They think he is out of commission. They don't know we've made contact. He would be the last person they would expect to knock at their door."

"It's what will happen once the door is open that concerns me," Samuel stated. "He is in no condition to protect himself."

"I disagree with that assessment of my abilities, Sammy."

"I don't care of you disagree, Joshua, I care if you live."

"Joshua, take the lead, but leave the action to your team. Pull in whoever you need. Find me the evidence I need to shut this down. Roc, you're his armor until he can protect himself."

"Sir..." Roc stammered. "I'm in-active Sir."

"Roc," JD spoke. "Your President is asking you to serve."

Lucy stood in the background and smirked. "He got you." Commando just looked at her.

"Yes, Sir," Roc hesitantly replied.

"Joshua, it's this or you sit on the bench. I can't afford to lose the one person in the CIA I trust." JD added, "By the way, your handler Ned, have you heard from him since the warning?"

Joshua glanced at Roc. "No."

"Put someone on locating him," JD ordered. "He may have an answer or two for us. Our point of contact will be Al."

"Yes, Sir," Joshua disconnected the call, then pushed another button. Monique's image appeared on the screen.

"Location?"

"Alive. You?"

"Alive. Ned?"

"Nothing."

"Melissa Sue?"

"Alive. Delivering her to my father."

"Will meet you there. Out."

Joshua sat back. Roc could see he was in pain when he spoke. "Lucy?"

"On monitor 3."

Joshua pushed a button bringing the scene on monitor 3 to the main monitor. A picture and a dossier on Jonas Gary appeared. Joshua reviewed the information. "Jonas Gary is a mercenary for hire. He's working for someone. We need to find out who."

"Start with the pictures you saw," Roc suggested. "Who was in the pictures?"

"McClintock, Alston and Gary."

"Lucy, get a location on all three," Joshua said as he tried to stand. Pain shot through his back.

Roc put a hand on his thigh. "Take it slow, and breathe."

He couldn't tell which was more intense, the pain in his back, or the heat from the touch of her hand. The memory of her hands massaging his body down that morning was still very strong and virile. He willed his mind to fight through both. Using the console, he stood slowly. "I'm good."

"Yeah?" Roc watched him carefully. "I can give you something that will allow you to function while taking the bite out of the pain."

"No. I have to work through this."

"All right. Where are we starting?"

"Al Day's place. I want to talk to Melissa Sue, if possible."

Chapter Fourteen
Richmond, VA

Watching the medical team work on Melissa Sue was more than Al could take. "Are they all dead?" he asked his daughter, Monique, who stood next to him.

"Yes." the ones remaining are. A few left before I gained entry."

"You believe this is connected to Joshua?"

"I do. They tortured her to get information she didn't have."

"Al." His wife, Ryan, walked into the room. "Tucker is waiting to speak with you and the President called. Joshua is en route."

Looking at his wife, Al said a little too calmly for her liking, "Would you prepare the conference room? We need all the parties at the table to decide who is going to retaliate for what." He walked down the hallway.

Monique and Ryan watched his back. "He is too calm," Ryan exclaimed.

"Yep, people are about to die." Monique followed the path her father had taken.

Ryan exhaled and prayed for the strength and wisdom to keep both of them out of jail.

Al walked into the secured office off his bedroom. He took a seat at the desk and pressed a button. Tucker, his right hand man, appeared on the screen. "How is Julianna?"

"Adjusting to her new life," Tucker replied.

"Is she adjusting to you being a part of that life?"

"I'd like to think so." He shrugged.

"Jonas Gary has surfaced."

Tucker sat up. "I'll be on the next plane."

They all stared at him as if he had three heads. Al, Ryan and Monique couldn't believe what had just occurred.

"What?" Joshua asked, tired of everyone gawking at him.

They all looked at each other, as Monique shrugged her shoulders and walked over. "We're not used to you actually walking through a door." She walked around him, surveying every angle. "You're hurt."

"Still better than you on my worst day."

Monique put her hands on her hips, and smiled. "Still as arrogant as ever." She looked up at Roc, raising a questioning eyebrow. "And you are?"

"With him," Roc replied.

"That's cute," Monique quipped. "Do you have a name?"

"I do."

All stared at her waiting, but she didn't offer anything more. Joshua spoke. "Manners, right. Roc, Al Day and his wife, Ryan." He then pointed to Monique. "That is Al's bratty daughter Monique."

Rarely did things surprise Roc, but the petite young woman standing in front of her with the wavy hair, black jeans, thigh high boots, and crisp white blouse did not appear to be an agent of any kind. She had to respect her game. She extended her hand. "Roc."

It was then Monique who was surprised. "You're Roc," she said unbelieving.

"I am," Roc replied with a smirk.

"Ha," Monique laughed and looked at Joshua. "Ha, I'll be damned." She nodded her head in acceptance. "Well, all right then." She looked Roc up and down. "I'm not even mad at you."

Roc laughed. "Glad to hear it."

"Okay, can we get this mutual admiration moment over so we can get down to the reason we are here," Joshua huffed.

"Is he on his period or something?" Monique asked.

Al had to smile at his daughter. "He does seem a little touchy, doesn't he?"

"Melissa Sue is in the back." Ryan nodded as she smiled at Joshua. "It's good to have you home."

"How is she?"

"Beaten." Al frowned as everyone followed him down the hallway.

Joshua stopped when he reached the doorway. The tall leggy blonde was beaten beyond recognition. "What are the doctors saying? Will she make it?"

Al nodded. "Monique pulled her out in time."

"They didn't want to kill her, just extract information." Monique shook her head as she spoke.

"Our military did that?" Roc asked.

"No, they weren't military. They were mercenaries."

"Jonas Gary?" Joshua asked.

"That was one of the names," Monique replied, "but before I pulled Melissa Sue out a call was made to someone named Holt."

"Holt? What did you find out about him?" Joshua asked.

"Nothing." Monique shook her head. "But I know the men who made the call are supposed to meet up with him in D.C. and I have the cell phone number the call was made from."

"We can get coordinates on that number and track the person who made the call," Roc offered.

"Good." Joshua looked at Melissa Sue again. She was there because she helped him. Whoever did that to her was going to pay. "Send me the number. I'll track it down." He saw Monique's expression change. She clearly wanted to stay on this leg of the case. Joshua shook his head. "I need you to find Ned."

Monique hesitated, then pulled out her cell. "Where's your device?"

Joshua turned to Al. "I need a secure means to communicate. Sally has been compromised."

"Done." Al turned to Ryan and nodded.

Al watched his wife walk down the hallway. Damn if she wasn't as sassy as ever. He turned back. "Are you in any condition to be tracking down people?" he asked as he gave Joshua a once over.

"I'll be with him," Roc responded.

"Are you any good?"

"She's the best," Joshua replied with a smirk, then walked off.

"Pissed at you, because you're not a man," Monique quipped.

"Is he ever." All Roc could do was shake her head and follow him.

Washington DC

The phone was traced to an apartment building in Southeast D.C. Joshua and Roc sat outside the building watching.

"How do you want to handle this?" Roc asked.

Joshua looked over at her and smiled. "We're going to walk through the front door."

"I'm cool with that, but can you handle it?"

"I can handle my own," Joshua mumbled as he got out of the vehicle. Why did her questioning his abilities piss him off? Hell, he was injured and her question was legit. For some reason, it pissed him off coming from her.

"Under normal conditions, I have no doubt that you could handle whatever," Roc explained as she jumped out of the vehicle to follow him. "However, under the circumstances, it may be better if you let me handle this one."

They reached the door. "I said, I got this."

"Joshua, don't allow your pride to put your behind in jeopardy."

"I got this," he snapped.

The door opened and a huge bull of a man stood there. "What do you want?" he all but hollered at them.

Roc put her hands up in surrender, then leaned against the wall with one leg crossed over the other and her arms folded against her chest. Her stance seemed relaxed, but she was ready to jump in if either of the other goons in the room decided to help their friend. Besides, she knew one punch to his left side and Joshua would be down for the count. But there were times when you had to let a man be a man, no matter how stupid it was.

The first punch Joshua landed was solid, not bad, the second decent, but when he tried to lift his left leg for a kick to the man's mid-section, the impact was weak. They were going to have to work on that, Roc thought. The man was able to recover sooner than Joshua expected, landing an upper cut into his midsection. That knocked the wind out of him. The man then kicked him, where...in the left side. The impact was so powerful it knocked him to the floor, propelling his body backwards until he landed right at her feet.

Roc looked down. "Is it all right if I get a little piece of this action?"

All Joshua could do was close his eyes and moan. Just as he did, the man came over to grab Joshua off the floor.

"Not this one." Roc kicked her leg out behind the man's knees, knocking him to the ground. Before he could recover, she punched him in the windpipe with her fist. One of the other men saw his friend was down and took a step towards her. Before he made the second step, she pulled a small round object from her pocket, with spikes on the end, out of her pocket and flung it at him. It landed in the middle of his forehead as if it was a third eye. The last man decided he was not taking any chances. He pulled his gun. Unfortunately, her trigger finger was faster. Her Glock was smoking, before the man realized she had shot the gun out of his hand. The man grabbed his hand, singing in soprano.

Roc walked over, grabbed the man by the neck, pushing him against the wall. "I don't have a lot of time. So I'm going to ask this question one time." She put emphasis on the words *one time,* by putting one finger in his face. "Where can I find Holt?" She applied more pressure to the man's neck while he was still screaming about his hand. "One time." She raised a brow as she spoke. When she was certain her meaning was understood, she began to release the pressure from the man's neck.

"Text number," the man whined. "All I have is a phone with a text number."

"May I have the phone, please?" Roc asked in the sweetest way. The man pulled the cell phone from his pocket with his bloody hand and looked at her as if she was crazy. "Thank you," Roc said, then punched the man, knocking him out. As the man fell to the floor, she turned back to Joshua, who was now standing and smiled. "We now have a lead to Holt."

Joshua said nothing, but the look in his eyes spoke volumes. He turned and walked out. Roc closed her eyes and exhaled. "Men and their pride." She blew out a deep breath then followed him out the door.

When she stepped outside, she fully expected him and the car to be gone. But he was sitting inside. She opened the door, sliding into the passenger seat and the moment the door closed he pulled off. Sensing the last thing he wanted to talk about would be the confrontation, she decided to start with the business at hand.

"Now that we have a means, should we contact this Holt guy?" A few seconds went by, no reply. She watched as he merged onto the highway. Traffic was backed up, as always. She tried again. "We could have Lucy put a trace on the cell, give Holt a call and pick up his location that way." Seconds went by, nothing. It was a rare occurrence, but her temper was about to show its ugly head. For three days she had done all she could to help this man to heal. Her mission was rescue and recovery. That meant that she wasn't finished until Absolute was back to his full capabilities. He had to be able to protect himself in combat. Absolute at half strength was an imposing man. However, her job was to get him back to his full strength and that's what she was going to do whether he liked it or not. Rather than stoop to his level of stupidity, Roc decided to take the high road and let him have his moment. She started singing, *If This World Were Mine,* Tammy and Marvin's version.

When they reached the house, Joshua stomped into the kitchen, slamming the door behind him. Lucy looked up, with her thin black reading glasses perched on the tip of her nose, as he stormed by her. "Where's Roc?" she asked to his back. She looked over at Commando. The dog put his paw over his eyes as if to say, *I'm staying out of this.* The sound of the door opening caused her to turn. "Hey." she said to Roc as she walked in, then nodded her head towards the now empty space where Joshua stormed through seconds ago. "What's up with him?"

Commando ran over to Roc and barked. Roc smiled and rubbed him behind the ears. "Hey man," she said to Commando then looked up at Lucy. "He's a little upset," Roc said as she pulled out the cell and gave it to Lucy. "Do you think you can trace the calls off this and get a possible location on this guy Holt?"

"Who is he?"

"I don't know, but he's involved in this conspiracy. I'm sure of it." She looked at Commando. Not in the mood to be questioned more by Lucy, Roc turned to Commando. "You want to check the perimeter with me?"

Commando barked. Roc smiled. "Okay man." She grabbed his ball from the corner and a flashlight. "Let's go."

After walking the perimeter, Roc decided to check on Joshua. She knocked lightly on his door. There was no answer. She cracked the door and Commando pushed it the rest of the way with his nose. "I'm going to tell him you opened that door."

Commando looked back over his shoulder as though to say, and what? Roc smiled and walked tentatively into the room. Roc stopped at the sitting area of his bedroom, which was furnished in burgundy with a leather sofa, recliner and a table. A large flat screen television was on. She followed the wall to her left, to the doorway leading into his sleeping quarters. She hesitated, until Commando came back to the door and looked at her as if to say what are you waiting for an invitation? She frowned at the dog, then he turned and walked back into the room. Roc walked over to the door and peeked in. "Joshua," she quietly called out. If he was already asleep she did not want to disturb him. The room was semi dark, but she could see Commando was getting comfortable at the foot of the bed.

"What do you want?"

Joshua was standing in the doorway of the bathroom. A towel wrapped around his waist and one in his hand. Why did he look more dangerous unclothed then he did fully dressed? "I came to close the wound that was opened tonight."

"I'm good." Roc stood there staring at him. "I think I'm man enough to take a shower, if not for anything else."

Roc wasn't going to play into his self-pity. "The wound is on your back. It would be difficult for you to reach. I need to close it again. Why don't you lay on the bed, I'll close the wound, then I'll be out of your hair for the night."

Joshua knew the wound had to be closed. But the thought of this woman seeing him as less than a man bothered him. He was sure Samuel was never this weak around her. He hated the fact that she made him feel inferior. He knew he could handle himself and protect her if need be. He just hadn't been able to show her that. He pulled the towel off, threw it to the side then laid on his stomach across the bed.

Roc walked over to the bed and just as she thought, the kick to his side had opened the wound. She walked into the bathroom and washed her hands. She then opened her kit, put on plastic gloves, and assessed the damage. It wasn't bad. His body had begun healing well. "I'm going to replace the dressing, then bandage you back up."

He didn't reply. The way he was positioned across the bed, made it difficult to reach the wound. Asking him to move was out of the question. She was lucky he was allowing her to do this much. The ideal position would be to straddle him, but...what the hell. She did just that. Getting comfortable, she placed her kit next to her and began singing, Natalie Cole's version of *Inseparable*. She had no idea why that song come to mind, but it did and it calmed her nerves as she began working.

Now she was in his personal space, and it felt strange, but nice. Her touch was more like a caress, than a rub. Her fingers were small and gentle. When she touched him before, she reminded him of his mother. Not this time. This time her touch was smooth, soft, sensual. Each stroke was like a tender, healing caress, reaching down into his soul. Then there was her voice, the tempo of her voice accentuated the rhythm of her hands and he found himself drifting. He felt the moment she slowly eased off of him, for he missed the warmth of her closeness. She must have thought he had drifted off to sleep.

"I'm usually pretty friendly, especially with women. Circumstances changed that." His voice was low and humble. "I want my life back."

His words almost brought her to tears. "Your wish is my command." She put the cover over him, then walked to the door. She found herself pausing.

"Thank you."

She smiled and walked out of the room.

Chapter Fifteen
Washington, D.C.
Day Four

The next morning, before sunrise, Roc had Joshua out running with Commando. The trio ran along the Potomac River, which bordered one side of his property. They stopped frequently to allow him to catch his breath, but she had him right back up to complete the five miles. Afterwards they hit his gym, and he felt like he asked Satan to bring him back to life.

"Okay what's your preferred training method?"

"Fencing." He grinned.

"Why?"

"It takes finesse, precision, and a touch of class to fence."

"Foil, épée or saber?"

"You know a little bit about fencing." He grinned as he stood and opened a cabinet on the wall. "Saber, of course."

"The gentlemen of the round table preferred swords." Roc stepped forward as he handed her a saber. "In the eighteenth century, the sword was symbolic of liberty. It represents liberty and strength." She circled swishing the saber through the air, as she took the battle stance. "The sword was often used as a symbol of the word of God. It reflected the high prestige and wealth of the owner."

"It's a shame the weapon is only used in ceremonies," he said as he took his stance. "This is the one form of battle that separates the men from the boys." They both bowed, then saluted each other. "Engarde" The battle began. "You see, the role of a gentlemen in the time of London societies, with the balls and aristocracy always intrigued me. Specifically, the monarchies, where titles and knighthoods were given."

The battle pressed on. "I take it you would have been a knight of the highest honor. A prince, oh no, wait, a king."

"No, I would have been a duke, in search of a duchess worthy of my status in life. The kings would call upon me when they were in need of defense of those who were weaker. Then all the maidens of the land would be at my feet bidding to do my will."

"Then you concede you are less than a king."

"I concede nothing. It is you who need to concede to me," he grinned.

"I'm listening." The battle became intense, for neither was giving the other a clear victory.

"You will concede that I am the more capable and you are merely a female, albeit a fine one, playing at being superior. And at some point, you too will be at my feet bowing to my superiority. For I am a man. God put us here to rule. He put women here to bear children."

The statement pissed Roc off. The hell with men and their pride. The battle raged on, with the sabers swishing through the air.

"I will concede nothing until you concede that you, Joshua, are not a king, but a king maker."

The statement caught him off guard, for it was the very thing his mother had said to him. Roc lunged, knocking him to the floor. She stood over him. "Until you can stop me from knocking you on your behind, I am superior."

Roc dropped the saber on the floor next to him. "Prove me wrong and I'll be out of your hair and on my way to my nice simple life, waiting to bear a worthy man's children." She turned and walked out of the room. She had reached the room her clothes were in, when she realized, she had lost her cool. That was something she never did and over a man who is arrogant, egotistical and a royal pain in the ass. For the life of her she could not figure out why in the hell she was falling in love with him.

Royce sat on a bench on the outskirts of the National Mall. People were moving about doing the things that most people took for granted, just enjoying life. As the head of Homeland Security, he knew there was a price to pay everyday for that freedom. There were those who were living the American dream, the one that promises life, liberty and the pursuit of happiness. Then there were others, like the man digging through the garbage can behind him, who dedicated their lives to making that dream possible.

"Is Absolute safe?"

Royce never looked over his shoulder to acknowledge the man, he continued to read from his tablet. "Battered, but home."

"Safe home compromised."

"Destroyed?"

"Affirmative."

"You?"

"Pissed. My system was infiltrated."

"Looking for?"

"Absolute."

"Any leads?"

"Level four clearance."

The response put Royce on edge. "Four?"

"I'll be in touch." With that, the man stumbled away.

Joshua was sitting at his kitchen table having his breakfast when Roc walked in dressed in jeans, a sweater, and flat black boots. She looked simple, sweet... good. That was something he had not noticed before. She didn't wear high heels, makeup, jewelry, the girly things like Monique or some of the other women he knew. She kept things simple and she still looked good. It suddenly hit him that he liked simple.

He knew he had offended her with his superiority talk. In truth he was joking, but she didn't know that because she'd never had the Absolute experience. She'd only known the wounded Joshua. It was time for her to be graced with all of him. Not as a way to seduce her, he told himself. Just as a way for her to see another aspect of him. Before he could even say good morning, Lucy walked into the room.

"We have a location on that number you wanted me to check out," Lucy announced with a pep in her step.

"Where?"

"Not where...who. The number is a part of a batch used by the office of the Vice-President of the United States of America. At the moment he is in the National Mall."

Joshua jumped up and grabbed his suit jacket with Roc in tow. "Send the coordinates to Genevieve."

"You strapped," he asked as they climbed into the SUV.

"Always." They pulled off.

"Good morning, Genevieve."

The console lit up. "Good morning Joshua. How may I serve you today?"

He grinned. "I love a woman who knows her place." He glanced at Roc as she turned to look out the window. "I'm joking here," he said. "Where is your sense of humor?"

"It left the moment I brought you home."

"That's a shame, for it takes a good sense of humor to make it in this world. Wouldn't you agree, Genevieve?

"I do not comprehend humor."

"That figures," Roc snorted.

"Don't snort, it's not lady like."

"I never claimed to be a lady," Roc replied.

For a moment, they drove in silence. Finally it was Joshua who spoke. "I was an ass earlier this morning."

"Just this morning?" Roc asked. "It seems to me that you've been an ass for a couple of days, now."

"Hey, hey, I was injured for some of those days. You know what happens when you have an injured wild animal. They tend to have a bit of a bite, so those days don't count."

Roc turned to look out the window.

Joshua looked over at her, and decided to let it go for now. "Genevieve, scramble my GPS."

"Scrambled."

"Thank you. Now, let's see what we can find out about what Eleanor McClintock is up to."

They pulled up on the monument side of the National Mall. People were walking, some sitting on the grounds with family. Some had dogs playing with Frisbees, and or balls. This was that time of the day when the mall was well populated. Which was probably why they selected this area.

Roc got out of the vehicle and began walking in the direction on the monitor.

"Wrong way," Joshua called out as he walked down into the subway.

Roc turned and followed him underground. "Where are you going?"

Joshua pulled open one of the service doors and walked through. Roc pulled her weapon and followed.

"We are going to a place where we can see them, but they will have no idea we are here."

The man had to be in pain, but to her it seemed he was in his element. He was literally strutting through the underground tunnel, as though it was his personal runway, dressed in a suit, with his trench coat flying out around him. *It's possible, just possible, working might speed up his recovery.* Roc watched him and wondered how a man could look good walking through a sewer in D.C.

The underground walkway was wet, musty, not the most pleasant smell in the world, but not enough to make a person gag. The trail was under the sidewalk where pedestrians steered clear of Frisbees, jumping dogs and running children. Joshua pulled out his cell to check the coordinates sent to him by Lucy. "They're this way." He pointed forward and continued walking. Every hundred feet there was a grid built into the side of the concrete allowing them the ability to see people in the Mall without being detected. Joshua stopped at one, but the view wasn't what he needed. They continued on to the next. He stopped, looked out between the bars of the grid. "Legs." He grinned. "Nice long legs." He reached inside his suit jacket and pulled out a pipe like object. Turning to her he asked, "You know how to run surveillance without being detected?"

The question was insulting and he knew it. "Patience is a virtue, did you know that?" Roc asked as she took the cell phone he extended from him.

Joshua gave her a crooked grin. "You're always so calm, at peace."

"I try to be," Roc replied as she watched the monitor for any movement by the target. Joshua extended the device, then tested the range by following a dog running after a Frisbee. "We have eyes and ears," he mumbled as he scanned the area.

"Aww, there is nothing like eyes and ears." Roc nodded.

Joshua grinned. "The best there is. Where is she?"

Roc looked down at the monitor. "To our left."

Joshua pointed the device to the left. "She's alone."

"Then we wait." Roc nodded. "Let's see who she can lead us to." She looked at Joshua. "Would you like for me to hold that?" She didn't want to get into another pissing contest with him, but she know if he held that arm up too long it would begin to cause him some discomfort.

The question was not meant the way he took it, yet it still gnawed at him that she thought he needed help. He did, he just didn't want her to think he did. Joshua closed his eyes to shake off the stupid thought. *What in the hell was wrong with him?* Since when did he give a damn what anyone thought of him. His hope was that the help was offered for medical reasons only. "I'm not used to someone trying to protect me. I'm normally the protector. I'm not saying this to be a smart ass, it just happens to be the truth. I know I'm limited at the moment. But I promise to let you know if I become uncomfortable. Fair enough?"

Roc looked at him sideways, then tilted her head,."Fair enough." She turned back to the monitor.

Joshua tried not to acknowledge her presence, but a few things kept coming to his mind. When he asked if she knew Samuel, her response was 'as well as a wife knows a husband'. Then, there was the easy way they had with each other.

Ten minutes of those thoughts was enough. "What's the deal with you and Samuel?"

The question surprised her. She adjusted her position under the pipe to get a better look at him. "Ask what you want to know." The woman held his glare.

"Are you sleeping with my brother?"

Never looking his way, she replied. "You must have a low opinion of your brother. He's a married man. It would be disrespectful to his wife if he participated in any extra-curricular activities." She looked away. "I've never known your brother to disrespect any woman."

"You believe I would?"

"You just did when you asked the question of me," she replied. "We have company at three o'clock."

Joshua looked up at the target. He watched as a man approached and embraced the woman they were following. "Hmm, that hug lasted a bit long for a casual acquaintance."

"Mrs. McClintock has a little a little extra-curricular activity going on." Roc grinned. "I wonder if the hubby knows."

"Not surprising, most married women have a side piece."

"You know that from experience?"

Joshua grinned as he ran his hand down his jaw line. "I've had a round or two with a wife here and there."

"Of course you have," Roc smirked. "Do you recognize him?"

Joshua took a picture with his handheld. "You don't seem to have a very good opinion of me."

"It's not my place to have an opinion one way or another." She looked up at him. "Just as it's not your place to question me on my sexual activity."

The phone beeped. Joshua was slow to drag his eyes from hers. There was something in hers eyes that made him feel guilty for treading into that territory. A glance at the screen showed a name to go with the face. "Face recognition is a wonderful thing." He turned the monitor to her.

Roc smiled. "Well, well, well, if it isn't the elusive, David Holt."

"Let's go," Joshua said as he turned, swiftly walking in the direction from which they'd come.

"Holt or McClintock?" Roc asked, wondering whom they were going to follow.

"Both," Joshua replied as they reached the door leading back to the subway.

"We can't take both, Joshua." Roc stopped him. "We," she pointed to him, then herself, "are going to follow one or the other, not both."

"Look, we have a lead in this case and I'm not going to blow it because you have some kind of unquenched thirst to play mother hen." He turned to walk up the steps, with Roc in tow. "I'm taking Holt, you take the woman."

Roc reached up and grabbed him before he took another step. She pulled him back into the subway.

"What in the hell is wrong with you?"

Roc put her arm around his neck and pulled his lips down to hers.

Joshua was stunned to silence, as her mouth demanded he open his. And he did. What a contrast. The woman was hard as nails on the outside, but as sweet as honey on the inside. It only took a moment for him to move closer to indulge further into the smooth motions of her tongue. That was when he felt it. The hard cold steel in her hand behind her back. He attempted to pull away, but she held him firmly against her. She fired two quick shots through the lining of his coat. Joshua turned to the sound of a body hitting the ground. He looked at the man, who had two holes, center mass in his chest, then looked back at her. "Well." He licked his lips. "That's one way to douse a fire."

Roc checked the man for identification. They both groaned the moment she pulled the black folded case from his pocket. She looked up at Joshua. "CIA." She looked back at the man with the gun still in his open hand. "Now why would our own people be after us? And how in the hell did they know how to find us?"

Two things he knew for sure, no make that three. His reflexes were off. He never saw the weapon the man had. Two, his own agency had ordered a hit on him and three, this being the most uncomfortable one of all, Roc, had some juicy lips.

"We have to get out of here." Joshua grabbed her by the hand. "I'm sure he is not alone."

They ran towards the next set of steps, then stopped. "Oh hell, more of the bad guys," Roc noted.

"This way," Joshua said.

Roc turned, but he was gone.

"Hey, up here."

Roc looked up to see he had climbed up into a vent and was holding his hand down to her. She grabbed his hand and he pulled her up seconds before two more men rounded the bend. They lay in the tight vent looking down at the men as they found their partner. Joshua snapped a picture of one of the men when he looked around.

The man pushed the earpiece. "We need a cleanup team."

Joshua and Roc looked at each other. They didn't have cleanup teams. At least, that's not how they referred to their counterparts who wiped a place new, as if nothing ever happened. Joshua nodded his head backwards. The two slowly moved down the vent, away from the action happening below them. They moved in unison until they reached another vent opening. Looking out, they seemed to be in a deserted part of the subway system. They were about to jump out when the sound of a Metro whisked by, nearly taking Joshua's arm with it. He'd pulled back just in time. They waited for the train to go by, then looked out again.

"We have bad news, and bad news. Which do you want first?"

"I'll take bad for twenty, Alex." Roc smiled.

In the dark, musty subway, with little light, her smile was bright. He couldn't help thinking about the kiss. The fact that their bodies were intimately fused together in the small vent did not help. "If I didn't know better, I would have the impression that you are enjoying this little venture."

"I am. This is a Jack moment. Do we go back and take our chances with the fake CIA agents or try to out run a train?"

"You look at *24*?" Joshua lay there in the vent with her body pressed snuggly against his.

"Every chance I could when it was on TV."

He grinned. "That's all right."

"I'm happy you are pleased with that bit of information. But I must ask, do you have a plan for our bad versus bad situation?"

"Hmm, what would MacGyver do?"

"Die."

"You don't like MacGyver." He frowned.

"Give me Jack."

"So what would Jack do in this situation?"

"That's easy." Roc grinned. "Jack would outrun the train."

Joshua laughed, a rich deep laugh. The first good laugh he'd had in years. "Super agent Roc, let's outrun the next train."

"This is when I miss Ned," Roc sighed. "He would be able to tell us down to the split second how much time we had before the next train."

Joshua nodded. "That he would, however, we don't have Ned. So by my calculation another train will be coming through in about seven minutes. Do you think we can make it to the opening before the train runs us down?"

Roc peeked around to get a better look at the distance to the next opening. "How's your back?"

"Non-factor."

"Wrong answer," Roc replied. "We'll wait until the next train passes, then we'll jump and haul ass to the opening."

"You should have children."

"A moment ago you were critical of my maternal instincts."

"Not in a derogatory way. I feel they are focused in the wrong direction. I'm not a child. I'm a grown man."

"That is evident," Roc replied as she adjusted her leg which was over one of his. "You refuse to accept you are an injured man, who has limitations. My job is to eliminate those limitations as soon as possible."

"Is it always about the job with you?"

"If that was the case, I would still be active."

The statement confused Joshua. "You didn't re-up?"

"No."

"Then what are you doing here?"

"You have people in high places who care about your well-being. They wanted you to have the best chance at survival so they commissioned me to come in."

"You're good," he acknowledged.

"Yes, I know."

"Arrogant, are we?"

"No more than you."

"I'll take that. Why did you leave the agency?"

They heard the Metro approaching. Roc looked up and turned her body to be lowered out. "To get married and have babies," she replied as the train rushed by.

Once the train passed, Joshua began to lower her down, head first. While he held onto her feet, she did a handstand, then flipped up right. She knew Joshua's back was not going to allow him to do the same, so to avoid the pending argument, Roc reached inside, grabbed his arms and yanked him through. They fell backwards onto the platform with him on top of her.

"Did you get married?" he asked as he lay there.

"No."

"Have babies?"

"No. Now if the personal inquiry is over we need to get off this track and through that opening."

He took a long look at her, then stood extending his hand to her. As they brushed themselves off, and began walking, he asked, "Why not?"

"Why not what," she asked as she looked back down the track over her shoulder.

"Why didn't you get married or have babies?"

She shrugged her shoulders. "Never found that God fearing man who loves children and a sense of adventure." The tunnel was getting lighter which meant they were getting close to the opening or at the very least, another station.

He stopped suddenly. "How did they get my GPS code?"

"What?"

"That's how they are tracking me. The night we were chased in the car, they used my GPS implant. To do that, you have to know the code. Only Ned has access to the code."

"Ned would not give up that info," Roc stated.

"No, he wouldn't." They stopped and stared at each other. "That means someone hacked into his system."

"Or, he's dead."

Joshua was thinking the same thing, but did not want to say it out loud. That concern had to be placed on the back burner for another train was heading right at them. Roc grabbed Joshua's coat and pulled him into a full speed run. "Train," she yelled.

They took off running towards the opening. Joshua flew by Roc grabbing her hand and pulling her behind him.

"Don't stare at it, run."

The train was coming at them full speed. As they rounded the bend, the end of the tunnel wall was only a few feet away. They had to haul ass to make it. Roc was laughing at the situation. Joshua thought she was crazy. He grabbed her by the waist, jumped from the track, rolled their bodies down the grassy hill and stopped. The two lay there breathing hard, the adrenaline pumping through their bodies and laughing as if they'd just come off a joy ride.

"Now that's what I call fun!" Roc laughed. "I have to do that again."

Joshua laid back on the grass, laughing, and breathing hard. Suddenly he stopped. The memory of another adventure came to mind. Akande crossed his mind. He sat up, causing the pain in his back to seep through. He stared at Roc. Her reaction to their brush with death was completely different. She was sitting there enjoying the moment. Did the fact that he liked that make him crazy? He stood, extended his hand to help her up.

"Let's get out of here," he said solemnly.

Roc stood and wondered what she had said or done this time. Wiping her pants off, she looked around. "Any idea where we are?"

Joshua looked around. "Yeah." He turned and began walking. "We have to remove the GPS or they will locate us again."

"I wouldn't remove it." She joined him in step.

He looked at her as they walked. "Explain yourself, Lucy," he grinned with an accent.

The other Joshua was back, just guarded. "What's better, we chase after them or have them come to us?"

He thought about that as they walked. "Okay." He nodded his head as they walked across the tracks where several hotels and other businesses were. "Let's grab a room. I need to think."

Chapter Sixteen
Washington, D.C.

The two checked into a hotel after picking up a few necessities. A change of clothes, toiletries, and a magnet, was all they needed. After entering the room, Joshua removed his coat and was pissed to find she had shot a hole in his coat. "I can't believe you shot the coat," he fussed. "You can shoot anything else, but not the damn coat."

Roc stood there in disbelief. She had saved his life and he was upset about a coat. "I can't believe you are prancing around about a coat."

Joshua stopped, then glared at her. "I do not prance. It is not just a coat. It is a survival tool. Built in the same manner as those of our ancestors. When our ancestors went to hunt, their coats were made with certain tools sewn in. I have everything I would need to survive inside that coat." He spread it open and pulled a button from the inside. He held it up. "A few inches over and we all would have blown up."

"I've seen your closet, you have at least a hundred coats in there." She sat on the edge of the bed. "I had no idea you were so finicky."

He narrowed his eyes on her. She was right, he was acting like a prick and he had no freaking idea why. "Don't you have something you should be doing?"

Roc stood, picked up her bag and walked towards the bathroom. "You're right. I need to take a shower." She stopped at the bathroom door. "I'm really sorry about your coat. I'll replace it. In the meantime, will you try to get information on David Holt?"

Why did she have to be so cool, calm, logical? He exhaled. "Sure," he huffed as she closed the bathroom door. God, she made him feel inadequate. He realized that was his problem and he had to find a way to deal with it. He pulled off his suit jacket, placed it across the back of the desk chair then sat down, placing his long legs on the edge of the bed.

Picking up his bag, he tried to shake off the feeling that he was missing something. This was one of those times, when he needed to talk to Ned. He hadn't said much about it, but the fact that Ned was missing concerned him greatly. He laid his head back and willed the subtle reminder of his injury to calm down. The crawl through the ventilation system of the subway did not help, nor did rolling down that hill. But damn if it wasn't fun. He smiled at the memory, then thoughts of the kiss came to mind. Damn if it didn't feel like the very first time. The kiss made his toes curl, it was clear it took over his mind, for he never heard anyone approaching. Did not sense anyone's presence or the danger. That was the one thing he always picked up on, danger. The thought bothered him. Then he realized, with Roc around, he didn't have to watch his back. He wasn't alone.

That was it. For the last three years he'd felt utterly alone. Yes, he had a huge family, but all of them expected him to be their hero and he liked it. He liked being the one everyone called when they were in trouble or needed help. It's just, when he was in trouble, he didn't feel he could go to any of them without diminishing his hero image. So he stayed away from home, trying to deal with the devastation of his country's betrayal. His head snapped up. That was the first time he'd thought of it that way. Every other time it had been Akande's betrayal.

Standing, he stretched, opened the bag. A stop at an electronic store gave him what he needed. A device that could scramble the signal from his implanted GPS any time he wanted to. Now was one of those times. He set the scrambler up and placed it on the desk. The water in the bathroom cut off, and that's when he heard it. Roc was singing again. This time it was *Stop, Look and Listen,* by Angela Bofill. God, she had a musical voice. Just the sound of it soothed him, regardless of how restless he may be. He shook the thoughts off. The last thing he needed or wanted was to need anyone, especially not a woman. He pulled out his tablet and began searching for any information he could find on David Holt.

Roc was thankful for the reprieve. She needed to get a moment away from Joshua. The adrenaline of the day had seeped through her pores and had her thinking crazy there for a moment. The second she saw the man turn towards them as they walked up the steps, the only thing she could think to do was to hide Joshua's face. That's when she decided to pull his head down and kiss him. Her eyes never left the man, who had pulled his weapon and was about to point it at Joshua's back. The look of victory was in the man's eyes and she saw his intent. His intent was to kill and she couldn't, wouldn't, allow that to happen. Not to Joshua. She would be lying to herself if she said the kiss or the closeness to him, crawling through the duct, did not have an effect on her. It did, but not as much as hearing him laugh when they were rolling down the hill. That touched her heart more than anything. Yes, she needed that shower, not just to clean the dirt and sweat of the day away, but to clear her mind of impossible thoughts. Funny, it was another Lassiter man that gave her those kinds of thoughts. Unlike his brother, Joshua didn't make her feel unsure about herself. She was comfortable, and didn't feel she had to think or be a certain way to be around him. She was just plain....no, she wasn't. She looked into the mirror, then wiped away the steam to take a good look. When on a mission, she was Roc— not herself—Roc. With that settled, she put on the robe she'd bought and walked back into the room.

"What did we find out about this David Holt man?" Roc asked as she came out of the bathroom in a white robe, and pulling the shower cap from her head.

Joshua watched as her hair fell around her shoulders. She looked down at the monitor in his hand as she talked. "Did we find a connection between him and the Gary guy?"

She was standing too close. He could smell her fresh scent from the shower. He took a step away and sat in the chair at the table. "Nothing. I wish Ned was in place. He has a program that would find the connection."

Roc walked over to the dresser picked up her brush and began to use it on her hair. She turned to him pointing the brush at him. "You know, if we can connect Gary with Holt, we might be able to keep those two trains from colliding."

The pose she had was too much for him to take. "Will you go dress, please."

Taken aback by the tone of his angry request, Roc, closed the top of her robe, confused. "Sure." She cleared her throat. "I'll, umm go into the bathroom to change."

Joshua's jaw clenched. He didn't mean to sound so rough. There was a battle within him and damn if he wasn't losing. He threw the device on the bed then walked to the bathroom door. He knocked lightly. "I didn't mean it to come out like that," he said to the door.

"Not a problem. This is only going to take a moment."

He exhaled and walked away from the door. He heard her when she began singing again, *I Try*, by Will Downing. She was trying to stay calm. He noticed that whenever she was nervous, she would sing to calm herself. What she didn't realize was that her singing, her voice, had a different effect on him. He laid his head back. He just couldn't understand why he kept snapping at her. The woman had saved his life, more than once. She did all she could to keep him comfortable even when he rejected her offers. Yet, he kept snapping at her. It's because he could feel her caring spirit sneaking a little further under his skin. She started another song. He couldn't help it, he grinned. He wondered if she realizes she switches up between Gospel and R&B when she's nervous or upset.

She came out of the bathroom in a pair of jeans and a big tee shirt. "As I was saying, I believe there is a connection between Holt and Gary."

He watched her under his eyelashes and wondered if she thought the outfit would be a turn off. It wasn't. He watched her under his eyelashes as he nodded. "I believe that as well." He saw her relax when he replied. He felt like an ass for making her nervous. Then she tripped over his bag. She bent over to move it and that was his undoing. He moved with the speed of a panther after its prey. He grabbed her under her arms and slammed her body against the wall. " I don't want you," he seethed.

The sudden jarring caught her off guard. What was about to happen did not surprise her for the tension had been building around them from the beginning. And the truth of the matter was she wanted him with the same passion he proclaimed not to want her. It was time to step over the elephant in the room.

"That's a shame, Joshua, because I do want you." She held his troubled brown eyes as he continued to fight the losing battle.

He slammed her against the wall again, trying to fight off the way her scent was drawing him in. "I don't," he said with his nostrils flaring and his body touching hers.

"Are you angry at me or the wall?" She watched as his eyes began to soften from the attempt at humor. "Either way, your strength is coming back." She shrugged as her lips curved up.

"I don't want to want you." His lips touched her throat.

She inhaled a soft breath and murmured, "I know."

His hands slid down her body to her waist as he eased her back down to her feet. "I can't let you get to me." He kissed the top of her breast.

"I know." She laid her head on top of his and gently rubbed his back. "I'll protect your heart," she moaned.

"Don't say that." He was struggling, but she felt so good, she tasted as sweet as honey and her touch, her gentle touch was torturing him.

She cupped his face with her hands. "I have your back Joshua, you can let go."

Her lips captured his in a sweet kiss. It was hot, carnal, and probably illegal in a few states. But damn if she could pull away. "Can I take my clothes off now?" she whispered against his lips.

His head snapped up breaking the intimate touch of her lips, saw the soft curve of her smile, then looked into her cinnamon brown eyes filled with desire. That was his undoing. His lips captured hers and a fierce battle of wills ensued. There was no preliminary feeling each other out. Both knew exactly what they wanted from the other. They needed to quench that thirst that was about to choke the life out of them.

Dropping onto the bed, her junction met his rock hard member, he was the first one to moan. Her mouth was so sweet he couldn't pull away if his life depended on it. In truth, he felt his life was just beginning anew at her touch. The temperature in the room intensified by at least twenty degrees when she removed his shirt, breaking the kiss only for a second. His lips were back on her with the urgency of a drowning man. Roc reached between them, unzipped his pants and pushed them down with her feet. She wrapped her thighs around him, encompassing his entire body in her warmth. Joshua never felt so protected. Roc flipped him onto his back, placed his arms above his head then slowly pulled away from his lips.

This was heaven. Joshua closed his eyes and enjoyed her making love to him. She kissed his chest, ran her tongue over his nipples, her hands massaging his sides, her lips kissing his stomach and then there was the heat of her mouth on him. Joshua damn near leaped off the bed when her lips closed around him. Her tongue worked up and down him as if he was her own personal lollipop, made especially for her mouth. He felt her mission was to bring him to completion. She was working like a wildcat at her job and there wasn't a damn thing he could do or wanted to do to stop her. For if she stopped, he would die right then and there. The sensation was building so fast, he knew he was about to explode and tried to pull away, but her lips tightened around him, as her hands squeezed his base. He exploded before he could pull away. Then something happened he had never experienced before. He heard himself scream.

Roc sat back on her legs and had the nerve to grin down at him. "Gosh, you're sweet."

Joshua couldn't do anything but lie there and laugh. He was drained, spent and wasn't the least bit embarrassed by it. "Do you ever let go? It's damn you're sweet. This is one of those times you can let a curse word slip out." God, she was a contrast. She was a tough woman, yet she sat above him looking like an angel.

Joshua reached up pulling her down to him. He stripped the t-shirt over her head exposing golden brown mounds that made his mouth water. He flipped her onto her back determined to give her as much pleasure as she had given him. His fingers expertly massaged around the tip of her breast, which came to attention at his touch. His tongue flicked across it, once, twice, then he took the entire breast into his mouth. He heard her moan with pleasure. That made him smile, but the taste of her skin took center stage. She tasted like cinnamon sugar with a touch of nutmeg. "You taste like my mom's sweet potato pie," he groaned. He devoured her mounds as if they were just that. He went from one to the other massaging, suckling and licking every inch of them until her body began squirming under him. Her hands were roaming his back, his waist, squeezing his buttocks and demanding he come into her. The heat was building all over, his heart was racing, every vein in his body was pumping, begging to be satisfied. He pulled away from her breast, kissing down her stomach, unzipped her jeans, pulled them off and threw them aside. Joshua sat back and looked down at her. She had a beautiful body, glistening with passion. He licked his lips as his eyes traveled from the dark hair at her junction, to the firm breasts that tasted so sweet, to her eyes. It took all of his resolve, not to show what he felt, but the look in her eyes took his breath away. He saw himself there. He blinked not believing, yet sensing...no, he shook the thought away.

Reaching down, he placed one of her legs over his shoulder, then did the same with the other. Taking her by the waist, he pulled her to him and entered her in one powerful swift motion. They both screamed. Her muscles blanketed him in her succulent juices, so hot, comforting, just like home. The sensation was so intense he stilled there with his eyes closed, savoring, but not believing the incredible feeling over taking him. He pulled out, then thrust into her again, still not believing, but knowing. He shook the thought off again and thrust into her again, and again and again until he realized it was her pushing up to him, meeting him half way. He wasn't alone, he now had her. The realization caused him to pause for a moment, but she wasn't having it. Her body slammed into his. Her legs dropped from his shoulders, his body covered her, pumping furiously into her over and over, fanning the spark until it became a flame that consumed them. He released, growling as his entire universe exploded. He felt her inner walls contracting around him, squeezing, not allowing him to hold back. Then she screamed. Her juice was hot, warming him, her muscles still comforting him. He felt as if he was being sheltered inside a cocoon...safe, warm, protected.

In that moment Joshua had never felt more content in his life. Her hand was lightly rubbing his shoulder. Her touch was soothing, caring, loving. Roc made him feel like a man who had just completed a journey. Her thigh was lying across his, her head on his shoulder and her lips on his neck. He closed his eyes thinking heaven must be like this. Then he did something strange...he slept.

Chapter Seventeen
Washington, D.C

Royce sat at a table in the lounge of a hotel in D.C. wondering why he had been summoned. It was rare for one of his agents to contact him for a one-on-one meeting, yet he'd had two such requests in as many days. The agent approached the table, then took a seat.

"This couldn't have waited until 6:00 or at least until the sun came up?" He raised an eyebrow.

"No," Roc replied as she sat up leaning towards him at the table. "I crossed the line."

Seeing she was serious, Royce sat up and leaned towards her. "What line are we talking about?"

Roc hesitated as she took a sip of her tea. She lowered her head, closed her eyes and exhaled. "I've fallen in love with the man."

Royce did not show any expression. It wasn't his place to chastise or judge. His role here, as the head of Homeland Security, was the mission. "Will this compromise the mission?"

"No," Roc replied, but offered nothing more.

He acknowledged her reply with a nod. "Any information to report?"

Roc looked around. "We followed up on a lead that led us to this David Holt guy who we think is connected to Jonas Gary."

"The man Absolute overheard."

"Yes." She nodded. "A funny thing happened when we went to follow him."

Royce raised an eyebrow.

"We were approached by fake CIA agents."

"You weren't at the National Mall yesterday at any time, were you?"

"Afraid we were."

"They weren't fake," Royce replied.

Roc looked surprised. "They drew on us."

"The report is Absolute opened fire on them."

"Who in CIA began this manhunt for him?"

"CIA did not initiate the hunt. They were asked to assist."

"By who?"

"Admiral McGary." Royce waved off the question before she could ask. "He's being watched, but he's not the leader. I'll handle the CIA connection. Stay on this Holt guy, Ned's doing an in-depth on him. He's involved, I just don't know how deep."

"Ned." Now she was pleasantly surprised. "He's good."

"He's pissed. Someone hacked into his system."

Roc and Royce both smiled on that note. "That would piss him off."

"Yes, it did. What he's discovered to date is what has me pissed off."

"Well, don't hold back."

"Whoever is at the top, has level four clearance."

"That could be a problem." Roc sat back and sighed. "Joshua will be happy to know Ned is good. Is Monique with him?"

"I'm certain she will be before sunrise."

"You know, you've done your job, you brought him home," Royce said to Roc. "You can go home now."

"He's weak." She nodded her head, "He's getting stronger, but he is not back to his level."

"Is that your professional assessment or personal?"

She thought about his question, then answered. "I haven't lost perspective."

"I'm glad to hear that." Now, the man, Royce, spoke up. "I've known you for a while, Roc. This is going to break a few hearts, including my brother's."

Roc smiled. "Grayson has women lined up waiting to get a taste of him." She sighed and sat back. "You would think I was old enough to know better."

Royce sat back and laughed. "You're talking to the wrong person on that, Roc. I fell head over heels in love at forty-five. Here I am three years later, still hopelessly in love with that woman." From the look on her face he could tell she was beating herself up inside. He had the pleasure of knowing both sides of Roc. He knew she would eventually figure things out. As for Joshua, he knew him just as well. While he hoped the man would see all that Roc had to offer, he knew what the man had recently gone through. Hell, he was a part of that situation. "You know, he's a good man. He was hurt deeply, by his country. It may be difficult for him to get pass that."

"The Akande situation." She nodded.

"Yes," he replied. "The one thing I do know is if it's right, it will come to fruition. Don't give up." He shook his head. "Don't let him give up."

Roc smiled at Royce. "Shelly is a very lucky woman."

Royce stood with a broad smile on his face. "That she is, and I'm fortunate to have found a treasure. Call her soon, she worries about you."

"Will do." Roc watched as Royce walked away. The question still bothered her. She wanted to believe she gave him an honest answer, but she just wasn't sure. Roc stood, leaving a tip on the table as she grabbed her tea cup and shook her head.

The pain was subsiding, he could tell when he rolled over. He didn't feel like breaking someone's neck. No, he felt remarkably comfortable. Roc was right, he thought as he turned over, he just needed to take a day to rest and his body would begin healing. It wasn't so bad having her around after all. He smiled at the thought then began drifting back off. There was a time not long ago when closing his eyes had been the last thing he wanted to do for he knew what was coming. What once was a precious memory had turned into a nightmare to him. He used to fight sleep, pushing his body to exhaustion, knowing the nightmare would soon consume him. He wasn't feeling that at the moment, no, he was relaxed, content, at peace. Now that was something different. He drifted deeper expecting the memory of a lost love to invade his sleep soon, but...there was something different. It wasn't Akande knocking him to the floor. It was Roc. He sat straight up in the bed. Eyes wide open. He wiped his hands down his face. "What in the hell was that?"

He looked around the room. She wasn't there. But damn if she hadn't been there. He could still smell the essence of their lovemaking in the room, feel the passion that had exploded. "Damn if she didn't put me to sleep," he said as he wiped his hand down his face, then fell back on the bed. The woman literally sucked the life out of him. He hadn't been that satisfied since...hell he'd never been satisfied to a point where he fell asleep. He's the one who puts women to sleep, then leaves. The thought caused him to sit up. Did she leave? "Roc?" he called out. No response. He got out of bed and walked into the bathroom, she wasn't there. He looked around. The bag from the store was still there, but that didn't mean anything, the woman was just like him, she traveled light. He jumped in the shower, all the while wondering whether she would leave without saying goodbye. Yes, she would, he knew because he had done it many times. Frantic now, he dried off, dressed then left the room to search for her. He hit the elevator button, decided it was taking too long, so he took the stairs.

Why was he acting like a woman who felt as if she had been laid and left? Because it was wrong. Wrong for her to just use his body, then up and leave. He began to slow down. No, that wasn't right. It shouldn't matter to him if she was gone. Hell, that meant he was ready to work independently again...right. He pushed the door open when he reached the lobby. For a minute there, he was angry. Not seeing her in the room made him feel some kind of way. The least she could have done was feed him breakfast, take him to the movies, leave twenty dollars on the table, something. But you don't just get up and leave. Walking towards the front desk he began to wonder why her not being in the room was affecting him. It wasn't like they were a couple. No, they were just comrades working to finding truth, justice and the American way. Hell, he sounded like a commercial for the Justice League.

He was about to approach the desk when he looked over and saw two people sitting at the table in the restaurant drinking. His heart skipped a beat, then settled at the sight of her. He exhaled audibly, stepping back so he would not be seen. Seeing her magnified the memory from the night before. Roc was definitely a contradiction. He leaned against the wall and watched her. She was as lethal as he was, yet was gentle and caring, like his mother. His body still tingled from the touch of her tongue. Yes, she was a contradiction indeed, but one he couldn't afford. The last time nearly killed him. No, allowing her to get close to him was not in the cards. He watched her a moment longer as she talked with the Director of Homeland Security, Royce Davenport. Roc could be dangerous to his health. He turned to walk towards the elevator, then leaned against the wall. The sun had just risen so there was no one around. He had to take a moment to assess what was going on with him.

There were three Lassiter men in her life. She did not know all the connections until their mother told her about all twelve of her children. There was the oldest, who she'd had a crush on for years, then the youngest one, whom she could never figure out why she had such a soft spot for him and now this one. This one was different from the other two, she thought as she walked out of the restaurant. Yes, this one she had lost herself with. With Samuel she could control herself, never would have crossed that line. With Joshua, she couldn't stop, didn't want to stop. From the moment he regained consciousness, she knew there was an attraction. The more she cared for him the deeper that attraction became. When the President ordered her to stay with him, a part of her was relieved, for she wasn't ready to leave him. Hell, as much as she loved her normal life, she knew when she returned it would not be the same after the Absolute experience. She walked around the corner to the elevator still thinking about the situation. All

"I...don't get jealous." He glared down at her as he pushed the elevator button. "Are you always so straight-laced?"

"Only when I cross the line."

The door opened and they both stepped inside. "Is that what we did?"

"Not we." She pushed the button to their floor. "I crossed the line. My duty was to rescue and recover. It was not to bed you."

"To bed me," he grinned. "Is that what it's called these days? I thought we had sex...damn good sex."

Roc held his gaze, then looked away. That in a nutshell was the problem. He called it having sex. She called it making love. "Davenport heard from Ned," she said in an effort to change the subject. Joshua raised a questioning brow. "He's good, pissed, someone hacked him."

"I figured as much." They stepped off the elevator and began walking towards the room. "He will have another built before nightfall."

They both stopped, glanced at each other, then pulled their weapons. They saw it at the same time. "Did you leave the door open?"

They moved, flush against the wall. "My darling, you know damn well, I'm not that careless."

Roc crossed over to the other side of the door, as Joshua slowly, pushed it open with his hand. Roc dipped low, Joshua went high as they rushed the room. They both checked the bathroom and closet, then stood in the middle of the room looking for anything that was out of place. There was nothing missing, however, there were two devices on the bed.

Joshua walked over, examined them. He picked them up smiling, "Ned's been here. He turned the device on. "Talk to me."

"It's good to hear your voice, Absolute."

"Same here, my geeky friend." Joshua sat on the bed.

Roc wondered if he knew the play of emotions running across his face. She gave him a moment, then realized he wasn't going to say it. Men. "We were concerned, Ned."

"Aww, Roc, my angel in disguise. You brought him home."

"That I did."

"Don't mind me I'm just sitting here."

"It's time for you to stop playing injured and get back to work."

"What in the hell do you think I've been doing?"

Ned laughed. "It is good to hear your voice. But we have a situation."

"Tell me about it. What do you have?"

"Someone high up is pulling strings with the Senate. They have a resolution about to hit the floor calling for the Attorney General to resign. If he doesn't, they are prepared to demand the President relieve him of his duties."

"If the President doesn't," Joshua added, "they plan to impeach him for not protecting the interests of the United States."

"Do we have any idea who's behind this?" Roc asked.

"Still working on it," Ned replied.

"What do you have for me?" Joshua asked.

"A connection between Jonas Gary, David Holt and the Vice-President's office," Ned replied.

Joshua and Roc glanced at each other. "Let me have it."

"I traced several money transfers to an account in the Caymans. Payments from the account have gone to both. Want to take a guess as to who the accounts belong to?"

"The Vice-President," Roc replied.

"That's where the paper trail leads me. Not sure that's where it originated."

"You think whoever is doing this is trying to implicate the Vice-President?" Joshua asked.

"I do. Too many coincidences leading one way tends to make me look in the opposite direction."

Joshua stood and began packing things into his bag. "You have a lead."

"Of course I do," Ned laughed. "I always have a lead." The device buzzed. "Jonas Gary is in Laredo. I've sent his coordinates to your device."

"Got it."

"Absolute, don't kill the man," Ned implored. "We need answers."

"You know my motto."

"That's precisely what concerns me. Keep in mind, the presidency may be at stake."

"I'll keep that in mind." Joshua terminated the communication then turned towards the door to see Roc packed and ready to leave. He walked over to her. "Does this mean we're going to Texas?"

Roc smiled up at him. "I think you're ready for a test run."

Joshua could not help remembering the taste of those lips, the feel of them on him. Nothing was as tempting as a woman first thing in the morning. "I did not have a chance to properly say good morning." He pulled her into his arms, parted her lips with his tongue then proceeded to give her a scandalous kiss. He slowly pulled away for the sweetness of her taste was wreaking havoc on his senses. "Let's keep this simple. I can't do anything more than that."

Roc pulled him by his lapel until their lips were a mere inch apart. "I don't recall asking for anything." She kissed him, long, slow and deep. No region of his mouth went untouched. When she was satisfied, she broke the kiss, turned and then strutted out of the room. "Let's go get Gary."

Joshua watched the sway of her hips in those black pants as she walked away. He shook his head as he closed the door. "Hurt me, baby, hurt me."

Chapter Eighteen
Laredo, TX

"The President is expecting you in the Oval Office sometime today. How do you intend to handle the situation?"

"I will simply indicate to him, my mission is at a critical point. Deserting my post at this time could cause deaths."

"Do you think he will buy that?"

"He's a bleeding heart liberal, of course he will buy it."

"Don't make a mistake by underestimating this President, McGary," the voice on the telephone cautioned. "Better men than you have made that mistake. Harrison is still standing."

"You handle the situation in D.C. I'll handle Harrison."

"Know this," the voice warned. "One wrong move, I'll have you taken out of commission. Do we understand each other?"

"You wouldn't dare? It would jeopardize your position."

"Stupid moves jeopardize my position. As I see it, I'll have nothing to lose. Release the serial numbers to those weapons to the press, then get those *weapons off U.S. soil before night fall." The call was disconnected.*

"It's time to disband, McGary." Jonas stood in the corner in the room listening to the conversation. "Your plan is falling apart and I have no intention of being around when it all crashes down."

"Send the serial numbers to your man in D.C. Then pack the weapons up and move them back across the border."

"I can do that, as soon as I receive payment."

"You'll get paid." McGary nodded.

"Now, would be a good time," Jonas added.

"You don't trust us?"

"No."

McGary watched the man for a few moments before realizing he was serious. He stood then walked over to the wall safe, which was behind a picture of a confederate flag. "Whatever happened to your patriotism, Gary?" He pulled out a small computer, powered it up then made a quick transfer.

"Patriotism is overrated," Jonas stated as he waited to receive notification of a deposit into his account. "My patriotism to my country ended the day my wife was taken from me. My loyalty now goes to the highest bidder."

"A man without a country isn't a man."

Jonas pulled a knife from his pocket, and with a flick of his wrist, he whirled the knife pinning the Admiral's pants to his chair. "A man without his genitals isn't a man. You want to question my manhood again?" Jonas let out a cynical laugh. He walked over and pulled the knife out. "You're a patriot, yet, you are trying to overthrow your government," he said soberly. "I believe my way of living is a lot more honorable than yours."

Sly watched as Jonas Gary walked from the hotel to his vehicle. From the conversation he'd just overhead him have with the Admiral, he knew Gary was instructed to move the weapons back to Mexico. The Admiral was about to be double-crossed.

"Ready to give up your post?" Joshua stood behind Sly as they both watched Gary.

"How's your back?" Sly never turned around.

Joshua wasn't surprised Sly knew he was behind him. The man taught him how to detect movement, without actually seeing it, among other things. "Tolerable."

"Roc?"

"Day by day."

"Gary," Joshua asked as he glared at Roc.

Sly did turn then. He looked from Roc to Joshua then back to Roc. He shook his head. "This man is dangerous." He glared at both. "Now is not the time for distractions."

Neither was going to insult the man's intelligence. "Understood," Joshua replied. "What's going on with Gary?"

"He's about to double cross the Admiral."

"How so?" Roc asked.

"He has a stock pile of weapons used to setup the Attorney General. The Admiral who is in cahoots with Gary has ordered him to return the weapons back to Mexico. Gary has other plans."

"He's made a deal," Joshua stated.

Sly nodded. "He made a deal." Sly began walking towards the building. "You two handle Gary. I'm taking McGary to the President."

With that, Sly was gone.

"You think Gary will lead us to the weapons?" Roc asked as she stood behind Joshua, looking over his shoulder at the man.

"Yes, he's going to take us to those weapons, then I'm going to kill him for what he did to me."

"I'm down with that."

Joshua turned to look over his shoulder at her. "You're after my heart, aren't you, darling?"

"He's the one who started this. He put you in this position. He has to pay."

"If you look at it that way, he's responsible for me meeting you." Joshua shrugged his shoulders.

"Once this is over with I'll determine if I want to kill him fast for that atrocity or let him suffer. He's moving."

Joshua turned back to see Gary get into a black sedan. "Let's roll."

They got into the black SUV they had rented and began to follow him. They held back so they would not be detected. The black sedan parked in front of a building that looked like a warehouse. Neither moved from the vehicle until they saw Gary walk inside.

Joshua surveyed the building. One of his specialties was being able to gain access to a building that seemed to be impenetrable. There were several entry points he could explore to see what was inside the building. "I'm going in."

Roc opened the door to step out, but Joshua put a hand on her shoulder. "You have to let me go at some point."

He was right. Roc nodded. "You have ten minutes. If you're not back, I'm coming in to get you."

Joshua smiled displaying the deepest set of dimples. "I know you will, Angel."

Roc grinned and watched as he crossed the street, then walked towards the back of the building. She scanned the area to get a feel for the layout. The people walking the block were mixed, but mostly

Hispanic. There was clearly a lot of illegal activity taking place, however, that wasn't their mission. Gaining control of those weapons was their number one priority. Joshua appeared on the roof of the building. She watched as he went undetected by those down on the street, then disappeared. He was indeed an amazing man, she thought as the feel of steel against her temple drew her attention.

"Use your left hand to open the door, then step out, slowly," the voice said.

Law enforcement. That was the first thing that came to Roc's mind. The person with the gun was law enforcement or had been at some time.

"Is there something wrong, Officer?" she asked while she opened the door.

"You're watching my building and I want to know why?"

Stepping out of the vehicle, Roc noticed people on the street looking at them, but no one made a move to interfere. "I like the building,"

A hand struck her across the cheekbone as she turned. "Wrong answer." Before the man knew what hit him, Roc struck him in the face with the back of her fist, turned, delivered a kick to his groin, then saw the fist of a second man right before it connected to her face. The blow drew blood, but did not immobilize her, she kicked out taking both men down. Roc ran across the street, dodging cars, ignoring the horns blaring and the angry words coming her way. She jumped on the hood of one car, slid across the top, dropping on the opposite side. Following Joshua's path she ran between the buildings, only to be stopped when she heard the magazine to an assault weapon that was pointing at her, click into place. She slid to a stop, narrowed her eyes, then put her hands up.

"Join us inside, why don't you," the man she knew to be Jonas Gary stated.

Roc did not resist. She turned then walked in the direction towards which the man pointed. Her jaw was stinging and she was sure her face looked a fright, however, she grinned when she saw the two men limping as they followed them into the building.

Joshua was right. There was a stockpile of crates around the walls. She did not have x-ray vision, but she was willing to bet there were weapons in each one.

Gary was disgusted with his men. He pushed her forward causing her to trip and hit the floor. "Who the hell are you?"

Roc wiped the blood from her nose. "Your worst nightmare."

He raised his leg to kick her, she grabbed it and pulled him off his feet. Roc jumped up, but froze when one of the men came back in with a gun drawn on her.

Jonas stood, then yanked up the gun he'd dropped. He raised it to hit her with the butt, when the sound of a bloodcurdling roar caused him to whirl around. He saw one man being thrown against the wall, while a knife sailed through the air landing in the other's forehead. When he recognized the man, he moved quickly, grabbing Roc up to shield him from the man in the suit, with murder in his eyes. "Hold it, right there." Jonas held the barrel of his gun to Roc's temple.

Joshua paid the man no mind. "You good?" He nodded at her as if it was only the two of them in the room having a conversation.

"I have a bit of a headache."

"Did he do that to your face?"

"Hey, up here. I'm the one with the gun."

The look in Joshua's eyes chilled her to the bone. "You're a non-entity."

Jonas cocked the gun. "You want to try that again?"

Joshua stood with his feet braced apart, arms folded across his wide chest, showing no emotion, other than a raised eyebrow. "You should have killed me when you had the chance."

He turned the gun on Joshua, tightening his grip around Roc's neck. "We can always remedy that."

With a flick of his wrist, Joshua flipped a round metal device with spikes at the man's arm, causing his hold on Roc to loosen and the gun to drop. Just as quickly as he hit the floor Joshua was over him pulling Jonas up by his neck. "Don't ever touch what's mine."

The anger was radiating so fiercely from him, it caused Roc to pause. She could see his body shaking. "Joshua." Roc touched his arm. "We need to take him back to D.C." He did not respond, in fact, his features hardened at her touch. "Joshua, the President needs information from this man. We need him alive."

"Do you believe in karma?" Joshua did not take his eyes away from Jonas. "I ask, because I believe when a man is about to meet his maker, he should at least know why."

"I believe you have me mistaken for someone who gives a shit," Jonas spat out.
"I'm sorry to hear that. Some say one's actions, in this and previous states of existence, play a role in deciding their fate in future existences. Your fate was sealed the moment you put your hands on my woman. Oh, you may not die at my hands this moment, but make no mistake, your hours are numbered." Joshua released his hold on the man's neck, and then hit him

with a powerful blow, which rendered him unconscious. He turned to Roc.

The gentleness of his gaze seared her right through to her heart. "It's not that bad."

He pulled a handkerchief from his inner pocket and gently took her face in his hands to examine the bruise. "No man should ever put his hands on what belongs to me." He began to wipe the blood away. His touch was like a warm caress. It was difficult for Roc to concentrate with him touching her in such a caring way.

"Does that mean we're going steady now?"

The sparkle in her eyes let him know she was kidding, but he felt compelled to clarify. "Went down that road," he held her gaze "not going again."

His words were contradicting his touch, but Roc learned a long time ago, take a man's words at face value. She took the handkerchief from him, then continued wiping her face. "You might want to contact Ned, to get this cleared out."

Joshua felt he had disappointed her with his words, but neither her face, nor her voice showed any reaction to his words. "Roc, there will not be more." He held her gaze to ensure understanding.

"You came through loud and clear." Roc watched as he nodded then turned away.

Washington DC

"It has come to my attention that key individuals have been detained and are en route. It could be detrimental when they reach their destination."

"We have a scapegoat if needed."

"Good to hear." The call was disconnected.

"Mr. President," Calvin greeted as he walked through the door of his office into the Oval Office. "The chopper carrying Admiral McGary has landed. Do you want him brought here?"

JD sat at the desk with his sleeves rolled up, suit jacket on the back of his chair and his tie lying on the desk. Papers were literally lying all around him. The events of the last few days had distracted him from the education bill and he was determined to read through every inch of it before he signed the document.

He looked up as Calvin spoke. "No, he doesn't deserve to step foot in this office," an angry JD replied. "Have him taken to the bunker." He threw the pen he was writing with on the desk, then sat back in his chair. "How could a patriot like McGary be turned against his country?"

Calvin sighed. "Let's be clear," Calvin said as he sat in the chair next to the desk. "If what Ned's team has discovered is true, McGary is no patriot. A man true to his country would never jeopardize its citizens the way McGary has."

"Could the man hate me to that extent?"

"Fanatics don't need a reason to dispense hate. But I think we have a more pressing situation." He pressed a button on the desk. Joshua's face appeared on the monitor on the desk.

"Good evening, Mr. President," Joshua spoke.

There was something in Joshua's tone that made JD smile. "It's Mr. President tonight, Joshua? Either you are about to blow up something or you are trying to soften me up for a blow. Which is it?"

Joshua smiled. "Soften the blow. Gary is not talking, however, according to McGary he received orders from the Vice-President's camp. Not the Vice-President, but his camp."

"Who in his camp, if not him?" JD asked.

"It doesn't matter," Calvin replied. "He is responsible for all actions taken on his behalf."

"Roc here, Mr. President. The Intel suggests the Vice-President may not be aware of this activity. According to McGary, he had a conversation with the VP where he alluded to the plan and it appeared the man knew nothing of it."

"I have to agree with Calvin on this one," Joshua stated. "He is responsible for whatever actions the people in his camp make. I say take them all down."

"It's wrong to hold one person responsible for the actions of another." Roc held his gaze then walked away.

"How did McGary communicate with the person?" JD asked.

Joshua's attention was still on Roc, who had walked away and taken a seat in the back.

"Joshua?"

"Cell phone. Ned tracked it. It's registered to the VP's office, the same with Gary and Holt." Joshua hesitated. "JD, I have to get a little personal here. Does this Holt guy have a connection to your wife?"

"They went to school together," JD replied as he sat forward. "But the history is with my sister, Ashley."

"How so?" Joshua asked.

"Family business, Joshua," JD replied.

"All due respect, Mr. President. Your family business may be at the very heart of what's happening here."

"How so?"

"It seems Holt approached both, Gary and McGary. He is also connected to the McClintock camp."

"Holt wouldn't have the clout to pull something like this off," JD stated. "There is no way he could persuade McGary to be part of a conspiracy against this country. He doesn't have the political connections to get the Senate to act so quickly and decisively." JD shook his head. "No, someone else is behind this, Joshua. I need to know who. Bring them to the bunker. I need answers."

Joshua stepped out of the chopper at a private airstrip near the Pentagon, with Gary in handcuffs, held by the arm. Roc had McGary the same way. They were walking towards the SUV Ned had arranged when a black sedan and another SUV pulled to a stop between them. Two men stepped out of the vehicle flashing credentials, while four armed men dressed in military wear, emerged from the SUV.

"Absolute." One man extended his hand and flashed his credentials. "Jackson, Homeland Security. We have orders to take your captives to the bunker. The President is eager to speak with them."

Roc pushed McGary to the ground, put a foot on his back, then pulled her weapon. The man seemed friendly enough, but something about the scene did not feel right. Joshua watched as the men from the SUV held the back door open, but never drew their weapons.

He looked over his shoulder at Roc. "What do you think?" he asked, certain she understood he was talking about the odds of six to two.

Roc shrugged her shoulder, still pointing her weapon at the military men. "I'm cool with it, but I was kind of looking forward to meeting the President in person."

Joshua smiled, turned back to Jackson. "I don't want to disappoint the lady. We'll see this one through." He stepped around the man. "You're welcome to join us."

"I'm afraid, I must insist," Jackson stated with a frown on his brow. "You've served your country by capturing these traitors. You and the lady will be honored for your actions." The man smiled.

Roc started singing the chorus to the song *Poison*, by Bell, Biv, Devoe. *Never trust a big butt and a smile. If I were you, I'd take precautions.*

While the burst into song confused the agent, Joshua grinned, then discreetly pulled a button from his coat.

"Get us the hell out of here," Gary sneered at the agent.

Joshua looked from the prisoner to the agent. The agent was clearly pissed by Gary's statement. "You two know each other?" He sounded surprised.

"Look around you," said Jackson, the friendly tone now gone. "I prefer this go down without bloodshed."

Roc shook her head. "We saw your face, you can't let us walk. Which means we will have to kill you and your men to leave here alive. And make no mistake, gentlemen, I have every intention of leaving here alive."

"There's six of us, only two of you," He smirked. "I like our odds."

Joshua laughed. "You think you have the advantage?"

Agent Jackson looked around the seemingly deserted airstrip, then smirked. "I do."

Joshua looked over at Roc. "Arrogant little roach, isn't he."

Agent Jackson took exception to that, nodded his head and his men immediately pulled their weapons.

Before any of them could pull the trigger, shots rang out. The first shot hit Jonas Gary center forehead.

Joshua didn't have time to wonder who, he flipped the button towards the SUV. It exploded on impact. Gunshots filled the air, taking out agent Jackson and his partner. Roc covered the Admiral. Not sure who was firing, Joshua took cover behind the sedan, then drew his weapon. "Let me see your face, Roc," he called out in desperation. "Roc!"

Hearing the desperation in his voice, she looked up. "Good, over here. Good guys or bad?"

"Not sure, but I would say good, since they took out the bad guys."

"I don't like working on assumptions."

"Get me the hell out of here," McGary cried out.

Joshua grinned at Roc, who was now behind the sedan, beside him. They both had their weapons ready as they looked around. "Should we leave him there?"

Roc looked at McGary who was on his stomach, with his hands strapped behind his back, in the line of fire. "Oh, I don't know, now that his partner is dead, he may be willing to talk a little more."

"I don't think he has much more to tell us."

"I do, dammit, I have information the President will want to hear."

Joshua and Roc looked at each other. Roc shrugged. "Oh, all right." She reached out and pulled the man behind the sedan with them.

"You two plan on sitting there much longer?"

Joshua looked up to see Al "Turk" Day, his wife Ryan and Tucker Donovan, standing with weapons drawn. "I'll be damned. The calvary has arrived."

Joshua stood. "How's Melissa Sue?"

"Healing," Al replied as he looked over at the SUV which was now on fire. "You still playing with explosives, I see."

Joshua grinned. "Never know when something needs to be destroyed." He looked at Tucker. "What are you doing on the East coast?"

Tucker walked over to Jonas Gary's body. He kicked it over. The man's eyes stared up at him. "Protecting what's mine." He looked at Roc. "He do that to your face?"

Roc touched the bruise she had forgotten was there and shrugged. "I'll live."

Tucker shot Gary's body again. "He won't."

Al did not give anyone a chance to question the statement. "Let's move before the other good guys appear."

Roc stood, pulling McGary to his feet. "How did you know we were coming to this airstrip?"

"Airway chatter."

They all walked towards the SUV left by Ned. "Who was on the box?"

"Homeland Security and the AG's office." Ryan replied. "My question is how did they know you would be here?"

Joshua placed McGary in the backseat of the SUV, closed the door then turned to Al. "I don't like not knowing all the players." He turned to Roc. "Too much is at stake. The President needs answers."

Chapter Nineteen

The bunker was filled with people wanting exactly what Joshua indicated, answers. They stood behind the glass partition, as Joshua questioned McGary.

Brian, James and Royce listened as Roc just looked on. While the men were focused on McGary's responses, her mind was on the man. No, not McGary, she knew that fool was going to spill his guts before it was all over with. No, she was watching Joshua. There was no denying, the man was back to full form. She was no longer needed. A sadness washed over her with the realization. Yet, a sense of happiness engulfed her as well. Joshua "Absolute" Lassiter was back. The United States' deadliest weapon was ready for duty and she'd had a hand in delivering him.

Joshua loomed over McGary as if he was nothing. Firing question after question, until the man had no choice but to tell all he knew. He was relentless and Roc was enjoying every moment for she knew her heart was going to take a long time getting over this Lassiter. Joshua touched her in a way Samuel never had. This man had a quality she just could not explain. He was charming, funny, arrogant, yet humble, kind but firm and he was fine. There was just no other way to describe Joshua, she thought as she watched him pick McGary up by the collar demanding names. There was nothing boastful about the man, for he could back up every word he used to describe his skills, from the battlefield to the bedroom. Roc sighed. She would not feel that again. She closed her eyes and shook her head as the memory of the night before filled her.

"Thinking about me, aren't you, Angel?"

Roc opened her eyes to see Joshua standing in front of her with those damn dimples. She stood straight. "What do we have?"

"A location for a meeting taking place." He grinned. "McGary is supposed to provide security. Care to join me?"

It was time for her to cut her losses. "You can handle it. It's time for me to move on."

Joshua had turned to leave the room when her words stopped him. A look of confusion was there for a brief moment then disappeared. "Move on? As in leave...now? You're leaving before the job is done?" His eyes narrowed.

"My job is done." She walked out to the open door as she continued. "You are able to function at your full capacity. You don't need a nursemaid." She wanted to tell him he needed her...the woman, but that was something he would have to conclude on his own.

Yes, she was right again, but he wasn't ready for her to go...not yet. "I believe the President ordered you to be backup on this case. The case isn't over. We have a man to take down." He opened the door and held it until she broke eye contact and walked through. Uncertain why the thought of her leaving cut...it cut deep.

The tide was turning. The connection in Texas had been interrupted. Word was McGary was in custody and Gary was dead. The only face the man knew was his. David had to make a move. He needed cash and lots of it so he could disappear. Hell, this job was all about the cash to him. Yes, the idea of bringing Tracy Washington-Harrison to her knees was a sweet incentive. However, it wasn't his driving force. He wanted to live comfortably. He made that clear when he was approached in prison last year. He had to admit, coming up with the plan was an ingenious way of using his skills. After all, being cunning is an art form. To say David was good would be an understatement. Working as a political operative you had to know how to dish the crap when needed and to whom. You had to be willing to sell your soul and David, certainly had no problem with that. The plan was really simple. Put JD Harrison in a compromising situation, one for which the nation would never forgive him. Well, the first thing a normal person would think of was an affair with a woman, better yet a man. Now that would raise a few eyebrows, but the nation would forgive and forget. It had to be something more. Something the country would never recuperate from, like a bomb on U.S. soil, under JD's watch. David stood in the window of his plush hotel room, provided by the McClintocks, grinning at the simplicity of it all.

All the players thought it was all about the weapons in Texas. Hmm, that was only the decoy. The real deal was happening in D.C. and the beauty of it was not even the man paying for it all, knew the details. You see, prisons are filled with education. You have nothing but time on your hands to learn about things you would never have imagined. There are valuable skills to learn inside of prisons. People of all walks of life are behind bars, from the brother on the street corner, hustling, to the man with a PhD in chemistry. A few questions here and there to open the lines of communication and all you had to do was listen. People love to talk about their accomplishments. Then there's one more asset in prison...networking. The largest network of illegal ideas is shared inside prison walls. All your experts are there. You listen to where they made their mistakes and what they would have done differently and poof, you have the perfect plan.

David had to applaud the man who hired him for coming up with the idea of making JD his own worst enemy. Getting Congress to sanction him would tarnish his presidency and possibly keep him from running for a second term. It was child's play. It had been fun watching it play out. But if you really want to do something right, don't half step. Carry the freakin' ball through the goalpost. That's what David planned to do. Something the country would not soon forget, or forgive their President for allowing to happen. First, it was time to have a little fun. David picked up his coat, threw it over his arm and thought. *A good prison education is a terrible thing to waste.*

Taking the girls was as easy as spreading butter on a hot biscuit. In fact, it was too damn easy to get that close to the President's daughter. You see, there's humble and there's stupid. The Harrisons pride themselves on being everyday down-home people. Their children went to public schools in D.C., their son, JC, was allowed to shoot hoops on the local basketball courts and their daughter, Jazzy, attended dance lessons with her cousin Jada every Wednesday at 4.

David dressed in a black suit, white collar shirt, black shoes, a chauffeur's hat and a pair of sunshades, drove the black SUV and parked in front of the dance studio. There he waited. He knew the regular driver was...delayed. It's amazing how much information a smile and a little sweet talk could get you. They were coming out of the door. David spoke to the agent as she walked the girls to the vehicle. A complaint about the detail always sparked a little compassion, for most agents hated being assigned to children. They all wanted the President's detail.

The agent checked the back, as she should, then allowed the girls to get in. David climbed into the driver's seat. The agent then hit the top of the vehicle indicating it was clear to pull off. David looked through the rearview mirror and smiled. Too easy. The agent took her place in the passenger seat, pulling the door closed. She never bothered to look in the seat. If she had, she would have seen the hypodermic needle pointing up. "Ouch," she gasped, then glared back at Jasmine, thinking the girl had pulled another of her pranks. The girls were on their electronic devices, paying no attention to what was happening in the front. The agent pulled the needle out and looked at it. Too late. She was rendered unconscious in seconds. *She should have checked the trunk.* David smiled and pulled off. Too easy. Within fifteen minutes he was in a part of D.C. he was certain the girls did not know and the people around there didn't care or ever see anything. He stopped the car, opened the back door then removed his glasses. "Hello, ladies."

Jada looked around. "Jazzy, this isn't right."

Jazzy looked at the agent then back to David. "You're the man from the basketball court. What did you do to Diane?"

"She's resting while I take you girls on a little adventure."

"We're not going anywhere with you," Jazzy said as she kicked as hard as she could between his legs just like her Grandma Lena told her to do to strangers. She grabbed Jada's hand. "Come on, Jada." She pulled her cousin, leaving everything inside including the panic button she was told never to part with, and ran down the street. They turned a corner, looking back to make sure the man wasn't behind them. They ran dead into something or someone, knocking them both onto their behinds. The girls looked up and saw the scariest man they had ever seen. Stunned at first, they did nothing but stare. As the man reached down to help them up, both girls screamed at the top of their lungs, and began crawling backwards on the ground. Jasmine scrambled to her knees, pulling Jada by the blouse. "Get up, Jada, get up!" the child screamed. Jasmine was pulling her and running so fast, the girl never had a chance to stand up.

"Stop Jazzy, stop," Jada cried out.

Jazzy stopped, pulled Jada up by the arms then ran around the corner, straight into David's arms.

"Come here, you little wench. You're a pain in my ass, just like your mother."

"Put us down," Jazzy cried out as she banged her fist into his chest.

"I'm going tell my Daddy," Jada cried.

"Good." David smirked as he walked up to an old row house, kicked the door open then literally threw the girls to the floor. He slammed the door and locked the deadbolt.

The girls clung to each other as they stared at the man. "My Daddy is going to hurt you and so is my Uncle Al. They are both going to whip you good."

"Yeah, what Jazzy said," Jada huffed.

"They are gong to have to find you first." He grabbed Jazzy by the arm.

"No, Jazzy," Jada screamed, clinging to her cousin so tight, David was pulling both of them.

He threw them in an empty room and stared down at them. "The two of you are just like your mothers. You see one, you see the other."

"So," Jazzy replied.

"Yeah, what Jazzy said."

David looked at the two and had to laugh. Damn if it didn't seem like deja vu. His cell phone buzzed. "Holt," he answered and dismissed the girls, closing the door behind him.

Jazzy jumped up the moment she heard the lock click on the door. Jada looked around. "Jazzy, how are we going to get out?"

Jazzy looked around. There was a window, but they couldn't reach it, and there were bars on it. She walked over and opened a door in the room. It was a small closet. "I don't know, Jada, but we will get out. I promise."

Jada believed her cousin. If Jazzy could get them out of a locked vault, she could get them out of the room too.

"Mr. President," Calvin called out as he walked into the Oval Office.

JD looked up from the education bill he was reviewing. "Are they done?" he asked as he went back to the bill.

"No. I received a call a moment ago. The House has issued an ultimatum. Attorney General Roberts resigns or appears before the House to testify on his involvement in the Texas weapons situation."

"What?" JD asked, incredulous. "The situation isn't three days old and they are demanding a hearing?" He stood angrily, pushing his chair back against the wall. "Who initiated the hearing? I want every name on the document. Now." JD wanted to punch something. "Where is Gavin? Is he aware of this ridiculous change of events?"

"He will know within the hour."

"Anything from Joshua?" he asked.

"A possible lead, but nothing concrete," Calvin replied.

JD held his head down, then hit the desk with his fist. He took a deep breath. "What in the hell is going to happen next?"

Just then Secret Service agents burst through the room. "We're going black," one agent said into his communication device as he quickly walked throughout the room. At least five other agents secured the doors in the Oval Office, covering every window.

"This isn't a good time for a run through, John," JD stated.

"Not a run through, Mr. President," John replied. "Special Agent Dumas will be here in two."

JD glanced at Calvin then back to John. "Are my wife and children secure?"

"The residence has been secured."

"What's happened?"

"Need a twenty on Dumas," John spoke into his device.

Special Agent Dumas burst through the door. "Mr. President, we have a situation. We should follow procedure and inform the Chief of Staff."

"Mr. Johnson is here." JD pointed to the corner where Calvin was standing. The agent looked around.

Calvin saw the look of distress in the agent's eyes and instinctively moved closer to the area where JD was standing. "What is it, Dumas?"

Special Agent Dumas turned back to JD. "Mr. President, at eighteen hundred hours, the SUV carrying your daughter and niece was found on the Southeast side of D.C. One agent was dead on the scene, the other is unconscious."

"My daughter?" JD's heart was about to pound out of his chest. "Where is Jasmine?"

The nervous agent shook his head. "We don't know Sir."

"What in the hell do you mean you don't know?" JD stormed towards the agent.

Calvin jumped between them. "JD, calm down," he shouted. "Has her mother been notified, Agent Dumas?"

"We came straight here, Sir."

"My God, Tracy." JD ran from the room out the door to the pathway leading to the residence. The agents stationed outside the door tried to stop him. "Get the hell out of my way."

A flurry of activity began all at once. Special Agent Dumas ordered the men to lead the way to the residence. He ran behind JD and Calvin giving as many details as he could.

Calvin pulled out his cell. "James, meet us in the residence, now!"

JC walked into the family room and smiled at his little brother who was walking around with one of Jazzy's hats on his head. He picked William up, kissed him on the cheek then took the hat off.

"Jazz." The baby laughed and clapped his hands.

"Yes, Jazzy." JC put William down next to Gabby who was sitting in a chair reading. His other sister, Brianna, was doing homework. There was a rule in their house. All homework had to be completed before any other activities. He had just finished his before walking into the room. Now it was his job to help the others. "Where's Jazzy?" he asked.

Gabby looked up from her book, and shrugged. "She hasn't come home yet."

"She was supposed to help me with my math." Brianna looked at her brother. "Can you help me?"

"Sure." JC sat at the small desk with Brianna just as agents burst through the doors. He looked up to see at least ten agents moving strategically through the residence. They closed doors, pulled drapes on the windows and surrounded the room.

"I have four in sight," one agent said.

"FLOTUS unaccounted for," another said.

"Lock it down," another agent ordered. "We're going black."

JC had seen the security measure before, but this time there was an urgency with their movements. "What's going on?" he asked.

"Your father will be here in a moment," an agent replied.

JC's gut told him something wasn't right. "Where's my mother?"

"Your father will be here in a moment."

"I didn't ask about my father. I asked you where is my mother?"

The agent touched his earpiece. "Affirmative."

William ran to his brother, frightened by the sudden rush of activity. JC picked him up and then gathered his sisters next to him.

"What's wrong, JC?" Brianna took her brother's hand.

"I don't know," JC replied.

Gabby stood next to her brother. "It's Jazzy."

JC looked down at her, then back up at the men and knew she was right. He gave the baby to Gabby. "Keep William quiet, okay. I'll see what's going on."

"Can I go with you, JC?"

JC smiled down at Brianna. "Not this time. You stay here with Gabby, okay."

"Okay."

"Come on, Bri, let's read to William until Daddy comes."

JC walked over to the door where two agents were stationed. He could see they were on alert. He reached for the door and was stopped.

"You have to remain in the room, son," the agent stated.

"I want to check on my mother. Make sure she's okay."

"Your mother is secure."

"How do you know?"

"We know, son."

He heard the rush of movement outside in the foyer. "Is that my Dad?"

"Yes," the agent replied.

"May I go to him?"

"No, son, you have to remain here."

He turned to see the frightened look on his brother's and sisters faces. He had just taken a step to console them when the door burst open.

"Dad?"

JD grabbed his son and hugged him as the other children ran to Tracy.

She fell to her knees and hugged each of them. William began to whimper as JD took him from Gabby.

"What's going on, Dad?" JC asked.

"John." JD turned to an agent. The agent cleared all the other agents from the room and closed the door.

"Dad?" JC looked up expectantly.

JD hesitated, almost choking as the words came out. "Jazzy and Jada are missing."

"Where'd she go, Daddy?" Gabby asked.

"We're not sure, Gabby, honey. That's what we are trying to find out."

JC stepped away from his father's embrace. "Dad."

Before he could say anything the doors opened. James, Ashley, Calvin and Brian walked through.

"Where are the other children?" JD anxiously asked.

"Home," Ashley replied as she ran over to a distraught Tracy. "Why? What's going on?"

JD glanced at Calvin, who shook his head. As much as he was hurting for his own child, JD knew he had to be the one to break the news to James and Ashley. He turned giving William to JC. "Take the children to the play area."

"But Dad,"

"Now JC, I need to talk to your Aunty."

JC did as he was asked.

"JD?" James gave him a questioning look.

"You're scaring me, JD." Ashley frowned. "What's going on? Is it Mom?"

JD shook his head as he looked up at James. "There's no easy way to say this. Jazzy and Jada are missing."

"Missing?" Ashley frowned. "No they're not. They're at the dance studio."

"No, Ashley, they aren't there. One agent is dead and the other is hanging on to life."

"How long ago?" Brian asked.

"They discovered the abandoned vehicle less than an hour ago," JD replied.

"Details," Brian asked.

"Dumas has the details." Calvin pulled Brian away.

As the men huddled in the corner discussing the situation, JD held Tracy and James consoled Ashley. There was no mistaking the murderous look in James' eyes.

"Did you say an agent is alive? Are they able to talk to tell us anything about the children? Give me what you know."

"Let's take a seat."

"I don't want to take a seat, JD. I want to know where my daughter is," James seethed.

"I know, James. I want to know where Jazzy and Jada are."

The two men held each other's angry glares, then James sighed. "I apologize. Tell me what you know."

"The Special Agent in charge placed a routine call when the vehicle did not arrive here at the scheduled time. When he received no response, he activated the tracking system on the vehicle. It was located in Southeast D.C."

"What in the hell was it doing there?" James asked.

JD shook his head. "Don't know. When they arrived on the scene they found one agent unconscious and the other in the trunk dead."

"No," Ashley cried out. "What about the girls? Was there any sign of the girls?"

"Their book bags were in the backseat as was Jazzy's panic button."

"Dad." JC walked over.

"JC, I need you to watch the children right now."

"Dad, listen," he yelled. "That man has her."

JD looked at his son as Tracy asked, "What man?" All eyes turned to JC. "The man from the basketball court," JC stated, then looked at his dad. "Dad, the man I told you about from school."

Brian turned when he heard JC's remark. "David Holt?" he asked as he walked back over.

"Yes," JC replied, relieved that someone was finally listening.

"Holt!" James yelled. "Holt has my daughter?"

Ashley and Tracy looked up. "Find him and kill him," Tracy demanded. "If David Holt is anywhere near those girls I don't want any questions asked. You kill him!"

"Tracy." JD reached out to calm her down.

"No, don't calm her down. She is right." Ashley jumped to her side. "You find him James. And you kill him. Do not leave Jada in that man's hands. How long has he had them?" She looked at JD.

"We don't know for a fact that it's him. Tracy." JD held her at arms length. "The children need you right now." He looked up. "John have Mr. Brooks' children brought here. Also, locate my mother. Do we have eyes on my mother?"

"Yes, Sir we do. She is en route," John replied. "We will have the other children in five." The agents moved with speed, not wasting a minute to gather the family.

JD turned to JC, along with Brian and several agents. "Son, tell me what you know."

JC proceeded to tell them about the run in with Holt at the basketball court. "He was talking to Jazzy and Jada when I approached him."

"A few days ago?" Brian asked.

"Yes."

"Was Elliott with you?" Brian pulled out his phone.

"Yes."

Brian walked over to the agents. "Run this plate." He then pulled up a picture of David Holt. "This is the man you are looking for. He's an ex-felon. Not known to have conventional weapons, however, if he has the President's child he is considered an enemy of this country."

"Keep this on the low," JD instructed. "If he gets wind that we are looking for him, he will disappear."

"The city is on lockdown, Mr. President. It's automatic when there is an attack on a principal protectee. Every mode of transportation is shut down. Police blocks are in place at every exit from the city. He will not get out of this city," Agent Dumas proclaimed.

"That doesn't prevent any damage he could do to the girls inside the city." James paced angrily. "I have to find my daughter." James ran from the room.

"Calvin." JD nodded towards the door where James exited. Calvin ran behind James. "Brian." JD pulled him aside. "Too much is happening today."

"You think it's connected?"

"I don't know." JD exhaled, anger radiating from him. "My daughter...Brian..someone has my daughter."

"We're going to find her," Brian stated.

JD closed his eyes, then looked at Brian. "Get with Joshua. Tell him I want my daughter back. My gut is telling me there's more in play here than what we know."

"It's all connected, Dad." JD turned to see JC standing behind him with a frown on his face.

"Don't you see it? One of your children has been abducted. You are in a compromising position as far as the country is concerned. If you received a ransom note ordering you to drop a bomb on another country or your child will be killed, what would you do? You would have to choose between your country and your child. They are pushing you into a corner. They want you to take the 25th amendment and step aside. If you do that the Vice-President takes your position." Every eye in the room was on him, but he didn't care. JC continued. "It's a conspiracy, Dad. I don't know who's behind it, but it is a conspiracy to get you out of office."

JD nodded to Brian, then turned back to JC. He walked with his son to another room. JD held a hand up asking the agents who followed to stand back. They stood in the back of the foyer, away from the windows. "Jon-Christopher, listen to me. Nothing in my life comes before my family. This situation will be handled. If what you say is true, all parties involved will pay."

"With their life, Dad?"

"Son, I took an oath to protect this country and its constitution."

"I didn't take that oath Dad."

JD pulled his son to him. It pained him to have his fourteen year old son thinking this way. "I'll handle it, son."

"I know you will Dad. Just don't give them what they want." JC pulled away and looked up at his dad. "Get Jazzy back, protect the AG, but don't give the Vice-President your seat. The country voted you in office, not him."

JD smiled at his son. "I will not step down. This is as far as you and I are going to discuss this. I love you, son, but this is my burden, not yours." He grabbed his son's shoulders, pulled him to his side and began walking. "Know what I need you to do?"

"Anything, Dad."

"I'm going to be a little busy with all of this. Will you help your mom?"

"I got her, Dad. But who's got your back?"

"Mr. President," Special Agent Dumas called from the doorway. "The FBI has arrived."

Chapter Twenty
Washington, D.C.

"**W**hy are you in a hurry to leave?" Joshua's voice was edgy, not as smooth as he wanted, as they got into the vehicle.

"It's time," Roc replied as she looked out the window.

"According to whose clock?"

"Mine, Joshua."

"You're not one of those women that thinks having sex...damn good sex constitutes a relationship, Roc. So what gives?"

"No. I am a person who believes in self-preservation." She turned to him. "You aren't ready for me because you haven't allowed yourself to heal. And I'm not a woman to be second to anyone." She turned away. "I'll work through this case, then I'm walking."

She's not walking anywhere. Joshua pulled the SUV into a parking lot behind a deserted building. He stepped out the driver's door, removed his trench coat then entered the backdoor. Closing the door, he placed the coat across the driver seat, reached between the two seats and pulled Roc to the back with him. "Sleep mode, Genevieve." The doors on the vehicle locked, the windows tinted to a dark shade, the back seats folded backwards into a bed.

"What the heck are you doing?" she hissed, as she looked around at what was happening inside the vehicle.

"Giving you an Absolute experience." His lips captured hers before she could release her next breath. His tongue captured hers in a fierce battle of control. An arm, strong as steel, circled her waist, pulling her tight to his body, as if he was trying to lock her in. His other hand grabbed her wrists, holding them together and above her head. Then his thigh covered hers, securing them between his. She was so thoroughly wrapped in his embrace, she felt as if she was in a cocoon. His kiss, so intense, it set her body ablaze. This wasn't good for her state of mind and she knew it, but there wasn't a darn thing she could do about the way her body was yearning to get closer to his. Heaven help her, she wanted this, her body was craving more of him. His taste was intoxicating, overruling her better judgment until the good sense God gave her vanished and the only thing that mattered was how his glorious tongue was making her feel.

The moment he felt her body begin to relax and move closer to his, he rolled her onto her back, taking his lips away from her mouth, planting kisses down her throat, to her breast, biting through the material of her blouse until the bud was hard, straining to be released. He let her hands go, opened her blouse then unsnapped the front hook on her bra. He pushed the material aside, then took the nipple into his mouth, sucking as if he was a baby nursing for the food of life. The life line of his was now straining against the zipper of his pants, but this wasn't about his pleasure. No, this was to mark his territory. He pulled up at the thought, then looked down at her, confused. But the look of passion on her face, made him want to see more. He grinned, then captured the other nipple into his mouth. Licking, sucking, feasting on it until she was squirming beneath him. Moving his thigh over hers, he felt the butt of her gun against his leg. He began to chuckle against her breast. He pushed his hard steel between her legs, pulled up then looked down at her grinning. "Is that your gun or are you that happy to be here?"

For a moment Roc didn't respond. All she could do was see that devilish gleam in his eyes. He was too fine for his own good. Her heart melted. "You realize I could kill...right?" she moaned as she reached down to unzip his pants.

The words were deadly, but the sensuous way she said them fueled his desire to have her. "Hold that thought darling." He unzipped her pants and pulled them down over her hips. "Give me two minutes and let me die a happy man."

Roc began laughing as she reached up and grabbed his suit lapel, pulling his lips down to hers. "You started this you better finish."

"Don't you worry darling." He slid easily between her legs into her wetness, not stopping until all of him was fully embedded inside her heat. They both moaned. He whispered against her lips, "Purify me, Roc." He slowly pulled out, then slowly pushed back into her. "Coat me in your sweet juice." He pulled out again, moving as if he had all the time in the world. He kissed her neck, as he eased back out, relishing in the feel of her silky walls closing around him, pulsing each time he entered. He didn't know which felt better, entering her or being fully enclosed inside her. The plan to mark his turf, was turning into something different...something more. It was her branding him, every time he pulled out and pushed back in. For the life of him, he couldn't stop. He thrust harder at the thought, and damn if that didn't feel good. She put her arms around his neck, and wrapped her thighs around his back pulling him deeper into her warmth. He put his hands on her hips and began pumping into her as if his life would end if he didn't fill her completely. Each stroke put him closer to a state of delirium, the feel of her was driving him to push harder, faster, deeper until he felt her body explode and all her glorious, juices flowed around him. He captured her lips with his, enjoying the scream escaping her throat. His tongue touching every corner of her mouth, as he drove fiercely inside of her, demanding that she surrender every fiber of her body to him. He refused to release his seed, until she gave him everything. Her walls began to pulsate around him again, and he was ecstatic, for he was ready. He pushed up on his hands, his lower body driving into her, absorbing every drop of her essence as it poured from her. He didn't stop. The feeling was so all consuming he couldn't do anything thing but explode. His body jerked, at the impact of his release. But he continued to move within her, determined to keep the exquisite feel of her around him.

He slowly lowered his body down to hers. He gathered her in his arms, as he moved to the side. They lay there, wrapped in each other's arms as if they had nothing more important to do than just be...

Finally, Roc whispered into his neck, "I'm thirty-five years old getting busy in the back of a car."

"State of the art automobile, darling, only the best for you." They both lay there laughing.

An hour later, he pulled into a space across the street from where the meeting was to take place. They watched the building in silence for a moment. "What do you think?"

Roc looked round. "It will be dark in a few. I say we wait."

He opened the door. "I say let's go in. They are going to wait until dark. We need to be in place before they arrive."

Roc got out of the vehicle and followed as he walked into the building. Instead of entering through the front door, Joshua walked around to the back. There were steps leading down into a basement entrance. Using a set of tools from his pocket, Joshua picked the lock. They both eased into the building closing the door behind them.

Roc pulled out her flashlight and slowly shined it around the room. As expected, the basement was vacant. "Shall we explore upstairs?" she asked, then turned to see she was alone. "Joshua?" she called out.

"Up here," he replied.

She shined the light in the direction of his voice, to find him inside the vent. "What is it with you and small places."

"I like it tight, what can I say." Then he had the nerve to grin displaying those sexy dimples.

"Cute." Roc looked around. "I'm going to check out upstairs."

"I'll meet you there."

Roc took the stairs as Joshua disappeared. The first level of the building was open space, as if it was a reception hall of some kind. She walked the area, with her weapon drawn. Some light was coming in through the covered windows, as she checked the few doors to ensure no one was there.

"We have eyes in place," Joshua advised from behind her.

She swung around. "You are going to get yourself killed doing that."

"You knew it was me. I can tell...your heartbeat increased the moment I walked in the room."

She tilted her head as she spoke. "You are not that potent, Mr. Lassiter."

"Yes I am." Joshua grinned

"Those dimples are going to get you killed." She turned, continuing her surveillance of the room. "Or me, before this night is out."

"I think we have a few minutes. Come look at what I found."

"You are having too much fun with this."

He stopped in his tracks. It hit him. She was right. He was having fun. This was the first time in three years that he'd had fun on a mission. The last time was with Akande. He waited for the anger to hit him, but it didn't. The thought of Akande didn't anger him. Why, he did not know, but damn if it didn't feel good not to hurt at the thought of her.

She stopped and turned back when she realized he wasn't behind her. "What's wrong?"

Joshua held her gaze. He saw the concerned look there, but there was something else there too. He saw him, the old Joshua reflecting through her eyes. He walked towards her. "When this case is over with, remind me to kiss you like the gift from God you are."

His eyes sparkled with mirth, as he walked by her. It took Roc a moment to gather her wits after his statement. Then she turned and followed him up a flight of stairs.

She looked around as she reached the top. The upstairs was another open area with windows all around. The place could have been an open loft with the great views of the city's skyline from any point in the room. "Wow."

"Nice, isn't it," Joshua said from a corner of the room. "Check this out." She walked over to where he stood. "We should be able to see who's coming and going from here."

Roc looked out of the window. "There's a blind spot. If the person doesn't want to be seen, they could enter from that direction." She pointed to the left.

"In that case, I have a set of eyes planted."

This man she could not figure out. He argued with her for shooting his coat, yet he was now on the dirty floor in his suit like a kid in a candy store. "You are getting your suit dirty."

Joshua looked up at her from over his shoulder, thinking how many times did his mother say that to him? It always seemed to be right before church. He was glad she was looking around and could not see the play of emotions her words caused. He continued to adjust the wire that had a camera at the tip, as thoughts of his mother and church filled his mind. The fact that he was lying on the floor getting his suit dirty was a testament of God's presence for him. It was the first time in a few years that he'd felt it. What caused this to hit him at this moment, he didn't know. But it felt damn good to have God's presence with him and know it.

> *No one will be able to stand against you all the days of your life. As I was with Moses, so I will be with you: I will never leave you nor forsake you.*
> **Joshua 1:5**

He felt as if the words were echoing in his ears. "I know now, you have always been with me."

"What?" Roc turned back to him.

"Nothing." He should turn the thoughts off. "Look at this." He sat up with the handheld in his hand.

Roc sat on the floor Indian style as he did and watched as the monitor showed the empty room below. "Do we have sound?"

Joshua pushed another button and a big smile appeared on his face. "We shall soon find out."

Roc couldn't help it, she smiled back. "You're nothing but a big kid, you know that."

In that moment, with her smiling up at him, he had the irresistible urge to kiss her. So he did. Just a quick peck on the lips. But her eyes asked for more and never let it be said that Joshua Lassiter did not deliver. His arms circled her waist, startling her, and lifted her across his lap. Neither spoke, as they sat face to face, their lips parted and a breath away from the other's, when it hit him like a boulder. This was the angel God sent him. He held her face between the palms of his large hands. "What God hath joined together, let no man put asunder."

"*King James Bible. Mark 10 verse 9*," Roc whispered. The smile in his eyes filled her with joy. She knew this man had no idea the havoc he was playing on her mind. But at this time, in this moment, she didn't care. She wanted this. She wanted him.

The kiss that followed melted his heart. Sweet, pure sensation flooded his body, as his tongue merged with hers. Every corner of her mouth was like another dose of medicine to heal his broken heart. The deeper he kissed, the stronger his heartbeat vibrated. His hands filled with the warmth of her body as he pulled the tucked blouse from her pants. Her skin was so smooth beneath his hands. He couldn't help but move one hand to the front, allowing his fingers to rub across the bra covered nipple. It came to attention at his touch. She clung tighter to him, matching his intensity, stroke for stroke of her tongue. He swallowed her moan, driving his tongue deeper into the sweetness of her mouth. Not able to wait another moment, he pushed the bra up, then took the brown nipple into his mouth. She gasped at the break from the kiss and melted at the feel of his mouth on her. "This is dangerous. We have to stop."

"Daring, darling is what it is." He returned to his taunting of her breast. "They're as tasty as before." He smacked his lips, then nipped her nipple, sucking harder.

Was it possible to get the big O just from his mouth on her? It didn't hurt to have twelve inches of steel pulsing between her legs. No matter how many times her mind told her to stop, she couldn't keep her body from rubbing, feeling, the heat of him there. The more he suckled, the more she squirmed against him. She heard the sound just as she knew he had, but neither was stopping the sweet torment they were experiencing. The bad would have to wait.

BOOM! There it was.

Joshua covered her mouth with his to keep her from screaming out. He held her body down, tight against him, until she rode the wave out. Then he kissed her gently on the throat as he caressed her back with his hands. Easing her heart rate down.

Her forehead fell against his. "We've got to stop doing this," she whispered.

"Not in this lifetime, Angel." He looked into her eyes. "You good?" he quietly asked.

She nodded as he sat her down next to him.

He stretched his long legs out, then peered down at the monitor as a second man entered.

Roc lay next to him watching and listening, but more so trying to ease her heartbeat that was still reeling from the Absolute explosion.

"Did you do this with the President's daughter? Are you responsible for this?" the man railed the moment he walked in the door. "All the pieces are falling into place. I can't take the chance of anything going wrong, not at this point. I've waited too long for this moment to let your stupidity interfere."

"Chill out, man. Everything is under control," Holt replied.

"Do you have the signed document from McClintock requesting the President's removal?"

"It should be on its way," David replied. "Once the document is signed by McClintock it is to be delivered to you. You will be the one to announce publicly that the President authorized the Vice President to approve the movement of the weapons into the country."

That seemed to have calmed the man down, but he watched David's every move. Finally, the moment he had been waiting for. It had been over 10 years now. It was time for JD Harrison to take his fall from grace. Oh yes, it had been a glorious ride for righteous JD. And he'd had no problem with hanging on to his coattail to get to the point of power needed to gather the troops to bring down the great JD Harrison.

The man still had not come into view. Joshua shifted, trying to get a better view. There was something familiar about the man. "I need to get closer. I need to see who Holt is meeting with."

Roc grabbed his arm to stop him. "You'll be detected before we have what we need. Let him talk." She exhaled. "This is his moment of glory. Be patient, you're going to get what you need."

"You could give me what I need."

The nerve of him. "You may want to back up off of that topic." She shook her head, then turned back to the two men meeting. "Pay attention to the meeting so we can wrap this case up."

"Gary is dead."

"Yes, and McGary is in custody."

"What about McClintock's wife? How're we going to keep her quiet?"

"She's under complete control." David replied. "What you need to be concerned with is how are you going to keep me quiet."

"I'm not concerned about that at all, Holt. You talk, you go back to jail. It's that simple."

He slapped the envelope in Holt's chest. "Here's your payment. Return Harrison's daughter back to her family or you will not see the light of day," he said then walked off

Holt looked inside the envelope, took the money out, flipped through the stack of hundred dollar bills, then placed them in the inside pocket of his suit jacket. He discarded the envelope on the floor.

Joshua and Roc looked at each other and smiled. That was the break they needed. They waited until they saw Holt leave the building then ran down the stairs. Roc picked up the envelope with a pin, stuffed it inside of a plastic bag. They left the scene running. "There has to be prints on that envelope."

"You get that to Brian," Joshua said as he jumped over the hood of the SUV. "I'm going to follow Holt."

Roc raised her hand for a taxi.

Chapter Twenty-One

Joshua watched Holt walk a few blocks, then pull off in an older model vehicle. "Genevieve."

"Yes, Joshua."

"There's a tan Oldsmobile three cars up to the right of me. Are you able to give me coordinates on previous trips within the last week?"

"Negative, the vehicle has no GPS system. It does have an antiquated bluetooth system."

"Lock into it. See if you can give me a location it's been to within the last week."

"Processing."

Based on the direction Holt was driving, Joshua knew he was heading towards Southeast D.C. He needed to know where, at least a general area.

"Complete."

Joshua looked at the map Genevieve provided. "Thank you, Genevieve. You are a genuine piece of art."

"Thank you. I know."

"It's dark, Jazzy," a frightened Jada whimpered.

"I know." Jazzy hugged her cousin as they sat in a corner in an empty room of a strange house. After the man locked the door, the two girls sat in a corner holding on to each other, but now they were cold and hungry.

"You think he forgot us?"

"I hope so." Jazzy was continuously looking around the room for anything that could help them get out. "Shoot, I'm tired of being scared. I want to go home." She went to stand, but Jada grabbed her.

"Where are you going, Jazzy?"

"To see if the light is working." She took her cousin's hand. "Come on, you can go with me."

"Okay."

They walked to the light switch by the door then turned on the light. Jazzy put her ear to the door. "I don't hear anything." She reached for the doorknob.

"No, Jazzy," Jada cried out. "Don't open it Jazzy the bad man is out there. I'm scared, Jazzy. Please don't open the door."

"Okay, okay, Jada. Stop crying. It's going to be okay. The door is locked anyway." She held her cousin tight just as much for herself as for Jada. She was afraid too. But she knew she had to be strong and protect Jada. It was also important that they find a way out of the house. Jazzy looked around the room again for about the hundredth time. "I'm going to do an SOS."

"A what?"

"An SOS. It's a signal you can send with sounds or lights to let someone know you are in trouble and need help. It's what people used before there were cell phones." Jazzy turned the light switch off. Jada grabbed her free hand. She turned the light switch on then off. "One, two, three." She turned the light on then off. "One, two, three." She did it again. On. "One, two, three." Then she turned it on and off three times quickly. "Okay, that's one set. We're going to do it again." She did the same routine. "Count with me Jada."

"Okay. One, two, three. On," Jada counted.

Jazzy could feel Jada calming down. She knew it was not going to last long, but at least she was okay for now. Man, she hoped her Daddy would find them soon.

Joshua pulled into the area Genevieve had designated as the likely destination for Holt. The area appeared to be deserted. There were rundown row houses on both sides of the street. A few had lights inside, most had nothing but boards or broken down porches. "Go stealth, Genevieve," Joshua requested. Genevieve's lights darkened. "Scan the area for the vehicle."

"Scanning...located, one hundred feet to the left of your current location."

"Thank you, Genevieve." Joshua looked around. "Do you detect any unusual movement?"

"Yes."

"Where?"

"Thirty feet away to the right of your current location."

Joshua stepped out of the automobile to look around. He missed it at first, thinking it was someone's television reflecting off the side of the house. But then he counted. "One, two, three." It's an SOS signal. Why in the hell would a distress signal be coming from a rundown row house? Then as if by osmosis, Joshua looked up to see all the helicopters flying above. He listened to the sounds of the night. Emergency vehicle sounds were in abundance in D.C., but tonight it seemed intensified. Joshua pulled out his handheld. "Ned, what's happening?"

"Joshua, where in the hell have you been? The President's daughter and niece have been taken. They believe David Holt is involved."

Joshua began moving toward the blinking light. "Give me ten, Ned." He went black again as Ned was calling out his name. His gut was telling him all hell was about to break loose.

Jazzy was getting tired. She knew they had to do something else. The SOS thing wasn't working. "Okay, look." Jazzy held her cousin at arms length. "You trust me right?"

Jada bobbed her head up and down. Her single ponytail bounced along with it. "I don't think the bad man is here. I think he is gone. We have to try to get away now. You understand?"

"Yes." Jada nodded.

"Okay, I'm going to unlock the door."

"No." Jada shook her head.

"We can't stay here, Jada, we have to get out. It's going to be all right."

Jazzy pulled a bobby pin from her hair causing the end of one of her braids to fall into her face. She pushed it aside, then began working the lock. To her, this was child's play. In fact, she had been picking locks since she was five years old. One could call it a family trait. It clicked. The two girls looked at each other, eyes wide with fright.

"Shhh." Jazzy put her finger to her lips, then slowly turned the knob and cracked the door. The room looked empty. She could see all the way to the front door. She opened the door a little further. "See Jada, he's not here. Come on." She grabbed her cousin's hand and ran full speed towards the front door. They had just about reached the door when Jada fell over something.

"Ouch," she cried out.

"Get up, Jada, we have to go."

"I hurt my leg Jazzy."

Jazzy bent down. She rubbed her cousin's leg. "It'll be all right Jada." She kissed her leg as her mother had done hers many times. How Jazzy wished her mother was here now. "We have to go."

A noise came from the back of the house.

Jada's eyes grew big. "Jazzy."

Jazzy grabbed Jada's hand and pulled her towards the door. "Come on," she cried.

They reached the door and it was locked. Jazzy pulled another bobby pin from her hair and began to work on the lock.

Jada kept looking towards the back of the house where the noise came from. When a man appeared in the doorway, all she could do was pat Jazzy on the shoulder. She couldn't speak.

"Stop, Jada. I almost have it."

The shocked child couldn't speak for the figure was overwhelming. "Jazzy," the child stammered.

"Jada." Jazzy pushed her hand aside.

"Jazzy." The girl's fingers gripped her.

"Jada." Jazzy stood and turned to the girl. "What?" The impatience clear in her voice.

Jada just pointed.

Jazzy saw the man standing in the doorway with his arms folded across his chest, his coat hanging open and a weird look on his face. Her first instinct was to protect her cousin. She pushed Jada behind her and just stared at the man.

Joshua stood there, not believing what he walked in on. Two little girls, who he was sure were the President's daughter and niece, were picking a lock on a door. What concerned him more was the item on the floor in front of them. He knew not to make a sudden move, for that would frighten them. "Jasmine, stay very still."

The young girl seemed indignant. With hands on her hips, she stood defiantly in front of her cousin. "How do you know my name?"

"I'm a friend of your father's."

"That's what the other man said."

"He lied."

"How do I know you are not lying?"

Joshua almost grinned. He instantly liked the little girl. Not only for her tenacity, but more for the way she put herself in front of her cousin. He wished the situation were different for he would take a picture of the two. The little one had her arms wrapped around the other's waist. The taller one had her hands behind her, holding on to the smaller one. Too cute, he thought, but dangerous. He knew he had to move them away from the item on the floor. "Fair question." He took a step towards them. They started to move. "Don't move." He held up his hand. "Jasmine, I want you to see something." He pulled out his handheld and pushed a button. "Ned, we have a situation. Connect me to the President."

"May be difficult."

"Do it...now."

Ned asked no questions, but did what Joshua asked.

"Joshua." JD's picture appeared on the monitor. "Tell me you found my daughter."

"Hold on Sir," Joshua turned the handheld to Jasmine.

"Daddy," the girl cried out and started to run.

"Stop," Joshua shouted. "Sir, tell her not to move," he rushed out.

"Jasmine, stop. Don't move."

Jazzy cried out. "Daddy."

"Don't worry baby, you're safe now. Stay still baby, stay still."

Jazzy cried. "Daddy come get me."

"I'm coming, baby."

"See, Jada, Daddy's coming."

Joshua kept an eye on the girls as he turned the handheld back to him. "Mr. President, we have a situation. The girls appear to be unharmed. However, there is a device at their feet."

The tone of JD's voice indicated he understood. "Joshua...that's my baby. Get her out of there."

"That's the plan Sir. Lock on to my location. Send the calvary, but do not enter. I need you to keep the girls calm." Joshua pushed a few buttons, and pointed the handheld towards the device. It read off the items that the device was made of, causing Joshua to close his eyes. Not only was the device explosive, as he had concluded, it was dirty. Meaning it contained substances, which would cause harm to anyone within miles if it goes airborne.

"Sir, it's dirty."

"We're en route."

"Sir, you can't come into this area."

"I'm on my way." The screen went black.

"Where's my Daddy?"

"He's on his way," Joshua replied trying to calm the child.

"Why can't we move?" Jazzy asked.

The last thing he wanted to do was frighten the child more. But he had to make sure she understood the situation. "Jasmine."

"Her name is Jazzy," the smaller child offered.

Joshua smiled. "Okay, Jazzy. I want you to look down." The girls did. "You see the wires?"

"Yes, Jada tripped over them."

"Okay." He bent down until he was eye level to them. "You see how they are spread out across the floor?"

"Mmm hmm."

"I need to lift you across the wires without touching them. Will you let me do that?"

Jazzy looked at the wires. "I can jump across them."

"No," he said a little more anxiously than intended. "It's not safe. I'll reach across to pick you up. Okay?"

"Okay. Do Jada first. She's scared."

"No," Jada cried out.

Joshua smiled. The loyalty between the two was adorable. "I tell you what. I'll get both of you. What's her name?"

"Jada." The girl peeked around her cousin to reply, then disappeared behind her again.

"Okay, Jada hold on tight to Jazzy. Jazzy, arms up."

Joshua reached across the wires, raised the two girls up and over the loose wires. His first responsibility was to get the girls out of that house. But he couldn't bring himself to leave them unattended in the vehicle. Nor could he bring himself to leave a dirty bomb unattended. He pulled out his handheld.

He knew Roc had gone black, so he called Brian instead.

"Anything on the fingerprints?

"Not yet."

"Damn. We have a bigger problem." He relayed the events to Brian as he stared at a bomb with enough power to clear the city block. "I need to speak to Roc."

Chapter Twenty-Two
Washington, D.C.

Joshua heard him before the man entered the house. He grabbed the girls up. "Shh, be very quiet." He placed them back inside the room and was about to close the door when Jada called out.

"No, please don't leave us."

"Shh, I'm not going to leave you," he whispered. He looked up at Jazzy.

"I got her." Jazzy nodded.

Joshua smiled and closed the door then disappeared into the woodwork of the room just before David Holt appeared.

The moment he entered the room he knew something was wrong. The device wasn't where he left it. The wires were out of synch. He walked over, adjusted the wires, restored the connection to the door, then he froze. He stood slowly reaching into his pocket.

"Not a good move."

David turned to see a tall dark man dressed in a suit leaning against the door of the room the girls were in. The lazy stance didn't fool him. The man had a sense of danger surrounding him. "You're in the wrong place, my brother."

"Put your hand in that pocket and this will be your dying place...my brother."

David's hand froze. "What do you want? There's nothing valuable here."

"I want information about that device." His eyes never left Holt's.

David's cynical grin appeared. "That little baby. Hmm, that baby is what's going to get me out of here."

"Umm...I don't think so." Joshua took a step forward.

David mistakenly took that as the moment to pull his phone from his pocket.

Joshua, on the other hand showed how wrong he was. He was on David and throwing him against the wall, away from the device. The phone dropped from his hand and landed by the door where the girls were. David proved to be a bit of a fight, which only amused Joshua. David kicked Joshua in the side knocking him backwards, momentarily giving him a chance to dive for the phone. It was just inches away from his fingers, when he felt the tall man's foot on his hand. He looked up to see the man looming over him. Joshua picked him up by the back of his suit jacket, holding him like a rag doll. He punched David with so much force his body bounced off the wall and fell to the floor. Joshua grinned at the sight, but when he turned, the vision of Jazzy standing in the doorway with the cell phone chilled him to the bone. He was sure the phone was the detonator to the bomb.

"Jazzy," he spoke cautiously. "Don't."

"I want to call my Daddy."

"No, don't push any buttons."

"Sweetheart."

Joshua did not turn when he heard the familiar voice.

"My name is Roc. Your parents are outside. They are so anxious to see you. They asked me to come inside to bring you out." Roc walked slowly towards the two girls. She held out her hand. "Will you come with me?"

"Is my mommy outside too?" Jada asked.

"Yes, your parents are outside also."

Jada ran to Roc and jumped in her arms.

Joshua slowly walked over to Jazzy who still had the phone in her hand. He had no idea what could trigger the device and did not want to startle the girl. He bent down in front of her and smiled. "We haven't officially met." He held out his hand. "My name is Joshua."

"It's a bomb, isn't it?"

Joshua held the girl's eyes. He never underestimated the intelligence of children. "Yes."

"Do you want to know the code?"

Joshua was a little surprised. He thought the girls would be a little squeamish, but this one wasn't.

"There's two you know." She pointed to the phone. "There's the code that he used to test and the actual detonation code." The girl shifted on her feet. "See these? The prints show they were used regularly, in sequence 274. That is probably the test code. Then see these ones, 872, that is probably your boom code."

Joshua couldn't help himself, he had to smile. The child had a logical reason for her choices. He held out his hand. "May I?"

"Sure." She hesitated, then tilted her head. "You know what they mean, right?" She asked as she gave the phone to him.

"No." He stood and looked down at her. "Ash and Trac. Both codes are connected to my mom and aunt." She walked over and took Roc's hand, then looked over her shoulder as they walked out of the back door. "Are you coming?"

Joshua smiled, then walked over to her. He kissed her on the cheek. "I'll be out in a minute."

"Okay. You can leave him in here."

Roc stared at him. "You got that?" She nodded towards the device.

"Child's play."

She held his eyes for a moment, then turned and took the girls out the back door.

JC watched as his parents gathered Jasmine in their arms. The scene was surreal. The sirens, the lights from the emergency vehicles, the Secret Service, FBI, local police, the television cameras, the helicopters above. There was a happy outcome. Neither Jasmine nor Jada were harmed. That thought brought a smile to his face. Then he turned. His eyes met David Holt's who was sitting in the backseat of a police cruiser. There was something in the man's eyes that struck him as odd. He wasn't frightened by his future in prison. There was no remorse in his eyes. There was a smirk on his face. And in that moment JC knew, if given the chance, David Holt would strike again. There had been too much violence against his family. Most of it caused by men like Holt. Men who wished to be like his Dad.

He didn't remember when his father was shot, or when his mother was beaten, or the time when David Holt tried to rape his Aunt Ashley, or when his Uncle Brian was shot four times in the back trying to save him. He did vividly remember the night his Dad was elected President of the United States. He remembered the stage being sprayed with bullets. He remembered smiling up at his Dad one minute, then the burning sensation that struck him in the chest. But most of all, he remembered his mother's scream. That gut wrenching sound still woke him up every morning. He never wanted to hear that sound from his mother again.

JC walked over to the vehicle where David sat. "May I have a moment with him?" he asked Joshua, who was standing by the door.

Joshua wondered if the boy knew his intent was written all over his face. He believed the boy had a right to feel as he did. Joshua sent a text to Brian as he spoke. "It's a dangerous line you are about to cross, JC. The outcome could change the course of your life. Do you believe you can handle the consequences of your actions? If that answer is no, then I want you to turn around and walk back over to your family."

JC looked up at Joshua. "Would you walk away knowing this man will return one day, in some way to harm your family?"

Joshua knew he should say yes, but he couldn't bring himself to lie to the boy. "No." He nodded to the Secret Service agent that was ten feet away. "Give us a few minutes here, would you?"

The agent gave Joshua a knowing look, stepped away then turned his back to ensure there were no witnesses to what was about to happen. Brian walked up behind JC, put his hand on his shoulder and squeezed. He was about to pull his weapon when Douglas walked up. He pulled his weapon, put the silencer on the tip then held it out to Brian.

Brian held the weapon as he turned JC to face him. "I want you to look at the faces around you."

JC looked up. There was Brian, Douglas and Joshua, who were all surrounding him. But it was the face over their shoulders that meant more to him than all of them combined. His father was there, in the distance, with his Uncle James standing next to him. He held his father's eyes. Eyes that told him, he understood the turmoil he was experiencing. But more than that, he saw the love his father had for him and that...was all he needed. He didn't take the weapon from Brian. He looked up at Joshua.

"Open the door."

Joshua opened the door to the cruiser and held it.

David looked out and grinned. "So what's this, the inquisition? I'm shaking in my boots." He laughed.

All the men turned their backs to allow JC to have his moment.

"Mr. Holt, why do you hate my father?"

"Your father," David spoke with a smirk. "I don't hate your father. I hate what he stands for. The great American way of truth, honor, loyalty. He's a damn boy scout." He looked away then turned back and looked the boy dead in his eyes. "Now, your mother, I hate that hoe. She ruined my life sticking her nose into something she had no right to. Now her, I'll be back for."

JC didn't doubt David's words for he could see the hate in the man's eyes. "You once told me I was like my father." JC smiled, but there was no warmth in it. "You are right, I am. He's a good man. I'm not a man yet. I'm still a susceptible child, especially in the eyes of the law. I could take your life and not a court in this country would convict me."

"You are your father's son. He didn't have it in him when he confronted the man who killed his father." David grinned. "You don't have the nerve." He leaned forward. "You'd be surprised what a man can accomplish while in prison. Know this little man, that bitch mother of yours will pay," he taunted.

JC held his head down, thought for a moment. "I want you to remember me every time you get on your knees in prison as somebody's bitch."

"Jon-Christopher," Tracy called out as she rushed towards the group standing near the vehicle.

The next chain of events happened as if in slow motion. David kicked the door open, pulled the gun from the Secret Service Agent's holster and pointed it at Tracy.

JC grabbed the gun from Brian, and before he thought to stop himself, he put two bullets in the kneecaps of David Holt. David's gun fired hitting the Agent who was now pushing Tracy back towards the other agents. They quickly whisked her away as she screamed for her son.

The man howled as Joshua reached him. Brian grabbed JC and quickly walked him over to his father. JD took his son by the shoulder, looked at Brian who shook his head no, letting him know JC did not kill Holt. JD exhaled, then was surrounded by agents who walked briskly to the waiting sedan leaving all the other men behind. The agents closed the door ensuring no danger to the President or his son.

Standing at the vehicle with a bleeding David, were Joshua, James, and Douglas. Brian saw the look on James' and Douglas' faces. He looked at Joshua. They both turned their backs as a single gunshot filled the air.

"What is taking so long dammit, it's been over 15 minutes," Monique exclaimed. "We should have a result by now."

"The security level of the person must be up there," Ned explained. "I've hit three security levels. There are only five." He looked over his shoulder at her. "We go any further and we may not be able to match the prints."

"Keep at it," Monique sighed. "You're the best. If anyone can do this, you can."

"We have to find out who the son-of-a-bitch is before 9 am tomorrow."

"What happens then?" Monique asked.

"The Attorney General has to make a resignation announcement or appear before the House to testify."

"Can they call the President to testify?"

"They could, but he will refuse to testify against the AG."

"He's loyal like that. If he refuses, can he be impeached?" Monique raised an eyebrow.

"According to the constitution they can sanction him. For this President, that will be a death sentence."

The computer beeped indicating a match had been found. They both gaped at the monitor and could not believe the reflection looking back at them.

"Oh hell," Monique exclaimed as she ran from the room.

Chapter Twenty-Three
Washington, D.C.

"**W**e have to get to the White House. I want to see this go down." Roc's excitement showed as she jumped into the SUV.

Joshua hesitated. He hadn't been back to the White House in three years.

"What's wrong?" Roc asked as she noticed his hesitation.

"Nothing." He shook it off and jumped into the vehicle.

When they reached the West Wing, Joshua's steps began to slow. The memories of the last time he was there came back full force. Pain he hadn't felt in days began to return in his back. His long black trench coat that had the windblown motion going on whenever he swaggered into a room was now limp. He stopped outside the Oval Office. "You can go in, Joshua," Mrs. Langston said.

He turned to Roc. "You go. I'll catch up later."

"Hey." She touched his arm. "We broke this together. Don't you want to see them slaughter him?"

"You can tell me about it later." He kissed her cheek then turned and walked away.

She looked at Brian who had just opened the door to the Oval Office. "What just happened?"

"The last time Joshua was in this office was three years ago."

Roc was confused for a moment, then it came to her. "The Akande situation," she sighed. She wanted to kick herself. The decision to leave earlier was the right one. She let his dimples and that tongue of his sway her thinking.

"Yeah, that. You coming?" Brian tilted his head.

"Sure." Roc knew how to control the feelings which were chasing around inside. Reality hit her like a brick. Joshua was still not over Akande. After all they had been through, their laughter, their talks, their lovemaking. He was still not over her.

"Thank you for coming, Gavin," Calvin shook his hand patting him on the back. "I can't tell you how much JD appreciates you standing behind him and supporting him the way that you have. He's anxious to speak with you."

"I always have JD's back, no matter what. Let's get this dirty mess over with."

Gavin walked into the room to find JD standing at the window with his hands in his pockets and his head down. He could see JD was in a distressed state with everything that had happened.

Gavin walked over to him. "It's been a hell of a day. Tell me what you need."

JD turned "Have a seat, Gavin. Thank you for coming over so late."

"Anything you need, you just name it." He pulled a document from his coat pocket. "I have this document with the Vice-President's signature accusing you of ordering him to approve the movement of weapons into the country. If you want me to destroy this document I will."

JD held out his hand. "May I?"

Gavin gave him the document.

"Say the word, and it's gone."

"That would mean destroying evidence." JD glanced at the document to ensure it was what they needed. "I wouldn't want you to do that." He handed the document to Calvin, then nodded to Special Agent Dumas, who opened the door. Calvin stepped out.

Brian took a step closer behind Gavin. Noticing a movement, Gavin looked over his shoulder. He turned back to JD. "JD."

"President Harrison." JD's eyes narrowed.

Calvin stepped back into the room. "The Vice-President states, this is his signature, but he did not generate the letter." Calvin gave the document back to JD.

Gavin looked around at the people in the room. "You are the Commander-in-Chief. I serve at your pleasure. You know my loyalty is with you. Can you say the same for McClintock?"

"I appreciate the support, Gavin. But I have a question for you. Did you really think you would get away with it?" A vein began to pulsate in JD's neck.

Gavin chuckled nervously as he looked around at the people in the room. "What, what are you talking about?"

The door opened and Secretary Davenport walked in. "Gavin Roberts, turn around. You are under arrest for treason against the United States of America."

Agents walked behind Gavin. "What the hell is going on here, JD?" Gavin stammered.

The door opened and in walked his wife, Carolyn Roth-Roberts. A distraught Carolyn looked at her husband. "Did you do this?"

"No, Carolyn, no." Gavin exploded, "JD, what is this?" He looked to Calvin and Brian. "What's going on?"

JD just stared at the man that he had considered his mentor, his friend for over 15 years. "Your plot didn't work Gavin."

"JD, stop this. Plot, what are you talking about?"

"You son-of-a-bitch." JD's simmering anger began to surface. "You put this country in jeopardy by planting weapons of mass destruction on U.S. soil, near homes and families. You put my children in jeopardy. You had a known rapist take my daughter. If it was in my power, I would have your ass disappear and no one would ever find you. Unlike you, I care about how this is going to impact your wife and your son. So I'm going to do what you didn't do for me and I'm going to make sure that your family is protected. But make no mistake, you are going to suffer for what you have done to this country and my family."

Gavin looked at his wife. "Carolyn," he pleaded.

"Why would you jeopardize my life, our son's life in this way? What were you thinking?"

Gavin held his wife's glare, then looked around the room and stopped at JD.

"What was I thinking? Give me a minute while I contemplate that question." He smirked. "The righteous JD Harrison," Gavin snarled. "I made you who you are. I was the one who brought you into the AG's office. It was me. I didn't have to, but I did. I made sure that you had a job because I felt guilty about your father's death. I mentored you. I taught you everything I knew about the law and how did you repay me? How did you pay me back when you had an opportunity? Did you do right by me? No."

"Gavin, what the hell are you talking about?" JD was genuinely confused.

"You had the opportunity to name your own Vice-President and what did you do? You chose a redneck Republican as your Vice-President and left me standing there with nothing."

"I gave you what you said you wanted. What I thought you deserved. Hell, Gavin, I made you the Attorney General of the United States."

"I should have been President, you righteous son-of-a-bitch. I did it the right way." He sneered. "I was Governor, then Senator, the next step for me was the Presidency. But, no, the sweetheart of the party, JD Harrison, got the blessing from the DNC. Leaving me with no choice but to settle for your hand me downs. Just like with my wife. Then you do the unforgivable. You gave the Vice Presidency to McClintock. That's what you did. You made a Republican the next man in line to run the country. You went outside of the party. Where was your loyalty when you made that decision, JD?"

"My loyalty was with my country." JD's anger rose. "I was trying to bring this country together while people like you were trying to pull it apart. I would still make the same decision. It's not what's good for the party. That's the way the people on the other side of the aisle think. I make my decisions based on what is best for this country. Your actions proved I put the right man in office. As much as you tried to put this in Jerry's lap, he would never stoop as low as you did, just because his feelings were hurt. That's something a bitch would do."

The agent began to move Gavin out.

"JD, wait, wait a damn minute." Gavin was heaving. "JD, you can't do this. Think of Carolyn, think of my son."

"Did you think of them? Once during the entire time you were planning this, did you think of them?"

Gavin stopped struggling and smirked as he turned to Carolyn to see tears in her eyes. "Don't worry darling." He glanced around. "Jeffrey Daniel Harrison is too decent of a man to put his mentor behind bars. After all, he found a way to pardon his brother-in-law. I'm certain he will find an acceptable deal for me."

"Get him the hell out of my office."

Roc watched as Gavin got his due, but her mind was on Joshua. She loved the man, with all her heart, but he did not love her. She stood as still as a statue as the boom came down on Gavin, never showing any emotion, but her heart had just been ripped out of her chest. It was her own fault. She should have listened to Samuel and never crossed that line. She should have listened. Her sense of self-preservation kicked in, just as the President turned to her.

"Roc, where's Joshua?" he asked looking around.

"You know Joshua, he pops in and out at will."

"Yes, I know." JD smiled. "Thank you for being an agent this Government can be proud of. You did a hell of a thing here today. Tell me what we can do for you."

Roc knew exactly what she had to do. It wasn't what she wanted, but it was what she needed.

Joshua was waiting out by the SUV as they walked Gavin out in handcuffs and put him in the back of the town car. He grinned as Secretary Davenport walked out of the doors. "Another one bites the dust." Joshua grinned.

"This was wild, and it's going to hurt us politically," Royce stated. "But right now, I'm going home to my wife and let her ease the roughness of the day out of my body." He laughed.

"You enjoy that," Joshua said as he held the door open for the Secretary to get in.

He then saw Brian and Calvin coming through the door. "You should have been in there, man," Brian said to Joshua. "You brought this one home for JD."

"Roc will give me the blow by blow."

Calvin and Brian glanced at each other. "Roc left." A helicopter flew overhead. Joshua looked up then looked back at Brian. "What do you mean, she left?" he asked confused.

"She went home, as you should too." Brian hit him on the shoulder as he and Calvin walked by to get into their vehicle.

"It's been a hell of a twenty-four hours. I'm going home to my wife and kids just to hug them tight," Calvin announced as he got into the vehicle.

"Yes, it has," Joshua replied.

"Hey, you want to come over for a few drinks?" Brian asked. "Lord knows you deserve one or two."

"I'm good. My bed is calling me. I'll catch you on the next go round."

"Then on that note, I hope my wife is waiting up for me. See you." Brian waved as he pulled off.

Joshua stood there for a minute, watching the cars pull away. He got into his vehicle and started the engine. He looked over at the passenger seat and immediately missed Roc's presence. "She could have at least said goodbye," he huffed as he pulled off.

Chapter Twenty-Four
Quantico, VA

The first few days weren't bad. Joshua hung out with his family who was ecstatic to have him home. The nights were hellish. Not in the way it was when things happened with Akande. In fact, tonight was the first time he had thought of her in weeks. Those tormented dreams of her had been replaced by the warmth of Roc's body next to his. Not just at night, but during the day, when they were hanging out, killing a few bad guys. He smiled at the memory, as he lay in bed. He missed her voice singing whenever she was nervous, and that's exactly what it was. It took him a minute to pick up on that, but whenever she was around him and became nervous she would just start singing and it would ease his soul as well as her own. He missed the way she would look at him whenever she knocked him on his ass and felt guilty about it. He missed the way she would make him work hard at getting back to battle form. He missed her lips, the way they curved into a little smile when she thought he wasn't looking. He missed the way they felt against his, against his chest, his thighs, his...hell, he missed her. Joshua threw the covers back. He was tired of everyone giving him the brush off when it came to her.

An hour later, at 4 am, Joshua was standing at the foot of Samuel's bed.

"You damn well better have a good reason for being here."

Cynthia stretched, as she turned out of her husband's embrace. "You knew he was coming sooner or later." She pulled the cover up around her. "You should have had this talk weeks ago."

Samuel kissed the back of his wife's shoulder as he got out of bed. He glared at Joshua as if he wanted to kill him. "We'll talk downstairs."

"You better not wake up the children," Cynthia cautioned as the men walked out the door. "You realize it's four in the morning," Samuel said as he turned the light on and walked into the kitchen.

"Did you sleep with Roc?"

Samuel's hand was on the refrigerator door as he turned to Joshua. "No." He opened the door, took out two beers and threw one at Joshua. "What difference would it make if I did? You're still in love with her and she is still in love with you."

"I didn't say..."

"You don't have to say it, Joshua. It's written all over you." Samuel pulled out a chair at the kitchen table, sat down then put his feet up in the other chair. After a moment, Joshua twisted the top off his beer and Samuel did the same. The two men almost looked like twins sitting there, drinking their beer at the same time, holding their heads back in the same way. They even began laughing at the same time. "So what are you going to do?"

Joshua huffed, "I'm going to go get my woman."

They saluted each other then took a drink. Samuel held his bottle. "Roc is a good person, damn good partner and not bad on the eyes. But she is vulnerable when it comes to you."

"How would you know that?"

"She told me." Samuel took another drink.

Joshua's bottle stopped mid-way to his mouth. "You talked to Roc?"

Samuel shrugged. "Yes," he smirked.

Joshua jumped up and rounded the table before Samuel could finish laughing at him. He grabbed Samuel by the lapel of his robe and pulled him up. The bottle fell to the floor crashing into several pieces. "Talk, Sammy, or I'm going to beat it out of you."

Samuel boxed Joshua's ears, causing his hands to loosen from his robe. He kicked out his long legs knocking Joshua's legs from under him. Joshua fell, grabbing Samuel's leg and pulling him down with him. The two began wrestling until they saw a pair of sexy legs standing over them with her hands on her hips and a very angry expression on her face. Samuel looked up with his arm around Joshua's neck. Joshua had his hand in Samuel's face. He spread his fingers apart so his brother could see his wife.

"Hi, sweetheart." Samuel smiled.

"Really, Samuel," Cynthia scolded. "Joshua, get up off my husband before I call your mother."

Joshua couldn't resist, he smushed Samuel in the face, stood, then extended his hand down to help his brother up. He walked over, kissed Cynthia on the cheek, then looked at Samuel.

"Handle your business like a man.

Joshua smiled. "I have no choice, I have you to live up to." Samuel turned to look at his wife and when he turned back, Joshua was gone."

Samuel took his wife's hand, turned off the kitchen light and for the first time in a few years, he did not have to worry about his brother.

"I think you are going about this the wrong way, Joshua." Royce offered him a drink. "Before you seek out Roc, I think you need to close out Akande."

"Akande has nothing to do with this."

"She has everything to do with your attitude towards Roc, and you know it." He sat down, took a sip of his drink then stared at Joshua. "You think you are still in love with Akande, but from what I saw, I think you were in love with the idea of being in love."

Joshua stood. "The more I talk to politicians the more I believe none of you have good damn sense."

Royce laughed. "Tell me this." He pointed at Joshua with his drink in his hand. "Did you ever tell her you loved her?"

"What?" Joshua smirked. "What kind of question is that?"

"One that you are avoiding answering." Royce sipped his drink. "Did you ever tell Akande you loved her or were in love with her? Did you ever use the word love in any conversation you had with her?"

"How many ways do you think you can ask the same question?"

"As many as it takes for you to ask yourself that question." Royce sat his glass on the table, then bent forward clasping his hands together between his legs. "Joshua, you came in here demanding information on Roc. Why?"

"I told you. I need to find her."

"Why? Why is it so important to find her? Are you planning on being in her life? If so, how? You know Roc wants the white picket fence, the children along with the husband. Are you ready to change your life to give her that?" He sat back. "Before you step to Roc, you better be damn sure what it is you're asking of her. More importantly, you need to know if you are ready to give her that. Again, I'm trying to lead you here, son. My advice is for you to close that door with Akande, before you attempt to open the door with Roc or anyone else."

Joshua left Royce's home empty handed, just like with Ned, he refused to give him any information on Roc's true identity. For some strange reason, he did not feel dejected. He had a renewed purpose. It was time for him to turn to a friend. The one he knew would always be there. He stopped and smiled. "Angel." He pulled out his Angel, then clicked on his Bible. He didn't know the exact passage, so went to the search box. His last search was there, *Healing the heart*. He now knew the answer, but needed guidance. He typed in the word love. Several passages appeared. He searched through them until he found just the right one.

> *There is no fear in love; but perfect love*
> *casteth out fear:*
> *because fear hath torment. He that*
> *feareth is not made*
> *perfect in love.* **1 John 4:18**

He wondered why he'd stopped dreaming about Akande, why he was no longer tormented by the mere thought of her. A smile of understanding appeared on his face. Without any fanfare, or drum roll, love had entered his heart. And its name is....that was the crux of his problem. He didn't even know her name. He started the vehicle.

"For now, you're going to continue to be Angel. And I will find you, my Angel. I will find you."

She looks like a Queen, Joshua thought as he stood in the shadows watching Akande. Strange, his heart wasn't beating furiously, he didn't have that feeling of doom that came over him the other times he had checked on her. He didn't want to kill the man playing with the little girl, who looked just like her mother. No, he didn't feel anything but happiness for the woman he'd once thought he loved. What he'd had with Akande was beautiful, but it wasn't love. What they'd had was two lost souls in search of something that made them feel special. Akande because she'd never felt loved or cared for, him because he'd never felt he could live up to his older brother in his parent's eyes. They'd filled a void for each other that neither had realized existed.

She sensed him, the moment he entered the room. There were other times, late at night when she thought he was with her, but when she looked around he was nowhere in sight. Today she knew he was in the room.

"Take Teddie to her father," Akande said to her maid. "Make sure he takes her to see her pony." She kissed her daughter's cheek.

The maid smiled as she took the child by the hand. "Yes, your highness, I will. Come along, Teddy, let's find your father."

"Bye, Mommy." The child giggled as she skipped behind her maid.

Akande stood there watching as the daughter she loved beyond reason smiled back at her. Once the door closed behind them, she inhaled. "I will never allow a day to go by without showing her the love you showed me."

Joshua stepped into view. "Hello, Akande." Her smile was radiant. She was as beautiful as the first day he'd met her.

"Hello Joshua." She stepped towards him then stopped. She looked towards the door, then back to him.

"He's downstairs in his library," Joshua replied to her worried expression. He leaned against the wall. "Is he treating you well?"

A soft smile appeared on her face. "Raheem is a good man. He treats me well." She looked him over. "What about you, Joshua? How are you?"

He leaned against the wall, in his suit, noticing how content she was. The young innocent girl he met three years ago had been replaced with a beautiful woman. No, that's not correct he thought. "You look like the Queen you are." Emotions played across her face that he could not decipher.

"I hurt you with my decision. For that I am sorry. In truth, I would make the same decision today. It was what was right for my country, for me and for you." She walked towards him. "You are not a King. You are a king maker." She took his hand in hers. "I have been watching and following you since that day in Washington. You have done well for your country. Not so well for you. Has that changed?"

"I'm well." He looked down at his hand in hers, then smiled up at her. "Did you love me?" Akande turned away, slowly releasing his hand. Her indigo and gold gown moved smoothly over her body. Strange, the sway of her body did not mesmerize him as it once did.

"I did." She turned back to him, "and I still do. However, it is a different kind of love now. I love the man who taught me how to love and how to make love. It is a memory that I will cherish all my life. I now care deeply for my husband. It was rough going in the beginning, I will be honest about that." She nodded her head. "I was not certain I could trust him," she said after hesitating. "Now, I understand the reasons for his actions were honorable and I've come to care for him."

Joshua watched the blush come over her face. He couldn't resist teasing her. "Really." He raised an eyebrow. "But you don't love him?"

Akande's chin went up in defense. "Why is that important to you, Joshua?"

Joshua shrugged. "I was wondering. Can he make love to you like I did? Does he make you scream and moan with the touch of his tongue? Do his lips make your mouth water when they are near." He walked towards her. "Can he make love to you with his eyes?"

Akande stepped away from him in a bit of a panic. "Joshua, stop that this instant."

"Are you hot right this minute for my touch?" He gently kissed her lips.

Akande pulled away, backing up until the wall stopped her. "Joshua," she almost cried. "I am a married woman. It is wrong for me to lust after another man."

Joshua leaned against the wall with his arms on either side of her. "It's okay, Akande. Things are as they should be. I just had to make sure, before I moved on."

She gazed into his eyes and that's when her breath caught. "You're in love with someone?" Joshua stepped back and smiled.

"Well." Akande began to breathe again. Does she like MacGyver or Jack Bauer?"

Joshua laughed, a rich deep laugh. "Jack Bauer."

"I see." Akande turned her head. "Will that be a point of contention in your marriage?"

"I did not say I was getting married."

"Isn't that your reason for coming here?" Akande stepped around him, to sit on the edge of the bed. "Destroying our cave wasn't enough?"

"In a way, it was. Putting your ring there was supposed to close that chapter in my life. But, it didn't. I carried that anger around for years. Now, I understand my time with you prepared me for her."

Before she could respond, she had to stop the word ring from bouncing around in her head. She stood, then looked down at him. "You destroyed the ring?"

"It was my way of putting the past behind me."

"Did it work? Are you now ready for your future?"

Joshua did not hesitate. "Yes, I am." He smiled, then nodded his head. "I can only pray I haven't lost her."

"If someone loves you, truly loves you, you will never lose them. They will always be there." She took a step back, then picked up the telephone. "Karin, would you place the black box on the dining room table in the west wing. I will be down shortly." She turned back to him. "Would you meet me in the dining room? I have something for you."

Joshua stood. "I could just walk downstairs with you."

Akande shook her head. "You have ways of getting in and out of rooms unseen. This is one of those times I need you to do that."

He walked over and opened the door. "I don't think the King would mind."

Akande rushed over, then pulled the door from him. "My husband knows all about you, Joshua. I think he would mind greatly." She stepped out of the door. "I'm certain you can find your way." She smiled then closed the door.

A few minutes later Akande walked into the dining room. On the table was a black box, next to it a gold serving tray lined with black velvet cloth. Akande opened the box, poured the contents out and smiled. She moved a few around with her hand until they were all lined up. She then placed another black velvet cloth over them, and took a seat, waiting for Joshua to appear. Her Joshua was in love. The thought pleased her for she knew he'd suffered at her hands. The woman, whoever she may be, was sure to be very happy. Joshua was a wonderful human being and a very passionate lover. She had no idea what she was giving up until she had to make love with her husband. Was he a considerate man, yes. But the passion was missing. She blamed herself for that. Her heart was lost to Joshua forever, but she would never tell him. The only way she could show just how much she loved him was to let him be happy.

"A penny for your thoughts."

She looked up. Those powerful legs, that wide chest, those dimples and the essence of the man, his lips, were all a reminder of what they'd shared. "I think it's time for someone to give back to a man who has given so much of himself."

Joshua pulled out a chair, sat, stretched out and then crossed his legs at the ankle. "What did you have in mind?"

"A small token of our appreciation, but something I believe will get you the response your heart deserves."

Frowning, Joshua watched as Akande pulled away the top layer of black velvet cloth from the tray on the table. To his astonishment, there were diamonds, all shapes and sizes, but raw diamonds.

"It would be my honor for you to accept any one of these to place on your wife's finger. "

He looked at her, then back at the diamonds spread out on the cloth. "You can't be serious."

"But I am Joshua." Akande stood. "I assure you they are of the finest quality there is. It would be my honor to know I had a small part in opening the next door to your future."

Joshua looked over the stones. One sparkled like no other. It was rough, uncut, exquisite. It was Roc. He picked up the stone, held it up to the light. Akande held out a black velvet bag. Joshua dropped the stone inside. "Will one be enough?"

"Yes," he replied. "Thank you." He kissed her on the cheek, then turned towards the windows he'd entered from. He stopped and without turning back he asked, "Your daughter's name is Theodora. Is she my daughter?"

Akande immediately replied, "No."

Joshua nodded his head, then walked out of her life.

Akande knew she had done the right thing. She prayed for the strength not to call him back to tell him the truth.

Chapter Twenty-Five
Atlanta, GA

"**P**rofessor Delany," Adam Lassiter called out as he ran towards his advisor. "Professor," he called out again.

Rochelle Delany turned to the young man she had been advising for three years now. He was a handsome devil. He reminded her of his brother. Tall, slim, nice body, beautiful smile. Dark chocolate, so sweet she would lick her lips and a few things belonging to him. Rocy shook her head. The child was barely twenty-one, a baby in her book. She needed one of him in an extra large, like his brother.

"Hello, Adam."

"Professor Delany." He gave her the letter in his hand. "I received this letter from the Centers for Disease Control and Prevention. They have accepted my proposal to develop the anti-childhood obesity program."

Rochelle read the letter, her smile increasing with each sentence. She had a bemused look when her eyes met his. "Adam, this is a formal letter of full funding for your research."

"Yes, that too." He smiled bashfully displaying those same dimples. She rubbed her stomach wondering if they ran in the family.

"Congratulations, Adam." She hugged him, then stepped back. "So...which offer are you going to accept?"

"Both are important in different ways." They started walking towards her automobile. "I mean the anti-childhood obesity program is really finished. It's just a matter of testing, which could take a few years. The creation of a combatant to a nuclear threat is exciting. Imagine developing a force field strong enough to withstand a nuclear attack. It's hard to turn away from that."

"True." They stopped at her automobile. "However, the CDC pays a lot more money than the US Government."

"There is that to consider." Adam grinned as he held the door open for her. "Now I have a question for you."

"Sure, what?"

"When are you due?" There was a look of surprise on Rocy's face. "Professor Delany, I've been studying your body for three years. Hell, I know the day your cycle starts. Of course I would notice the difference now." He dropped his head. "I'm heartbroken."

Rocy laughed so hard. "No, what you are is too observant and you need to stop. I see all these women on this campus chasing you down like dogs in heat."

Adam laughed. "You know I only have eyes for you. But seriously, congrats?" He raised an eyebrow.

"Yes, I've always wanted children."

"Well, he or she is a lucky baby and he, whoever he is, is a very lucky man."

Rocy smiled. "Thank you."

Adam blushed. "I have to go. Need to call my parents about this."

"You do that and congratulations again." She smiled as she watched the young man walk away. The smile disappeared once she was inside the automobile. "Genevieve, will you call Shelly please?"

"Home or cell?"

"Cell please."

"Calling."

"Hey stranger," her best friend's voice came through the speaker.

"I'm pregnant."

"What? You're pregnant. What is wrong with you? You can't just hit a sister with something like that without prep work," Shelly Davenport screamed. "Who? When? How?"

"If you have to ask how, Royce is not doing his job."

"Oh believe me, brother is handling his business. You know he put a pole in the extra bedroom."

Rocy laughed. "Get your freak on girl, I'm not even mad."

"Are you okay? Are you happy about this? Who?"

"Yes, I"m okay. Yes, I'm happy about it. The who is a little tricky."

"Does the father know?"

"No. That's what's bugging me." She watched Adam Lassiter talking to another student.

"I know you well enough to know you will make the right decision on that. And you know I'm here any time you need to talk."

"I know. Do me a favor. Don't mention this to Royce just yet."

"Okay...he ain't the daddy is he? I mean you be all over my man when you come home."

Rocy laughed even harder. "Get off my phone. You are a sick woman."

"Hey a sister has to ask these questions." Shelly hesitated. "I'm so happy for you. I know how much you love children."

"I love you, girl. You always know how to make me laugh."

"That's what friends are for. Talk to you soon."

Rocy disconnected the call and pulled off.

She was good. He was better, or more determined to find her. He stood in the shadow of her bedroom watching as she walked in the door. She hit a button on the remote and music filled the house. There it was, one of the things he missed about her. She began singing *No Air* by Jordin Sparks and Chris Brown.

He listened to the words and it made him realize he had hurt her deeply. This was the third day he had watched her from afar. But today he knew he would have to make his intentions known. He followed her to her classes this morning, then to the doctor's office, then watched as she talked with his little brother. She cut the song off.

"No more sad songs." She changed the CD. *Purify Me* by India Arie filled the house. She nodded her head. "Oh yeah." he began singing and dancing around the room.

Watching her smile as she wiped tears of joy from her eyes, he could only pray those were tears of joy because she had just found out she was carrying his child. He knew she would turn him down now if he approached her and for the first time in his life, he was at a loss as to how to get a woman.

"Who called the family council?" Phire asked as she looked into the dining room to see the ballot box on the table. "Mom," she called through the house.

"You will stop with the yelling."

Phire looked up to see her brother Adam at the top of the steps. "Adam, when did you get home?" She ran up the stairs and jumped into his arms almost knocking him down. He hugged her, then sat on the landing to the second floor of their home.

"I just arrived." He smiled down at the one person in this family younger than him. "How was cheerleading practice?"

Phire shrugged. "Boring. All they want to do is show their a... um, behinds. And now, they want to show more butt. They want us to wear the boy shorts up the crack of our butts. Hmmm." She rolled her eyes. "My stuff ain't for everybody to see."

"Isn't," Adam corrected her.

"Okay, isn't for everybody to see."

"They still giving you a hard time about staying a virgin?"

"Yes." She looked up at him. "Is it a bad thing Adam? I mean, you're a guy. Do guys give you a hard time about being a virgin?"

"No, but then again, it's not the main topic of our conversation." He touched her nose. "You do what you feel. Don't allow those girls in your school to bully you into anything you don't want to do."

"I don't, but you know, ZsaZsa is catching it."

"Who is ZsaZsa?"

"Princess ZsaZsa." She looked at him as if he should know. "Prince LaVere's little sister. She came to live with him after Joshua rescued her. She goes to school with me."

"A princess is going to John Marshall High School?" He tried not to laugh. "I bet she is catching it."

"They don't know she's a princess. All they know is she is different, talks proper and is still a virgin. You should see the guys betting on who is going to pop that cherry."

"You need to stop talking like that. It's not lady like."

"Who ever said that Phire was a lady?"

The two looked down the steps to see their sister Opal and her twin Timothy walking through the door.

Phire ran down the stairs and jumped in Timothy's arms. "Is everybody coming home?"

Opal answered her while Timothy whirled her around. "Yes, when Mother calls we all come running. Put her down." She hit Timothy on the arm. "She is too big for you to be swinging her around like that." Opal turned to Adam. "Where's Jade?"

"She's upstairs on her phone," Adam replied.

Opal began walking up the stairs. "When did you guys get in?"

"We flew in about an hour ago," Adam replied as he met Timothy at the bottom of the steps.

"Hey little brother." He gave a pound to Adam. "How're the buildings at Morehouse? Still standing?"

Adam smiled. "Man, that was freshman year. I haven't blown up anything since."

"How're things at Hampton?"

"Wrapping up." He grinned, displaying dimples similar to his brother's. "Thesis goes in next week and it's a done deal."

The door opened and in walked their brother Luke. "Aww, snap, Luke." Phire went through another round of another brother's loving hug.

"Look at you." He beamed down at Phire. "I bet you are giving the boys a fit."

"She better not be." Timothy frowned at Phire, then turned to Luke. "Man, you should be on the field practicing. Ya'll didn't do too well in the big D last season."

"Hey, man don't talk about the team." He shook his brothers hand. "Besides, looks like I may be coming back to the East coast."

"What?" Adam looked surprised. "The Lions are letting you go, averaging twenty yards a carry? Are they crazy?"

"My new agent has been shopping me around. He has two teams in a bidding war."

"That's what I'm talking about, Luke." Timothy grinned. "Don't tell Matthew."

"Tell Mathew what?" Their older brother walked out of the kitchen eating a sandwich.

They all looked up at him, and laughed. "Man, do you ever stop eating?"

"I'm burning calories all day long running up and down the court with the team."

"The basketball team, be running up and down the court," Phire smirked. "All you do is yell at them all the time."

"Little girl," Matt huffed, "Go in the kitchen and help your mother and stay out of grown folks conversations."

With hands on her hips she rolled her eyes. "When I see grown folks, I'll leave. All I see are my big head brothers who are about to get their butts kicked on the field as soon as my other sisters get here."

"We playing today?" Luke asked, excited at the thought of having an impromptu flag football game with the family.

"I don't think we are going to have time for a game," Jade said as she and Opal joined their siblings in the foyer. "Mother called a family council for one of us?" She looked around.

Everyone shook their head. "Not me," Adam offered.

Jade looked at Timothy.

"Nope, I'm good."

"Not me," Luke offered.

The others gave the same response as she eyed them. "Then who is the council for?"

"We'll find out soon enough," Luke replied. "Where's Dad?"

"In the family room with Diamond, Zack, Samuel and Cynthia," Matt replied between bites.

"Is Cynthia pregnant, again?" Opal asked.

Phire laughed. "We would be having a council every nine months if that's the reason. They act like they don't know anything about birth control."

"As long as you know..." Jade gave her a knowing look.

"Ain't nobody getting my cookies," Phire declared.

"Okay, it's time for me to walk away," Timothy said. "I do not want to be a part of that conversation."

"I'm with you," Luke said as he followed his bother.

"Come on you." Jade pulled Phire along with her as the others followed the group.

Sitting around the dining room table, Sally smiled at her family, then up at her husband who was taking a seat next to her at the head of the table.

Ruby, their oldest daughter, had arrived and, the next to the oldest daughter Pearl, who was in Washington D.C. serving as Press Secretary to the President, had called in via FaceTime, to be a part of the family council.

"Okay, Mom, who called the council?" Pearl asked.

"Yeah, Mom," Ruby asked. "Who needs help?"

"Your brother," Sally replied.

Everyone looked around the table, except Samuel.

"Okay fess up," Pearl laughed. "Who got somebody pregnant?"

Phire pointed. "Samuel is the only one around here who doesn't know how to keep his zipper up."

The family turned to look at Samuel and Cynthia.

Cynthia, Samuel's wife of five years and mother of their two children, shook her head. "Oh no, it's not me."

They then looked at Diamond. "Well, since we are all here together." She smiled at her husband Zack. "We just found out today. We are expecting."

The family cheered and offered congratulations. Samuel shook Zack's hand. "Oh hell, you're stuck now."

"I was stuck anyway." Zack smiled.

Luke frowned. "You just found out today?"

Diamond nodded her head. "Exactly three hours ago."

"But Mom called me yesterday about the meeting," he stated as he looked over at his mother.

"Same here," Jade replied.

"So, who is the meeting for?"

"I think that would be me."

All eyes went to the doorway where their brother Joshua stood. They all rushed him at the same time. For all, except Samuel, Pearl and Sally, this was the first time they had seen Joshua in years. They were all talking at once, as Joe and Sally sat back watching their family showering their brother with love.

It took the family fifteen minutes to settle down from the shock of seeing Joshua. When they finally allowed him to take a seat, all he could do was smile. He had missed the security of their love. There was no doubt in his mind that the people around this table loved him beyond reason. If he had to get guidance, these are the people who would steer him in the right direction.

"Joshua," Pearl spoke from the electronic tablet sitting in the middle of the table. "The President sends his gratitude."

He sat forward, serious for a moment. "How are the children?"

Pearl sighed. "Jada, that's James and Ashley's daughter isn't handling things too well. She's retreated into herself. Pretty afraid to go anywhere without her father."

Joshua nodded. "I'll have to go by to talk with her. How's Jazzy?"

Pearl laughed. "Eating up all the attention and telling anyone who will listen how she helped you rescue them."

Joshua laughed. "Yeah, JD better get a few big guns to keep that one in line. And JC? How is he doing?"

"Hmmm, it's hard to day." Pearl hesitated. "He seems to be okay, but I have a feeling that incident is going to haunt him for a while."

"Nope, I was there. JC is going to be okay. The President is doing a good job with him." Joshua sat back.

"Don't you want to know what happened to the Attorney General?"

"Don't care," Joshua replied. "I have other things on my mind."

"So, what gives, Joshua?" Phire asked looking up from her brother's lap, which she refused to vacate when he sat down. "You okay?"

He looked at her, she still had tears in her eyes. He kissed her forehead. "I'm better than okay." He hugged her then looked around at his family. "I'm in love with a woman and I don't have the slightest idea how to tell her."

The room was stunned to silence. All eyes were on him with shocked expressions on their faces. No one seemed to be breathing or thinking about taking a breath.

Sally looked up at her husband with a knowing smile. Joe rubbed her arm, reassuring her what she just heard was right. Her Joshua just said that he was in love. The last time they talked about a woman, he never said he was in love. This time, she knew it was right.

Matthew slammed his hand down on the table. "Man," he yelled angrily. "Why man? Why you go and do something stupid like that?"

The girls all turned to him and frowned.

"Not you, Joshua." He shook his head. "Don't do this man. Why? Why?"

Zack and Samuel couldn't help it, they both burst out laughing at the outrage on Matthew's face. Luke came out of his stupor and joined them laughing at Matthew.

"Matt," Ruby laughed. "It's not the end of the world."

"Yes, it is. It's the end of the world as we know it as men," he almost cried. "Joshua, man, don't do this to me. It's like a legend's life coming to an end." He huffed, "You're my hero, man."

The entire family fell out laughing. Joshua looked at Phire and shook his head.

"That's your brother." Phire shook her head.

"Matt, man it's okay." Adam patted him on the shoulder. "That leaves more women for you." He raised an eyebrow.

Matthew thought for a moment. "Hmm, you may have a point there." He looked at Joshua. "How can I help you?"

Sally laughed at the children. "Joshua has a situation and he has requested our input. Let's listen to what he has to say...shall we?"

"Sorry, man, you just messed with my head there for a minute," Matt stated. "Go ahead, man. How can we help?"

Joshua smiled. He told them the story of how he and Roc met, and how they parted. "She left thinking I was still hung up on Akande."

"Are you?" Samuel asked.

"No," Joshua replied. "Akande was put in my life for a season, not for a lifetime. She fulfilled her purpose which was to give me the ability to recognize love when it came my way. I will always care about her, but I wasn't in love with Akande. I am consumed with this woman. It wasn't until she was gone that I realized just how ingrained she was in my life. It's her smile that wakes me up every morning and her voice." He closed his eyes. "That sweet voice of hers that puts me to sleep at night. I can't move on with my life without her." He sat back. "With all the women I've had in my bed, I've never wanted one of them in my life. Even with Akande, I never dreamt about a home, with children all running around singing. I'm telling you, I've been touched by an angel. I just don't know how to bring my angel home."

The room was silent.

"That's nice, man." Luke smiled knowingly at his brother. "I'm happy for you."

"There is nothing like having the right woman in your life," Samuel smiled at Cynthia.

"I'll second that." Zack kissed Diamond's cheek.

"Does she have a suction cup or something between her legs, cause she just sucked your playa card right from under you?"

"Phire," Pearl censored her little sister. "Mom, you better do something with that child."

"I'm going to send her up there with you," Sally replied as she gave her youngest daughter a stern look.

"I'm just saying..."

"You are just saying your last words," Joe cautioned.

Ruby smiled. "I have the feeling Joshua is done with the playa card. It takes a real man to be able to express his feelings like that. I'm proud of you, little brother. What's her name?"

Joshua looked over at Adam. He knew his answer was going to have an impact on him. He held his brother's eyes. "Her name is Rochelle Delany."

The look in Adam's eyes was confusion at first, then understanding. He sat forward. "You know, that's interesting." He held his brother's eyes. "I have a professor named Rochelle Delany." There was a touch of anger in his voice when he spoke again. "Did you impregnate her?"

Eyes around the table went back and forth between Joshua and Adam. Joe and Sally glanced at each other in surprise then turned back to the children.

"Did you?"

"I knew somebody was prego..." Phire exclaimed, throwing her hands in the air.

Adam stood angrily. "Did you?"

Joshua stood, placing Phire on her feet. He never took his eyes from Adam. He knew his little brother had a crush on his advisor, he just didn't know how deep it went. "Adam," he spoke softly. "I'm in love with her. I want her to be my wife and I need your help to do that."

"Why would I help you with that?" He pushed his chair away from the table.

"Adam," Joe cautioned.

"No, Dad," Joshua spoke then walked around the table to where his little brother stood. He had grown into a formidable young man. Joshua recognized that as he watched him on campus with Roc. He also noticed how Adam looked at Roc. It was clear to anyone who could see that Adam was infatuated with his professor. "Adam," he spoke in an understanding tone. "She's a beautiful woman and believe me, I understand. But you're not in love with her and she's not in love with you."

Adam pushed his brother in the chest. "How the hell do you know?"

Samuel stood, with the intention of separating the two. He knew Joshua would never strike Adam. However, he wasn't sure what Adam would do.

Jade, Adam's twin, then walked around to him. "Adam." She stepped between her two brothers. "I would never take anyone's side against you." She looked over her shoulder. "Not even Joshua's" She took his hands. "You know Professor Delany is cool people and she cares for you. But you also know, she doesn't feel the same way. You told me yourself, that you hoped she would find a man deserving of her love." She looked at Joshua. "Who is more deserving of a love like hers than Joshua?"

Adam inhaled as he pulled his hands away from her. He looked around the table at his family, who all displayed concerned expressions. He looked up at Joshua. "She's a good, God fearing woman."

"I know," Joshua continued, treading lightly as Jade stepped away. He stood face to face with his brother. "I promise she will never have a day go by without knowing how much I love and cherish her."

He took his brother's shoulders between his hands. "I love you too Adam. I would never intentionally hurt you. But, I love her and I need your help to tell her that."

Sally watched as her sons squared off on each other. Her heart was breaking for Adam, but filled with joy for Joshua. Her Adam was so smart, yet very sensitive. To her knowledge, he had not been involved with any of the girls on campus. Now, she knew why. Glancing at Jade, she could see the concern on her face. The twins were close. Jade was a few minutes older than Adam and felt it was her responsibility to protect him, even from their own brothers. She knew Jade would be there to help Adam through this.

"You called this council together for me...didn't you?"

Joshua nodded. "Yes. I didn't want you to deal with this alone. I tried that and it's not the answer. There are times when even as men we need the love and support of family to help us though rough times."

Adam inhaled, then looked around at his brothers. "Go ahead, Matt, get out all your virgin jokes, so I can move on."

"No jokes, man." Matt held his brother glare. "All I can say is she must be a fine sister to pull two Lassiter men."

"Three," Samuel added.

"Excuse you," Cynthia interjected.

"I know Roc and at one time I too was attracted to her."

"Is that why you and Joshua were fighting in my kitchen?"

"Yes, and no," Samuel replied. "He wanted to know how to find her and I wouldn't tell him."

"Who is this woman, that had three of my brothers' attention?" Opal asked.

"She's the woman who rescued Joshua and nursed him back to health," Pearl offered.

"So is that what you call it now," Phire smirked. "How do you know it's not the Knight in Shining armor syndrome? You know when you think you are in love with the person who rescued you." She looked at Adam. "Just like Zsa Zsa, you know she thinks she is in love with Joshua. This Roc person could be just a little side piece that has you distracted."

"Say one more word," Joe stared at his daughter, "and you and I will be having a private conversation that your behind is not going to like."

"Daddy, I'm eighteen years old you can't spank me."

"He can't, but I can and will. Now sit down and be quiet."

"Look." Joshua was getting a little frustrated. "I'm the one she is in love with."

"Again, I ask how do you know?" Adam asked.

"Because I said she is."

Timothy laughed. "Now, that's the Joshua I know."

"Arrogant to the bone." Opal smiled.

"I only speak the truth." Joshua smiled.

Samuel watched the expressions playing across Joshua's face. He was joking, but glanced Adam's way. He was concerned about his little brothers. This was a new Joshua, a man secure in who he is, yet insecure about the step he was about to take. Then there was Adam. He had all the book sense in the world, but was unskilled in the art of women. He still wore his heart on his sleeve. Samuel glanced at his mother. She smiled and nodded her head indicating to him all would be well. Samuel sat back down. "Well, Adam. How do you think Joshua should approach Roc?"

Adam hesitated, then shook his head. "I guess if I have to lose her to someone it might as well be you."

His little brother wasn't so little anymore. Adam was standing six-two and a solid one-hundred-ninety pounds. Joshua shook his brother's hand, then pulled him into a bear hug and whispered so only he could hear, "Thank you for trusting me with her." He pulled away, holding his brother at arm's length. "I will love her as I love the church."

Adam could see Joshua was serious, but that didn't ease the hurt. He knew Professor Delany didn't have those feelings for him. For the last few years, she had inspired him to become the man he was today. He would do whatever he could do to contribute to her happiness. He also loved his brother and would give his right arm to see him settled and safe. He exhaled. "I have your back. What do you need me to do?"

Epilogue
Richmond, VA

"Why did I agree to this?"
Laughter erupted from the front seat of the vehicle. "Because you love him," Shelly replied. "Everything else is secondary."

"If you hadn't agreed the President was ready to charge you with crimes against the Country." Royce smiled at his wife, then looked in the rearview mirror at Rocy.

"Besides you will have to eventually tell him about the baby. Might as well get it all out in the open now. You are too old to go through this pregnancy alone."

"You make it sound like I'm ancient."

Shelly turned in her seat to look at her best friend. "I didn't mean it that way. I just want you happy." She smiled. "Royce believes Joshua is the man to do that." She turned back in her seat. "Hell any man who can give you multiple O's in one day is worthy."

"And you know, he can." Rocy laughed. She sat back thinking about that day in the backseat of his automobile when he introduced her to the Absolute Experience. The man had her so shaken she could barely walk straight. It took every ounce of will power she could gather to get into that chopper and return home. It wasn't long after her return that she realized the Absolute Experience had very little to do with his sexual powers. No, it went much deeper than that. The experience revolved around the essence of the man known as Joshua Theodore Lassiter. The danger, the charm, the faith, the loyalty and yes, the overpowering sex appeal of the man is what the experience is about. The more she thought about it the more she knew she couldn't and would never get over him. She started singing *I Can't Get Over You*, by Kem.

Royce and Shelly smiled as they continued the drive, for they were certain things would end as they should tonight.

"What the hell do you mean no?"

Everyone in the room's attention was on the couple in the center of the floor. They did not know if they should laugh or run for cover. The cool collected Joshua was pissed by the reply they were certain he did not anticipate. The woman, who they just learned was Rochelle Delany, their brother Adam's professor did not seem to be one bit fazed by Joshua's displeasure.

It all started out like a fairy tale.

The Lassiters had gathered to celebrate several accomplishments. Luke had learned he was traded to the Washington Redskins, with a very lucrative new contract thanks to his new agent, Nicholas Brooks. Opal and Timothy had completed their Master's programs at Norfolk State and Hampton, respectively. Jade had graduated from Spelman. However, the biggest celebration of all went to Adam. He had been awarded a contract with the United States Defense Department to design counter-terrorism weapons.

The family had reason to celebrate and they decided to do it in grand style.

The night began in the ballroom at the Davenport Estates. Zackary and Diamond were the hosts, using their estate for the celebration. A beautiful May night enhanced the open doorways to the ballroom, displaying the city of Richmond's skyline as the backdrop to the event. The warm breeze, coming from the James River, mixed in with the jazz sounds of Thasaint, delivering a romantic atmosphere for the attendees.

Secret Service agents discreetly remained vigilant in the background as President Harrison conversed with Joe and Sally, raving about Pearl, Samuel and Joshua. They were all valuable to him in different ways. Also there, was Prince LaVere' who owed the Lassiters so much for saving his little sister Zsa Zsa from kidnappers. Of course, the architect who designed Davenport Estates and the brother-in-law to Diamond, Xavier, was there to show his support of the family, for they had accepted him as a part of them, no questions asked. James and Ashley Brooks were in attendance, to show their appreciation to Joshua for saving their daughter Jada. What highlighted the night was to see Douglas Hylton there with Karen Holt, the ex-wife to David Holt. She was absolutely stunning. It looked as if David's death took ten years off of her life. Samuel and Cynthia were there talking with Pearl and her friend Dr. Prentiss. Everyone was shocked the two were still going strong. And of course, all the Lassiter children, Matthew, Luke, Opal Jade, Ruby, the ever-adorable Phire and her friend Zsa Zsa rounded out the people in the room.

All was going well, when a beautiful woman dressed in a royal blue off the shoulder dress, hugging every curve on her luscious body walked in with Secretary Davenport and his wife, Shelly.

Adam was the first to greet her with a hug. "Professor Delany, it looks as if you came dressed to break my heart."

"Sounds as if you have been taking charm lessons from your brother." Rocy smiled as she kissed him on the cheek.

"You still have a chance to fly with me to the South of France. We can get married there and he will never find us."

Shelly looked from Adam to Rocy and laughed. "What did you do, seduce the entire family?"

"Just a few of the brothers." Royce laughed as he took his wife's hand and pulled her away.

Rocy watched as her so called friends walked away laughing. "Okay, Adam," she exhaled. "No promises, but I'm here."

"Thank you. He loves you more than I do." He took her hand and placed it in the crook of his arm. "You have no idea how much it pains me to admit that."

Rocy smiled. "You will always be my little bomber."

"Ha," Adam laughed as he walked over to his parents.

Joshua knew the moment she walked in the room. He watched from the French doors which led to the garden. She was more beautiful than he remembered. Her hair was up in curls, with a single strand of diamond earrings hanging down. There was nothing on her neck, just her smooth skin shimmering from the touch of the light in the room.

"I never thought I would see the day when the great Absolute was afraid."

Joshua knew it was Monique behind him. For only she would have the nerve to approach him in that fashion. "I'm not afraid. Just..."

"A little nervous?"

"No. I got this."

"Looks like your little brother has her to me."

Just then Rocy laughed at something that Adam said, then turned towards him.

The moment stopped her in mid-laugh. It seemed everything and everyone in the room stopped. There were no voices or music heard, just the crackle of tension filled the room. People stepped out of his line of vision as if the red sea was parting. Adam and his parents stepped back, leaving Rocy there in the middle of the room alone.

Joshua knew it was on him to take that first step. So....he did. The strut was so arrogant it made the men in the room groan.

"Humble, my brother, humble," Samuel whispered as Joshua passed him.

Unfortunately, Joshua Theodore Lassiter did not have a humble bone in his body. He walked right up to Roc, pulled her into his arms and kissed her with a passion that had the women in the room fanning.

Rocy did not flinch, not once. She gave as good as she got. People in the room were downing water in gulps and holding their glass out for more, the heat radiating from the two was so hot.

Finally, Joshua ended the kiss, took her hand then dropped to one knee.

There is no fear in love; but perfect love casteth out fear: because fear hath torment.
He that feareth is not made
perfect in love.
1 John 4:18

"God planted a seed when he sent you to me. You pushed away my fear to love and opened my heart. I trust that God has granted a perfect love. I believe you are that love for me." He held out his other hand. Inside was a stunning five carat solitaire diamond, encased in a platinum band. The brilliance of the ring sparkled in her tear filled eyes. "Be my wife, Roc."

You could hear the intake of breath echoing around the room. All eyes were on the couple, with bated breath.

Rocy was overwhelmed with his proposal. "No."

Gasps of disbelief filled the air as shocked faces looked at each other.

"Oh, hell no," Monique yelled. "Wrong answer." She started to walk towards Rocy, pulling off her earrings, when a set of strong arms circled her waist stopping her. She swung around and stopped mid-swing when she saw the sexiest set of brown eyes staring back at her.

"Joshua will have to handle this," Luke said to the short, spitfire of a woman.

"What the hell do you mean, no?" Joshua stood.

"Would you like to talk about this in private?" Rocy asked in her quiet way.

"Hell no, I don't want to talk in private," an angry Joshua yelled. "I just poured my heart out to you."

"And it was beautiful, but I need more, Joshua."

Joshua ran his hands down his face looking up to God, not understanding what had gone so wrong. He had planned this, wrote every word of what he wanted to say. Rehearsed it over and over, just so it would be right. "What more, Roc? You have all of me. What more do you want?"

It was very seldom Rocy ever lost patience with anyone, but this man standing in front of her dressed in his tailor made suit, fitting like he just walked off of

Fashion Avenue in New York, could try the patience of JOB. She took her clutch, popped it upside his head then kicked his legs from under him sending him to the floor. The Lassiter girls could be heard in the background.

"Oh hell no, she didn't." Several of the men in the room had to hold them back.

Rocy put her high heel clad foot in his chest and looked down at him. "I want to hear you say it."

Joshua looked at her, then remembered when they were in a similar position. He began laughing with relief. "Aww Roc, do I have to?"

Rocy simply raised an eyebrow, then put pressure on his chest. "Repeat after me."

Joshua laid his head back on the floor and repeated what he had once said after her.

"You will concede that I am the more capable and you are merely a male, albeit a fine one, playing at being superior. And at some point you too, will be at my feet bowing to my superiority. For I am a woman. God put us here to rule. He put men here to love us."

Joshua reached up with lightning speed and pulled her down to him. She kissed him as they laughed together and the crowd sighed in relief. "I love you, Rochelle Delany. Will you marry me?"

"You and those darn dimples." Rocy smiled. "Yes, I'll marry you."

Joshua placed the ring on her finger then looked down into her loving eyes. "I will love and cherish you all the days of my life. All I ask in return is that you trust and believe in me."

46551139R00172

Made in the USA
San Bernardino, CA
10 March 2017